7

D1589570

TIES OF BLOOD

TIES OF BLOOD

GRAHAM REID

faber and faber

LONDON · BOSTON

First published in 1986
by Faber and Faber Limited
3 Queen Square London WC1N 3AU

Phototypeset by Wilmaset Birkenhead Wirral
Printed in Great Britain by
Whitstable Litho Ltd Whitstable Kent
All rights reserved

British Library Cataloguing in Publication Data

Reid, J. Graham
Ties of Blood
I. Title
822'.914   PR6068.E43/

ISBN 0-571-13877-2

For James Ormerod

The publisher acknowledges with thanks the financial assistance of the Arts Council of Northern Ireland in the publication of this volume.

CONTENTS

The following were involved throughout the production of the *Ties of Blood* series of plays:

Director	James Ormerod
Producer	Tim Ironside Wood
Executive Producer	Keith Williams
Designer	John Armstrong

The series was first broadcast on BBC Television during November and December 1985.

McCABE'S WALL

Cast:

SEAN MCCABE	J. G. Devlin
MARY MCCABE	Bernadette McKenna
LIAM MCCABE	Tony Doyle
TRISH MCCABE	Dearbhla Molloy
GRUNTER MAGUIRE	Mark Mulholland
WILL PRYCE	Kenny Ireland
BOB DAVIS	Sion Tudor Owen
MURIEL DAVIS	Bronwen Williams
CORPORAL DANIELS	Terence Budd
PRIVATE JOHNSTONE	Jonathan Phillips
PRIVATE DOBSON	Steve Delaney
INTELLIGENCE OFFICER	Richard Bartlett
SECOND LIEUTENANT	Tony Boncza
MAJOR 2IC	Ian McElhinney
SOLDIER A	David Huntley
SOLDER B	Dai Jenkins
SOLDIER C	Aidan McCann
TERRORIST	Trevor Moore

1. INT. DINING ROOM/KITCHEN, OFFICERS' MESS
PRIVATE JOHNSTONE *clears plates in dining room and enters kitchen.*
WILL PRYCE *is preparing a large cut of meat for cooking. He sips a cup
of tea. One of the mess waiters,* PRIVATE JOHNSTONE, *is scraping
leftovers into a bin.* WILL *is Welsh, in his early thirties. He is about
five-foot-seven, plump, rather ordinary . . . not by any means a ladies'
man. He is an intelligent, well-read man, sensitive, emotional.
Essentially he is a loner. His Welsh accent is not a very pronounced one.*

WILL: (*Pausing, watching* JOHNSTONE) Why is so much being
　　left this morning?

JOHNSTONE: Everybody seems to be in a hurry, Corporal.

WILL: They shouldn't sit down if they haven't time to eat
　　properly . . . it's waste. Typical army . . . they're never
　　doing anything, but they do it at the gallop. I mean, if
　　they're going to show so little appreciation of my
　　cooking . . . why don't I just make sandwiches the night
　　before and leave them for them?

JOHNSTONE: They're doing searches this morning.

WILL: I don't know why, no one was hurt. If these silly people
　　want to blow holes in the road and inconvenience
　　themselves . . . let them get on with it. (*Pause.*) Culvert
　　bombs throw up plenty of worms for the fishing. Do you
　　fish?

JOHNSTONE: Not over here . . . too risky.

WILL: I don't know . . . I think the fish are neutral, by and
　　large. (*Pause.*) It's a great country for fishing.

JOHNSTONE: (*Conversational*) You're a fisherman then,
　　Corporal?

WILL: (*Looking at him*) No . . . can't stand it myself . . . I find
　　it boring.
　　(*Pause.* WILL *returns to his task,* JOHNSTONE *goes to sink.*
　　SERGEANT BOB DAVIS, *a fellow Welshman, enters. His accent
　　is more pronounced than* WILL's.)

BOB: Will . . . how goes it?

WILL: Bob . . . fine . . . and you?

BOB: Oh not too bad you know. Try complaining and somebody lists the things you should be grateful for . . . so what's the point? (*Pause. Watching* WILL) I thought your meat came up cooked and all?

WILL: Cooked! I've just decided I'd like a proper piece of meat . . . properly cooked . . . for a palate of discernment . . . namely, mine.

BOB: Crafty enough, Corporal Pryce . . . and big enough.

WILL: The sort of helping that keeps our lads winning the Triple Crown.

BOB: Do you give yourself these special little treats every day then?

WILL: Just now and again . . . birthdays and that sort of thing.

BOB: I didn't know it was your birthday.

WILL: It's not . . . (*Placing his meat on plate*) . . . but I'm sure it's somebody's . . . and I'm a great believer in the human family.

(*He now turns his attention to his garnish and side salad*.)
You know I'd like to have a spy in the main cookhouse. I'm convinced they cook the meat by flamethrower.

BOB: I called to check up for tonight . . . you're still coming I hope?

WILL: I don't know, Bob . . . I've such a lot to do . . . letters to write . . .

BOB: Listen . . . we've organized a Welsh night . . . don't let us down.

WILL: Don't welch on the Welsh, eh?

BOB: Right . . . a little civilized company now and again's just what you need. You'll enjoy yourself.

WILL: I'd just decided on a night with my Welsh choirs.

BOB: You can send yourself to sleep with them.

WILL: You're talking like an Englishman . . . nobody falls asleep when a Welsh choir is in full voice. Anyway, after a night of an Irish danceband, it'll take months for my musical ear to recover.

(PRIVATE DOBSON *enters.*)

WILL: That was a long tea break, Private Dobson.

DOBSON: Sorry, Corporal.

WILL: Never mind the sorry . . . stop smoking king-size cigarettes.

(*As they gather their cleaning materials.*)

BOB: Are they sharing your special repast?

WILL: Give ove. . . . properly cooked food would be the death of that lot.

BOB: You're never going to shift all that lot yourself, are you?

WILL: Would you like me to make you a video?

BOB: Well . . . sit downwind of me tonight, that's all.

WILL: I'm sure your mother give birth to you on a daytrip to England. Run along now and let my privates clean the floor.

(BOB *laughs.* WILL *gives him a mock disapproving look as he leaves.* PRIVATES JOHNSTONE *and* DOBSON *begin work.*)

2. INT. THE KITCHEN OF THE MCCABE'S FARM

MARY *and her father are at breakfast. The youngest son,* LIAM, *and his wife,* TRISH, *are home on holiday . . . but still in bed.* MARY *is the youngest in the family . . . a late baby, she is in her thirties, an extremely plain woman.* SEAN, *in his seventies, a thin, sour-faced, wiry man. Although never active, he is a fierce Republican supporter. His nephew, an active IRA man who worked the farm with him, was shot dead by the British Army.* SEAN *hates them for the 'murder'.* MARY *hates the farm, the bitterness of her father, and what is going on around her.* MARY *dreams of leaving the farm, Ireland . . . finding a man who'll take her away from it all. Her father wants this little bit of Ireland . . . his bit to remain in the family. She will, he thinks, with the lure of the farm, find a man who'll keep her right where she is.*

SEAN: I hope them two's not going to lie all day.

MARY: They are on holiday, Da.

SEAN: There aren't any holidays on a farm. When do we ever get any holidays?

MARY: But Liam doesn't work on the farm.

SEAN: Naw . . . three sons and not one of them on the farm.
Not one of them left in the bloody country.

MARY: Trish is looking well . . . don't you think so?

SEAN: Trish! . . . Trish! . . . I could laugh at that one. Patricia
Kelly . . . since when did that become 'Trish' I'd like to
know. And the way she dresses . . . somebody wants to tell
her she's a middle-aged bloody woman. That's England for
you . . . don't know what they are . . . and everybody
trying to be what they're not. Notions about herself that
one.

(MARY *rising and going to the sink to start the dishes.*)

MARY: They've invited us out with them tonight.

SEAN: Oh aye they're great ones for that. They'll take us out
and buy us drink . . . but I'm damned if they'll rise from
their beds and give us a hand with the work. Anyway, he
knows I wouldn't go to that place. I'm not working myself
into the ground up here, to go and hand it over to any
Orange barman . . . you wouldn't catch me dead in that
place.

MARY: Do you think I should make them a bit of breakfast and
call them?

SEAN: (*Rising. Drains his cup.*) Let them get their own
breakfasts and call nothing at them.

(SEAN *exits, wiping his hands down his trousers.* MARY *collects
his dishes from the table and takes them to the sink. Goes over
and tends the fire. Goes to living room door, collects a basket
and is leaving as* TRISH *comes downstairs.*)

MARY: Morning, Trish, help yourself to breakfast.

(TRISH *has a slight trace of an English accent. She is a good
looking forty-four-year-old, she dresses, makes up well. Kettle
on stove.* TRISH *starts to wash the dishes. Pause.* LIAM *enters.
He is forty-seven, but looks ten years older. He has an ample
beer-belly, his hair tousled, scruffy. He wears ill-fitting pyjama
bottoms, shirt and pullover. He smokes and scratches himself.*)

TRISH: (*Disapproving*) Will you take your hand out of there, it's
disgusting.

LIAM: (*To fireplace*) It's itchy.

TRISH: (*To table*) Look at the state of you . . . at least comb your hair and get properly dressed. Come on, before Mary walks back in.

LIAM: That's all right . . . she lives here.

TRISH: It doesn't show much respect for me, you running about like that.

LIAM: So that's it . . . not consideration for Mary at all?

TRISH: If you don't respect your own sister it's a bit late for me to teach you now.

LIAM: Ah ha, that's wrong. (*Thinks*) Wait now, did you say 'teach' or 'learn'?

TRISH: (*Dismissive*) I said what was right.

LIAM: Talking polite with an English accent doesn't mean talking right.

TRISH: Will you go and get dressed before I pour your coffee.

LIAM: Give me a drop of coffee and then I'll go. (*She pours his.*) This oul kitchen hasn't really changed since I was a wee lad. If I close my eyes I can just picture my mammy there, baking bread.

TRISH: Mammy! . . . for goodness' sake at least talk like a grown-up.

LIAM: Not a damn thing wrong with saying mammy . . . is there?

TRISH: Your father'll not approve of us lying on.

LIAM: I'm on holiday. I'll lie as long as I damned well like.

TRISH: You should be out there helping him. You're not really on holiday, since you're not working over there now. I'm on holiday.

LIAM: Oh aye . . . what about the holidays we came on before you started working eh?

TRISH: I was working . . . just then it happened to be as a housewife.

LIAM: You'll have to watch the way you sit in front of my da.

TRISH: What's wrong with the way I sit?

LIAM: He'll expect you to keep your legs a bit closer together . . . he doesn't approve of flighty women.

TRISH: Liam McCabe how dare you . . . I'm a decent

respectable woman. If your da sees my legs open it's because the dirty oul get's looking for it. You didn't take that habit after strangers. The cheek of you and you sitting like that . . . I can see all you've got. Will you go and change before they walk in on top of us?

LIAM: I'm going, 'cause you'd hurt my ears listening to you.

TRISH: Put on a clean shirt . . . (*As he goes*) . . . and have a bath.

(*She inspects herself and self-consciously closes her legs.*)

3. INT. FARMHOUSE

LIAM *is bathed and dressed. He wears an ill-fitting, old-fashioned suit and still doesn't look the right partner for his wife.* MARY *enters, the basket full of eggs. She places it on the table.* LIAM *at window.*

LIAM: You should have said . . . Trish could have collected those for you.

MARY: Not at all. Trish didn't come all this way to run after me collecting eggs.

TRISH: I'd be afraid of the spiders in the hen houses.

LIAM: You're all right, we've stopped collecting spiders' eggs. (*She glares.*)

MARY: Did you get breakfast?

TRISH: We had coffee . . . we never bother with breakfast. (MARY *???*)

LIAM: An English habit. I think an Ulster fry'd kill me now. (*Pause.*) What happened to the wall out there?

MARY: There was a new driver on the meal lorry . . . near a month ago. Easy enough done . . . I don't know how they manage those big lorries half the time.

LIAM: And you're driving your own car now. When did this all happen?

MARY: Sixteen or eighteen months. I took lessons in Limavady.

LIAM: (*Broad*) Many's the lassie tuck lessons in Limavady, especially in my day.

TRISH: Pay no attention, Mary . . . your brother grows coarser with advancing years. (*Pause.*) I'd love to drive. Did you pass first time?

MARY: Indeed now I did not . . . fourth time . . . I was on the verge of giving it up altogether.

LIAM: Sure you've been driving a tractor near since you could walk.

MARY: There's a wild difference between driving that round the farm, and passing the driving test.

LIAM: Aye . . . but the principle's the same.

TRISH: Anyway you've got it now, that's the main thing. You've given me hope. I'm taking lessons, but I find it very difficult. He won't let me near our own car.

LIAM: I think not. I don't want to be reported to the NSPCC.
(MARY *???*)
National Society for the Prevention of cruelty to clutches.

MARY: (*To* TRISH) You can take a go or two in mine while you're here.

TRISH: Thanks very much.
(LIAM *scoffs. She glares at him.*)

LIAM: You may tell my da to keep the livestock well locked up. (*Pause.*) What's he up to anyway?

MARY: He's down fixing at thon oul wall.

TRISH: Go you down and give him a hand . . . and you a bricklayer.

MARY: I'm sure he'd appreciate a hand right enough. He's that short tempered now . . . anything that doesn't go right gets kicked and sworn at.

LIAM: Jasus if that's the way he is I'm staying away . . . I can do without being kicked and cursed.

TRISH: Honestly you . . . will you go and give him a hand, and him an old man. (*Pause.* LIAM *is uncomfortable.*) Well . . . what are you waiting for? Away and give your father a hand out.
(*He goes, resentful.*)
Sometimes I could give him a good shake.

MARY: He was always a bit like that, our Liam. That's why him and my da never got on.

TRISH: It's why him and me don't get on most of the time.

MARY: What . . . there's no real bother between you, is there?

TRISH: No, no . . . just an old marriage, creaking with wear.
(*Laughs to disguise truth.*) What about you . . . no young
men chasing after you?

MARY: There aren't many young men and if they're chasing it's
not after me.

TRISH: I heard your father mentioning Grunter Maguire.

MARY: Grunter . . . sure he's the life pestered out of me. I
think him and my da think I'll just give up in the end. My
da likes the idea of the two farms being joined up.

TRISH: But you're not keen?

MARY: For goodness' sake, Trish. Like I know I'm no oil
painting . . . but God knows I'd like to think I could do
better than Grunter Maguire. His habits turn my stomach.

TRISH: He's not bad looking . . . I mean he'd clean up.
(MARY *gives her a look. They both laugh.*)
Did you never think of trying England?

MARY: Aye . . . once upon a time, when I was in my twenties.
What on earth could I do in England now, at my age?

TRISH: You're not old, Mary.

MARY: I'm thirty-three, and as plain as the local paper, and
know nothing but farm work. Naw . . . I'm stuck here by
the looks of things.

4. INT. THE KITCHEN, BARRACKS
The steak is cooking. WILL *moves to* DOBSON *and* JOHNSTONE.
PRIVATES JOHNSTONE *and* DOBSON *standing while* WILL
inspects their efforts.

WILL: It won't do . . . it just will not do. (*Pause.*) Dobson, I
want this floor mopped again . . . use hot water this time.

DOBSON: I used hot water, Corp.

WILL: Well use more, hotter water. Try some elbow grease as
well, lad . . . soap it then rinse it . . . you can't mop a floor
in one wipe. Another thing . . . it's Corporal . . . not
Corp . . . got it?

DOBSON: Yes, Corporal.

WILL: Johnstone . . . look at the scum round this sink, lad . . .
gunge isn't it?

JOHNSTONE: Yes, Corporal.

WILL: Yes, Corporal . . . well it shouldn't be, Private. Do you know what a metaphor is, sonny?

JOHNSTONE: Yes, Corporal.

WILL: Well, I'm a Welshman see . . . this kitchen is my valley . . . and I want my valley green . . . do you understand?

JOHNSTONE: Yes, Corporal.

WILL: Get on with it then.

DOBSON: (*With barely suppressed glee*) Corporal . . . I think your meat's burning.

> (WILL *squeals and dashes for the oven, slipping on* DOBSON'*s soapy floor. He retrieves his meat, burnt. He is seething with anger and close to tears.*)

WILL: (*As the* TWO PRIVATES *seek to hide their merriment*) Ruined . . . like a bloody flamethrower'd hit it. (*He goes and tips it into the slop bucket. Then he does the same with his garnish and side salad.* DOBSON *laughs aloud.* WILL *grabs him tightly by the collar with both hands. There is a tremble in his voice and tears in his eyes.*) One more sound, Private . . . just one and I'll put your stupid English head into that mop bucket and drown you. Do you get me? Johnstone . . . (DOBSON *nods and* WILL *pushes him aside.*)
> Do me four pieces of toast. Bring it to my room. Tea and lots of cheese as well. Hurry it up.

JOHNSTONE: (*Jumping to it*) Right away, Corporal.

WILL: (*As he goes*) Tonight's going to be a disaster . . . I can feel it in my bones.

> (*They watch him leave then fall about laughing.*)

DOBSON: I should have nutted the fat Welsh bastard.

JOHNSTONE: (*Mimicking*) I want my valley green . . . and covered in toast and cheese. (*Laughs.*)

DOBSON: (*Inspecting the slop bucket*) Lovely bit of steak . . . we could have ate that . . . few chips . . . just the job, stupid Taff bollocks.

5. EXT. THE FARM

SEAN *is organizing himself to start repairing the wall.* LIAM *comes sauntering along.*

SEAN: Oh, so you did decide to get up after all.

LIAM: The old place doesn't change much, does it?

SEAN: It's falling down round me. I can't keep things going the way I used to. Mary works hard, but sure she's a woman at the end of it all. If she'd get herself a man, we'd get things sorted out before it's too late.

LIAM: Could you not pay a man?

SEAN: I'd a bloody good man in Declan . . . before them murdering bastards came along. He was more of a son to me than any of my own.

LIAM: None of us were ever that keen on farm work.

SEAN: None of you were ever that keen on work of any description . . . that's the truth. I'm surprised you could manage a holiday at all, and you not even working.

LIAM: I'm nearly as well off on the dole.

SEAN: Aye . . . England can afford to pay more out than she brings in . . . with her blagards all over the world taking the food from everybody else.

LIAM: Sure if I hadn't been paid off I'd have had to leave. I was getting the old dermatitis . . . handling bricks and cement just doesn't agree with me.

(SEAN *looks at him.*)

SEAN: (*Sarcastic*) Isn't it just as well I didn't ask for help . . . as a refusal often offends.

LIAM: Sometimes I get a longing to come home . . . settle here.

SEAN: Huh. I couldn't see fancy pants agreeing to that . . . she'd be like an orchid in the nettles over here.

LIAM: She's got a good job over there . . . good money . . . secretary to a big business tycoon.

SEAN: So when did she start all this Trish business and all the fancy dressing up?

LIAM: The English like Trish . . .

SEAN: She's Patricia . . . why not Pat?

LIAM: (*Ignoring that*) And then with the job and that she needs to be well dressed.

24

SEAN: Your sister Mary can be well dressed . . . without
    looking like a mantrap.

LIAM: Can you not claim against the firm for him doing that?

SEAN: Mary was directing him . . . she must have forgot there
    were two sides to the bloody lorry.

LIAM: If it wasn't for the hands I'd put it up for you in no time.
    I was one of the best.

SEAN: You must have been, seeing as they got rid of you.

LIAM: It was a pay-off . . . I wasn't the only one. There's a
    recession. Blame Mrs Thatcher.

SEAN: That oul whore's a lot to answer for . . . but even she
    can't be blamed for making a lazy shite out of you.
    (SEAN *is gazing intently towards the farm, sees* CORPORAL
    DANIELS, SECOND LIEUTENANT *and four other soldiers
    approaching front door.*)
    Look at them bastards . . . Jasus if I was a young man
    again I'd blow the whole lot of them into hell.

LIAM: (*Looking*) Where? . . . Who?

SEAN: Brits . . . over there . . .

LIAM: Have they their faces blackened?

SEAN: With half of them the black's permanent . . . that's the
    quare insult, sending that lot over here with guns to shoot
    us.

LIAM: What are they doing?

SEAN: Snooping and prying. It's not enough to have murdered
    Declan . . . we're pestered with them. They'll have a great
    time this morning . . . questioning you and her ladyship.
    Come on away up for a cup of tea.
    (*They amble off,* LIAM *glancing back towards the soldiers.*)

6. INT. THE FARMHOUSE KITCHEN
A SECOND LIEUTENANT *is scribbling in his notebook. A* SOLDIER
stands guard, other SOLDIERS *are searching the farm buildings and
vicinity.* MARY *and* TRISH *are in the kitchen.* TRISH *is looking very
glamorous, showing a provocative amount of leg.*

LIEUTENANT: (*Stopping scribbling*) It's rather odd, Mrs McCabe,
    not to know when you're going back.

TRISH: It's up to my husband. We can stay for three weeks, but he could decide to go back tomorrow.

LIEUTENANT: (*Pause.*) What does your husband do?

TRISH: (*Shakes her head*) Not much, Officer. He's a bricklayer – unemployed.

(*Pause.*)

LIEUTENANT: (*Looking appreciatively at* TRISH) Have you no relations left in Ireland at all Mrs McCabe?

TRISH: Distant relatives . . . but nobody I bother with any longer. I've lived in England for a long time . . . I moved with Liam, my husband, the minute we got married.

LIEUTENANT: (*Scribbling again*) Liam. Could I ask you what your Christian name . . .

(*Before he's finished* SEAN *and* LIAM *enter. Pause.* SEAN *glares sullenly around, hatred burning in his face.*)

(*To* LIAM) Are you the unemployed bricklayer?

(LIAM *glares at* TRISH, *who instinctively covers her legs.*)

(*To* SEAN) What happened to your wall, Mr McCabe?

(SEAN *crosses to windows, ignoring the* LIEUTENANT.)

MARY: A lorry reversed into it, Officer.

LIEUTENANT: Thank you. (*To* TRISH) I was asking for your Christian name, Mrs McCabe . . .

TRISH: Trish.

(SEAN *grunts.*)

LIEUTENANT: T.R.I.S.H. (*Writes it.*) That's a nice name.

TRISH: (*Smiling warmly*) Thank you, Officer.

LIAM: (*Exploding*) Her name's Patricia over here. She only uses Trish in England because you bloody people won't say Patricia. So write it down properly, Patricia.

(LIAM *moves across to look in the book, the* SOLDIER *at the door moves towards him.* LIEUTENANT *holds up a hand to restrain the* SOLDIER.)

LIEUTENANT: P.A.T.R.I.C.I.A. . . . (*looking into* LIAM's *face*) . . . no need to get excited, Mr McCabe.

(LIEUTENANT *holds* LIAM's *gaze until* LIAM *moves away.* CORPORAL DANIELS *enters. He stares straight at* TRISH, *taken by her. She smiles at him, he grins back.*)

26

(*Pause.*) Anything, Corporal?

CORPORAL DANIELS: No . . . ah, no, sir . . . not a thing.
(*His gaze returns to* TRISH. SEAN *grunts and mumbles. Hold.*)

7. INT. THE OFFICERS' MESS

The INTELLIGENCE OFFICER *and the* SECOND LIEUTENANT
from the search are there, drinking coffee.

INTELLIGENCE OFFICER: The McCabes virtually invented the
IRA in this area.

LIEUTENANT: I think that's going a bit too far, sir. The old
fellow's a bit of a die-hard . . . but he's never actually been
active himself.

INTELLIGENCE OFFICER: The nephew, Declan Mulgrew . . .
shot dead when sniping, his rifle in his hand. We've had to
turn the farm over countless times . . . usually as the result
of a tip-off.

LIEUTENANT: Yes . . . but we've never actually found
anything. Tip-offs are more often the result of a feud
between neighbours.

INTELLIGENCE OFFICER: Interesting set-up though. (*Thinking*)
The son could be a nasty . . . a team . . . good looking
wife, lures you in . . . snap . . . he has you.
(LIEUTENANT *smirks.*)
Smirk, Lieutenant . . . you can afford to . . . you haven't
had to deal with these people as long as I have . . . you
don't know what they're capable of. Believe me, I've seen it
all. We've buried a few good men who took the Irish at face
value.

LIEUTENANT: Sir . . . she's a very friendly, pleasant, attractive
woman . . . she has a good job back in England . . . she's
almost lost her Irish accent.

INTELLIGENCE OFFICER: Yes . . . (*Pause, rising*) . . . I must
go. Well done, Lieutenant. An efficient platoon, and an
alert platoon commander make my life a lot easier.
(*He goes.* WILL *comes through, carrying a newspaper. The*
LIEUTENANT *is watching the* INTELLIGENCE OFFICER
going. WILL *gazes after him too for a moment.*)

WILL: Would you like a *Guardian*, sir?
   (*Passes it over.*)

LIEUTENANT: Thank you, Corporal. (*Folds it carefully and
   shoves it in a pocket.* WILL *smiles.*)
   Interesting man the Intelligence Officer.

WILL: Fascinating.

LIEUTENANT: Damned important job he does.

WILL: Crucial.

LIEUTENANT: Mind you, he's not very trusting.

WILL: Suspicious.

LIEUTENANT: Do you think . . . I mean no disrespect . . . do
   you think he's perhaps a little too imaginative?

WILL: His problem is he reads James Bond, in the original.
   (LIEUTENANT *???*)
   Intelligence reports . . . sir.

LIEUTENANT: (*Trying not to smile*) I must be off . . . thanks for
   the coffee, Corporal . . . (*As he turns back*) . . . oh, and the
   paper. (*Taps his pocket.*)

WILL: (*Picking up the cups*) You're welcome, sir.

8. INT. WILL'S ROOM

A Welsh choir is blasting out from the music centre. WILL *is dressed
in underpants and shirt, his socks are on. He is conducting the choir.
They are singing, perhaps, 'The Battle Hymn of the Republic' and*
WILL *is conducting the different sections of the choir. Hold. After a
moment he stops and listens, crosses over and turns the music down.
There is loud rapping on the door.*

BOB: Come on, Will.

WILL: (*Calling*) Just a minute. (*He pulls on his trousers and
   fastens them.*) Come in.
   (BOB DAVIS *enters, he looks around.*)

BOB: Good God, man . . . you'll burst your ear drums with that
   noise.

WILL: Noise! (*Flabbergasted*) That 'noise' just happens to be one
   of the greatest male voice choirs in the world . . .

BOB: Come on . . . we've been waiting.

WILL: Philistine.

(WILL *goes and turns the music centre off completely, removes the record lovingly and restores it to its sleeve. Hold.*)

9. EXT. HOTEL. NIGHT
BOB's *car approaches hotel, and stops.* BOB, MURIEL *and* WILL *walk to entrance.*

10. INT. THE LOUNGE
LIAM, TRISH *and* MARY *sitting drinking.*

TRISH: I've never been drunk in my life. Women can hold it better than men I think.

LIAM: Rubbish . . . hard drinking's a man's job.

TRISH: Huh . . . give me a penny for every time I've had to put you to bed and I wouldn't have to work.

LIAM: (*Grinning*) Stick to the drink . . . not your sex lust.

TRISH: Stop the smutty talk . . . have some manners.

LIAM: It was a joke.

TRISH: That's how I try to pass you off too.

MARY: I don't know what people get out of a whole lot of drink.

TRISH: Have you never, Mary?

MARY: I've had lager and lime . . . at weddings and that . . . but I've no real liking for it.
  (TRISH *looks off right.*)
  (*Four people up steps to bar.* BOB, MURIEL, WILL *entering,* MURIEL, WILL *to table.* BOB *exits left.*)

TRISH: (*Looking around*) Not much by the way of talent here tonight. Maybe later we'll have a wee dance . . . maybe the big fish come later. (*Pause.*) Have you been to a dance here, Mary?

MARY: I haven't been to a dance for years. I used to go regular with Bridie and Shivaun. But sure Bridie's married and living in Coleraine. Shivaun went to the nursing in England. (*Pause. Drinks.*) I wish to God I'd gone with her when she asked me.
  (TRISH *and* LIAM *look at each other.*)

LIAM: Sure the da can't last for ever . . . then the farm's yours. You're your own woman then . . . You'll have the pick of the men.

MARY: I think if he was away tomorrow I'd have it in next week's auction . . . but then what would I do with myself?

LIAM: I'll come back and be your farm manager, eh?

MARY: I don't think you'd be much of a manager. Would you come back here to live, Trish?

TRISH: Oh God, I'd die sooner . . . or I'd die soon after I arrived, if I . . .

LIAM: There's a lot to be said though for ending up where you belong.

TRISH: You know, Mary I get this nonsense all the time. As soon as he puts the glass to his lips, the tears come into his eyes . . . then it's all the oul sod . . . he even dresses like somebody hankering to go back.

LIAM: I was born on that farm . . . it's been in our family for generations. I can't tell you how to live your life, Mary, but remember that's the old family home . . . we all feel for it.

MARY: None of you ever felt enough to stay and help my da to run it.

LIAM: My da was impossible . . . you know that. Sure it was slave labour. I worked on that farm from when I was big enough to stand. And the most I ever got for it was a boot up the arse, every time I dropped an egg, or spilt a drop of milk. My da was never going to pay any of us a living wage for working. And don't give me any old eye-wash about sharing the profits.

MARY: It was our Joe's place to stay and work it, the eldest son. I know my da virtually took it out on you and Michael when Joe ran off . . . but you never really tried.

LIAM: He wanted us all to join the IRA . . . do our bit in the struggle. Jasus, it didn't half dent his old ego when his oldest son ran away with a local Orangeman's daughter. (*Laughs.*)

TRISH: Keep your voice down . . . the whole place'll know your business.
(*Pause.*)

MARY: Do you know where our Joe is?

LIAM: Damned if I do. Canada was the last place I heard.

MARY: My da says it killed my mother.

LIAM: She took a long time about dying if it did.

TRISH: Every time two McCabes get together you go over the same old things. Another few of those and we'll be having the few tears for Michael. It's like stale vomit.
(*They both look at her, surprised.*)
Well . . . let's have a night out for once, when we just try and enjoy ourselves. Why would your da not come with us, Mary?

MARY: This place is owned by Protestants, and the Brits use it.

TRISH: It's a hateful term that . . . Brits . . . it's worse than a swear word I think.

LIAM: Don't we get Paddy all the time?

TRISH: That's not as bad . . . you can almost spit, Brit . . . and a lot of them do. I could never live in this place again . . . it's unhealthy.

LIAM: Unhealthy . . . Christ's sake woman . . . we lived for months just waiting for the Yorkshire Ripper to slit your throat . . . that's unhealthy.

TRISH: That's different though . . . that's just ordinary murder . . . but this!

LIAM: Different . . . I'll tell you this, will I? Listen . . . if the boyos here were as efficient as that Ripper fella . . . there'd be no bloody population left here in a couple of years.

MARY: Could I have another orange juice, Liam?

LIAM: What! . . . oh aye . . . right. (*Rises. To* TRISH) Is it still vodka for you.

TRISH: Unless they've changed it . . . I haven't.
(*He goes.*)

MARY: Is all that just creaking with wear?

TRISH: He's your brother, Mary . . . but, well . . .

MARY: What'll you do if he does decide to come home?

TRISH: Sell up and move down to London. You have to live outside this place to really see it for what it is. I used to think of myself as an Irishwoman . . . you soon learn. Saturday nights being a doormat for a lot of yobs in the Irish Centre, it soon taught me. Now I'm just a woman.

MARY: One of these liberated ones?

TRISH: I wouldn't go quite that far . . . Not married to your Liam. It's like having one of the anchors of the *Titanic* for a necklace.

11. INT. LOUNGE. HOTEL

LIAM *and* WILL *move from the bar*.

WILL: Pity about David and Marion.

BOB: He welched on the Welsh.

ALL: Cheers!

MURIEL: You know, Will we can't have you buying a round every time . . . there are two of us.

WILL: It's no problem.

MURIEL: It's a principle though. I mean if David and Marion wcrc here you'd do the same.

BOB: Maybe the womenfolk should start paying their way, eh?

MURIEL: Fine by me . . . provided there's allowance made for it in my wages.
(*Music starts*.)

BOB: Anyway . . . we're not going to be drinking that much.

MURIEL: Talk cash and Bob's ambitions immediately shrink.

BOB: No . . . I'm just saying . . .

MURIEL: I know what you're saying, love . . . anyway, Will didn't come for a night out to listen to us bickering.

BOB: Are we bickering?

MURIEL: No . . . but we're preparing the ground for it . . . I've learnt to read the signs.
(*All smile*.)
Have you been here before, Will?

WILL: Once or twice actually . . . just for a pint in passing as it were.

MURIEL: It's nice to get out now and again . . . into the community. It makes you feel that you at least still belong in the real world.

BOB: This is real?

MURIEL: The rural Irish are very like ourselves I find.

BOB: Nev . . . er . . . absolute rubbish. What do you say, Will?

WILL: I suppose there's something in that . . . we're both peasant races.

BOB: The Welsh are aristocratic peasants. Look what we've given to the world . . . Dylan Thomas, Richard Burton, Tom Jones . . . artists.

MURIEL: Max Boyce.

WILL: Lloyd George.

BOB: Who have the Irish given? Eamon Bloody Andrews and Danny Frigging La Rue.

MURIEL: He's not Irish. I like him.

BOB: Born in Cork. Talking of drag artists you know, they say there's a transvestite in B Company.

WILL: He must be the only normal one amongst that lot.
(*They laugh.* BOB *rises.*)

BOB: Must visit the wee house.
(*He goes.*)

MURIEL: It's nice to have you with us, Will. I wish you'd come more often.

WILL: The thought of going out never appeals to me much. Bob just wears me down . . . and I enjoy it in the end. (*Looks to* MARY.)

MURIEL: How's your mother?

WILL: She's fine again. It took a while to get over Dad . . . These things do. (*Looks to* MARY.) My sister lives close by, that helps.

MURIEL: You haven't come round yet to cook us that special meal?

WILL: I must do that soon.

MURIEL: Bob was saying you were doing yourself something rather special today . . . I'm afraid it made my macaroni cheese seem less than ample to him.

WILL: Take consolation from the fact that mine didn't work out quite as I'd hoped.
(WILL *is not comfortable with women, even a friend's wife and fellow countrywoman. The conversation dies.*)

12. INT. THE FARM KITCHEN

SEAN *is sitting with* GRUNTER MAGUIRE, *a neighbouring farmer in his mid-forties.*

GRUNTER: I thought the Liam fella would have throwed that oul bit of a wall back up for you in no time at all.

SEAN: He can't work at the bricks any more . . . dermatitis.

GRUNTER: Boyso . . . he'll get a right claim for that.

SEAN: Not from the dole he'll not.

GRUNTER: (*Alert*) Oh . . . on the dole. I thought that fella'd the great job.

SEAN: Paid-off. Sure that woman Thatcher's putting all the Irish on the dole. Trying to drive them out by the way.

GRUNTER: Isn't thon the sly oul bitch. You know I sometimes think to myself that one was born in a litter.

SEAN: Had you them Brits round the day?

GRUNTER: Aye they were mootching about there for an hour or more. They were civil enough.
(SEAN *looks at him.*)
I give them a pot of tea and a handful of jam sandwiches.

SEAN: You give them more than I would.

GRUNTER: You know I don't think they half feed them young ones . . . maybe that's what makes them so aggressive.

SEAN: Why do you give them tea?

GRUNTER: Now they're always civil with me, Sean. Besides . . . I be nice to them, before they can be nasty with me . . . they give me no bother that way. Besides, thon sister of mine's that much jam made I could open a wee shop.

SEAN: I'm tired, Grunter.

GRUNTER: I'll run away on, if you want to lie down.

SEAN: I don't mean just tired tonight . . . tired. I'm seventy-six you know. I'm not able for this place any longer. Mary's a great girl . . . but a farm needs a man.

GRUNTER: I didn't realize you were that far on, Sean.

SEAN: With three sons I should have been able to put my feet up at fifty.

GRUNTER: I couldn't see you being the man for that . . . sure you've never stopped.

SEAN: Still . . . I never had the option . . . that's the difference.
(*Draining his bottle.*) Neck another couple of them bottles.

GRUNTER: (*Opening two more*) There's nothing to beat the
Guinness.

SEAN: As the man says, there's nothing to beat the bottle of
Guinness . . . bar two bottles.
(*They chuckle, like men hearing a good joke for the first time.*)

13. INT. THE DANCE HALL

There aren't many there. Some are on the floor. WILL *and* MARY
are sitting quite close. BOB *and* MURIEL, TRISH *and* LIAM, *are
dancing.* WILL *and* MARY *occupy an almost deserted side of the
hall.* WILL *keeps looking across at* MARY. *When she returns his
look, both drop their eyes, embarrassed. The others are dancing.*
WILL *and* MARY *are stealing glances at each other.* WILL *drains his
glass, pauses a moment, rises and crosses to* MARY.

WILL: (*Embarrassed*) Excuse me . . . could I have a dance please?

MARY: (*Shy*) I'm sorry, no thank you.
(WILL *stands as though unable to move. Not sure what to do.
He turns away.*)
I'm not really very good . . . (*Pause.*) . . . Perhaps we
could try? (*She looks around. Rises.*) All right . . . but I'm
really not very good.
(*They go on to the floor, apologizing to each other.*)

14. INT. THE FARM KITCHEN

More empty bottles around.

SEAN: No . . . no . . . I find it hard to forgive.

GRUNTER: But they're like our own lads . . . that oul bitch has
left them without jobs to go to. Most of them haven't a
notion what it's all about.

SEAN: They know how to shoot them bloody guns . . . how to
kill.

GRUNTER: So do I . . . brought up on a farm . . . and so do
you.

SEAN: Why are they here . . . this is our country?

GRUNTER: Do you know . . . they don't know why they're

here . . . they haven't a clue. Talk to them . . . they
can't understand it at all.

SEAN: Do you know what . . . I fancy a bowl of porridge . . . a
bowl of hot porridge and a mug of good strong tea, how
does that sound?

GRUNTER: Like a feast, Sean . . . come on, get cracking.

15. INT. THE DANCE FLOOR

MARY *and* WILL *have just stumbled to a halt. Both laugh,
embarrassed.*

WILL: Sorry . . . my fault again.

MARY: No, I think it was me . . . I left my left foot in too long.
(*Pause. They get going again.*)
Are you a soldier?

WILL: How did you guess?
(*They laugh.*)

MARY: Welsh are you . . . you sound Welsh?

WILL: I am . . . from the valleys.

MARY: Are you an officer?

WILL: Not quite . . . but I try to be a gentleman.

MARY: I'm sorry, I suppose I shouldn't ask questions. I suppose
you're all top secret.

WILL: There's a stamp on the sole of my right foot . . . this side
up, confidential.
(*They stumble again and giggle again.*)

16. INT. THE LOUNGE AREA

BOB *and* MURIEL, *now sitting.*

BOB: I don't believe it . . . she must have threatened him.

MURIEL: (*Dreamy*) It's lovely to see him happy.

BOB: They're not exactly the most graceful couple on the floor.

MURIEL: But they look like one of the closest . . . they're really
looking at each other.

BOB: Give over, woman . . . I think I'll cancel your subscription
to *Woman's Own*.

MURIEL: We just take each other for granted . . . we don't look
at each other like that anymore.

BOB: Hey, where are they off to?

MURIEL: Well come on, give the lad a chance . . . he's probably away for a drink . . . then the twenty formal questions . . . then the date . . . have you forgotten how it happens?

17. INT. THE LOUNGE AREA

LIAM *at bar,* CORPORAL DANIELS *and* SOLDIERS *also at the bar.*

LIAM *moves from the bar.*

LIAM *joins* TRISH.

LIAM: (*As he sits*) They're going to sit down, thank God. (*Pause. Looking around.*) Christ, I hope people don't realize she's with us.

TRISH: What's wrong with you?

LIAM: People were laughing at them, did you see?

TRISH: So what . . . they seemed happy enough and they didn't seem to notice.

LIAM: One fall, one submission, or a knockout to decide the next dance.

TRISH: You're not quite Gene Kelly yourself.

LIAM: Why not Fred Astaire? If I didn't know you better you'd be telling me Gene Kelly was an uncle.

TRISH: I don't know why I bother coming out with you.
    (WILL *and* MARY *go to dance.*)

LIAM: Nobody else's prepared to buy you drink. (*Head in hands.*) Ah Jasus . . . they're on the floor again . . . look . . . he's fat . . .

TRISH: Well . . . she's skinny . . . so what?

LIAM: So what . . . it's like watching two of the frigging Mister Men. (*Rising*) I'm away for a pee . . . (*He looks on to the floor.*) . . . a long one.
    (*He goes. Pause.* CORPORAL DANIELS, *a good looking, younger man, starts eyeing* TRISH. *She smiles. He approaches. He was one of the search team earlier. He has an English accent.*)

CORPORAL DANIELS: Can I have a dance please?

TRISH: (*Takes a sip from her drink and rises.*) Certainly . . .
    (*He leads her on to the floor.*)

18. INT. THE FARM KITCHEN

SEAN *and* GRUNTER *sitting. The empty porridge bowls sitting.*
Pouring themselves more tea.

SEAN: We'll be pishing all night.

GRUNTER: Cleans out the system. I'll nip across in the morning
and we'll put that oul wall together.

SEAN: Good man. (*Checking his watch*) I wonder what time
they'll roll back in?

GRUNTER: There's a dance and all down there I hear.

SEAN: Devil the dance Mary'll go to. Mind you that other one
looks game for that sort of carry-on. (*Pause.*) England spoils
them. Kills a good Catholic upbringing.

GRUNTER: The young ones now like their bit of fun.

SEAN: Young . . . are you drunk? Thon one's near as old as you are.

GRUNTER: I know that . . . but she was younger when she went
across.

SEAN: A quare nice, quiet, girl too, Patricia Kelly. None of this
oul Trish business. You know what I'm going to tell you,
Grunter?

(GRUNTER *looks questioningly.*)

SEAN: The English are the laziest speaking people in the world.
Give them a word and they'll shorten it. Sure you watch
them Brits . . . you'll not get a word out of them where a
grunt or a nod'll do.

GRUNTER: Right enough . . . mind you, I think sometimes
they've trouble with the accents.

SEAN: Aye . . . their own . . . (*Exaggerated laugh.*)

19. INT. DANCE FLOOR/LOUNGE

The band play the last bars of the National Anthem and finish. The
people are leaving. BOB *and* MURIEL *go to their table.* TRISH *and*
CORPORAL DANIELS *go to* TRISH's *table.* WILL *and* MARY *go to*
another table. WILL *and* MARY *are sitting together, away from their*
respective company.

MARY: I'd like to right enough . . . but it's not always easy.

WILL: (*Scribbling on a piece of paper*) Here's my phone number
. . . you could ring.

(MARY *reluctant.*)

If we make an arrangement now . . . you could ring if anything comes up like.

MARY: I'm not very good about this . . . I mean I never go out much.

WILL: Nor me . . . but I've never had so good a reason before.

(MARY *drops her head, embarrassed.*)

We'll just be friends, Mary . . . I mean . . .

MARY: I know . . . aye . . . (*Looking at him, shyly, smiling*) . . . well why not?

(MARY *takes the paper.*)

20. INT. LOUNGE AREA, HOTEL

LIAM *and* TRISH, *obviously strained.*

LIAM: You could have told him to clear off.

TRISH: I felt like a dance . . . and you'd gone for a long pee.

LIAM: I was back in seconds.

TRISH: Well you were too late.

LIAM: I should have come over and knocked him out from behind his stupid grin. You should have seen yourselves . . . and you old enough to be his ma.

(MARY *enters.*)

TRISH: (*Furious*) Thanks to you I'm nobody's ma.

LIAM: (*Pointing*) Now you listen to me . . .

(MARY *comes over.*)

MARY: (*Sensing the atmosphere*) Sorry if I've held you up.

LIAM: (*Rises*) Don't worry about us. If we'd known you were falling in love we'd have got a taxi.

MARY: Don't you dare talk to me like that.

LIAM: I suppose yours was a Brit too . . . thank Jasus my da didn't come.

MARY: Liam McCabe, you'd better guard your mouth . . . (*She lifts the remains of the drink she left and throws it round him.*) . . . otherwise I'll break it.

(*She storms off,* TRISH *laughing in her wake.* LIAM *wipes himself. Notices he's being watched. Gives the two fingers and storms after the ladies.*)

21. INT. LOUNGE AREA

MARY *and* TRISH *hurry out of the lounge.* BOB, MURIEL, *and*
WILL *ready to leave, immediately after* LIAM.

BOB: That's a real little charmer for you.

MURIEL: You're sure that wasn't his wife you were dancing
with, Will?

WILL: No . . . his sister as a matter of fact.

BOB: The other one must have been his wife . . . they seemed to
be narking at each other half the night.
(MURIEL *digs him, he laughs.*)

MURIEL: She was dancing with that lovely dark haired corporal
from B Company.

WILL: He needn't worry about him . . . from B Company the
worst that can happen is he'll borrow her dress.
(*They go laughing to the steps.*)

22. EXT. THE CAR PARK OUTSIDE THE HOTEL

TRISH, MARY *and* LIAM *going back to* MARY'S *car.* LIAM *still
furious. The corporal who danced with* TRISH, CORPORAL
DANIELS, *is also there.*

CORPORAL DANIELS: (*When* TRISH *has passed*) Goodnight,
Trish.

TRISH: Goodnight, love.

LIAM: What the hell . . . (*Rushing to the* CORPORAL) . . . hey
you, Brit balls . . . come 'ere.
(*As soon as he reaches* CORPORAL DANIELS *he punches him on
the face.* TRISH *and* MARY *scream and rush across.* DANIELS
and LIAM *are swinging punches at each other.* DANIELS *rushes
at* LIAM *and they tumble to the ground.* SERGEANT DAVIS *and*
WILL *rush across and drag them apart.* LIAM, TRISH *and*
MARY *go to their car.*)

23. INT. THE FARM KITCHEN. MUCH LATER

SEAN *sitting with* MARY, TRISH *and* LIAM. LIAM *has a bruise on
his face.*

LIAM: (*Inspecting his hand*) I think I've broken something.

SEAN: I hope it was that Brit's jaw. (*Pause.*) They come over

here and think they've a licence to molest our women. You
did right, Liam.

TRISH: Did he . . . did he?

SEAN: Course he did . . . you're his wife.

TRISH: I'm me . . . me . . . I've the right to dance with whom I
please.

SEAN: You've no right to dance with a Brit.

TRISH: Brit . . . what do you know about Brits? You've set up
on this hill, festering, for years. You've never done nothing
for anyone.

LIAM: Here you . . . that's enough.

TRISH: Why . . . do you think you'll break your other hand on
me? It would be the first and last time let me tell you.

SEAN: (*In a voice meant to silence opposition*) You shouldn't have
been dancing with no lousy Brit. And as for you, Mary . . .
you . . . have you no shame?

MARY: (*White*) Yes, Da . . . I'm ashamed of you. I'm sick of you
and I'm ashamed of you.

SEAN: Is that so . . . do you forget those bastards murdered
your cousin? Do you forget they gunned him down in cold
blood?

MARY: He was in the IRA.

SEAN: He was fighting for his country's freedom . . . don't you
dare slander a hero in my house.

MARY: Hero . . . a cruel, vicious thug . . . a lout who could
barely write his own name. He was lying behind a wall with
a rifle when they shot him.

SEAN: He was wounded and the scum riddled him with bullets.
A quiet, civil, God-fearing Catholic lad.

MARY: Da you're not talking to a reporter from the *Belfast
Telegraph*. I knew him . . . I know what he was. He was the
one who'd murdered in cold blood . . . Why didn't you tell
them that? No . . . when they brought that up you threw
them off the farm.

SEAN: I'm warning you, lassie . . . you will not talk like that
about Declan in my house. You'll not do it.

MARY: I had a few dances with a quiet, respectable, Welsh

cook. If my 'big' brother hadn't caused a whole row you'd
have known nothing about it.

SEAN: There is no such thing as a quiet, respectable Brit soldier.
They're the dregs of every prison in that God accursed
country.

TRISH: Don't you talk rubbish . . .

SEAN: It's a fact . . . a well known fact . . . do you read your
history? What were the Black and Tans?

TRISH: I wasn't dancing with a Black and Tan . . . (*Pointing to*
LIAM) There's the closest I ever came to a Black and
Tan . . . because half the time that dirty, lazy, frigger
won't even wash. And if the British Army was recruited
from the prisons then the most of them would be bloody
Irish.

LIAM: Trish . . . you show some respect for my father.

TRISH: Do you . . . I didn't tell him a whole pack of lies about
dermatitis. (*At* SEAN) That lazy bastard never had
dermatitis in his life. He threw up a good job because he
wants to come home and pick up his inheritance. (TRISH
claws off her wedding rings and flings them at LIAM.) Well
he's on his bloody own. I can't breathe over here . . . (*At*
SEAN) People like you has the air polluted. (*Flouncing out*)
I'm going to bed . . . and you'd better find somewhere to
sleep down here. (*She goes upstairs. Silence.*)

SEAN: I warned you about those bloody Kellys . . . an ill-bred
pack.

MARY: You'd better pick those rings up before they're lost.

LIAM: Let them lie . . . they mean nothing anyway. (*Inspecting
his hand again*) I think something's broke. I'll maybe need
to get it X-rayed. (*Pause.*) If you give me a day or two, Da,
I'll do that wall for you.

SEAN: I think you've enough to rebuild, without worrying about
my wall. It wouldn't surprise me that one's away home
tomorrow.

LIAM: That peeler said they could slap an exclusion order on
me.

SEAN: You're a bigot if you stand up for yourself. I don't hate

without good reason. It's all right . . . none of you know
what it's really been like here over the years. We've had this
all our lives you know . . . first the B Specials, now these
pimply faced jailbirds . . .

MARY: For goodness sake give it a rest.

(*Pause.* LIAM *rises and picks up the rings.*)

LIAM: I'm away up . . .

(*Pause. He goes.* MARY *and* SEAN *sit across the fire from each
other.*)

SEAN: (*Quietly*) It was just a dance? No harm in that I suppose.
It was just a one night thing?

MARY: Da . . . I've the right to enjoy myself. I've the right to
lead my own life.

SEAN: So you're intending seeing him again?

MARY: I intend seeing him again.

SEAN: When you come into this farm you can have your pick.

MARY: I think Liam's back for the farm.

SEAN: That fella couldn't work a farm . . . talk sense. We
agreed it all a long time ago. You stayed with me . . . and I
promised you this place.

MARY: We'd better go to bed. (*Rises.*) I'll rinse these few things.
Away you on up.

(*She goes to the sink. He rises, stops.*)

SEAN: They'll not let you . . . the neighbours round here . . .
there are some things you just can't do.

(*He stands. She carries on, ignoring him. He turns and trudges
off.*)

24. INT. THE MAJOR 2IC'S OFFICE

CORPORAL DANIELS *is standing, his beret under his arm. The* RSM
stands behind him. The MAJOR *is furious.*

MAJOR: You are supposed to be a soldier . . . you're supposed
to exercise control . . . set an example . . . not go rolling
about the gutter with a local savage . . . and McCabe above
all.

CORPORAL DANIELS: Sir . . .

MAJOR: Quiet, Corporal . . . there is no excuse for what

43

occurred . . . I'm not interested in your explanations . . . it happened and it should not have happened. Your action could result in soldiers being confined to barracks. I don't want this sort of behaviour . . . I will not tolerate it. Do I make myself clear?

CORPORAL DANIELS: Yes, sir.

MAJOR: You're an NCO . . . I could have those two stripes off you for this. (*Leafing through a report*) You have an excellent record . . . You've been a good soldier . . . (*He stares at him*) . . . however, I'm going to make an example of you. Every man on this camp will know this type of outrage will not be tolerated. (*Pause.* MAJOR *prepares to write.*) You will be stopped five days' pay and three days' leave, clear? (CORPORAL DANIELS *visibly balks.*) Is that clear, Corporal?

CORPORAL DANIELS: Yes, sir.

MAJOR: Thank you, Sergeant Major.

(*The* SERGEANT MAJOR *opens the door.* CORPORAL DANIELS *marches out.* RSM *exits.*)

25. INT. THE SMALLER HOTEL LOUNGE

MARY *and* WILL *are sitting drinking.*

MARY: I'll make a picnic. It's a beautiful spot . . . so long as it doesn't rain.

WILL: I'm used to the rain.

MARY: But I want you to see it at its best.

WILL: I will . . . I'll see it with you.

(JOHNSTONE *and* DOBSON *pass the table, carrying pints.*)

DOBSON: Evening, Corporal . . .

(*They pass sniggering.* WILL *is furious.*)

MARY: (*Embarrassed*) Who are they?

WILL: Mess waiters . . . they work for me . . . I'll . . .

MARY: I know nothing of your world . . . and you know nothing of mine. We should be able to get to know each other's worlds.

WILL: You can come home with me . . . I've told you.

MARY: I work on a farm . . . I'm all my father has.

WILL: We can go to the barracks . . . I have my own

44

quarters . . . you wouldn't have to mix . . . if you didn't
want to.

MARY: Will . . . you don't really understand, do you? If I was
seen going into an army barracks . . . you don't know this
place.

WILL: What are we asking from these people? All we want is to
be left alone . . . to have our own little romance . . . it's
not going to shake the world . . . (*Thumping the table*) What
is wrong with that?

(MARY *places her hand over his closed fist.*)

MARY: It's not us . . . not just us . . . it's what we represent
. . . you to your side, me to mine.

WILL: I'm a cook . . . that's all. I don't carry a gun . . . I don't
beat people up, or interrogate them . . . I'm not a part of
that.

MARY: That's not the way people round here think.

WILL: People round here don't think at all . . . that's half the
problem, as far as I can tell. Look at us . . . two grown up
people who want to be together . . . we meet once a week
. . . twice on a good week . . . in a run-down rural hotel –
earth-shattering I don't think.

26. INT. THE FARM KITCHEN. DAY FOUR

MARY *is in kitchen at window.* TRISH *and* LIAM *are going back.*
TRISH *comes downstairs with case. Walks to table.*

TRISH: You don't have to take us the whole way to the airport
you know.

MARY: I think my da would quite like to see all the planes. He
wouldn't admit it though.

TRISH: I won't be glad to leave you . . . that's not what I
meant . . .

MARY: I know what you meant . . . I don't blame you. (*Pause.*)
Are you and Liam all right?

TRISH: Me and Liam are as we've been for years, love. We go
our own ways, more or less. We don't stick around as much
together over there. But you know what appearances are
over here.

MARY: Why did you come over at all?

TRISH: I'm not altogether sure . . . a mixture of daft notions in Liam's head. Also your dad isn't getting any younger.

MARY: Or any easier.

(*They smile.*)

He'll go suddenly . . . I know that. I'll hear a tap running somewhere and find him face down in the mud. Or he'll fall down in the ditch, in the corner of one of his fields. The Brits'll find him . . . I hope he's dead when they do for all their sakes. He'd think he was in hell.

(*They laugh.*)

TRISH: What about your Brit? (*Pause. Angry.*) Christ, I hate that term. What about Will?

MARY: He's fine . . . we meet . . . he sends me letters in plain brown envelopes. My da thinks I'm running up bills somewhere.

TRISH: Do you think he'll die before you fall in love?

MARY: (*Pause. Softly.*) He hasn't.

(TRISH *reaches out and covers* MARY's *hand with her own.*)

27. INT. THE OFFICERS' MESS KITCHEN

PRIVATES JOHNSTONE *and* DOBSON *are standing stiffly to attention.* WILL *is angry.*

WILL: Two stupid little wankers . . . what are you, Dobson?

DOBSON: Stupid little wankers.

(WILL *stamps down hard on his toes and screams at him.*)

WILL: Stupid little wankers . . . Corporal. What are you?

DOBSON: (*In pain*) Stupid little wankers, Corporal.

WILL: Stand up straight. I could have been with anyone. How did you know people knew who I was . . . breach of security . . . I could have you two up on a charge. Section 69 of the Army Act 1965. Conduct prejudicial to good order and military discipline in that you two little wankers did endanger my life. I could have you pair confined to barracks for the remainder of your tour . . . is that clear?

BOTH: Yes, Corporal.

JOHNSTONE: We're sorry, Cor –

WILL: (*Loudly*) Shut it . . . shut it and keep it shut . . . that's the whole trouble, isn't it . . . big bloody mouths. Now, I want this whole place so clean that the officers are going to get down from that table and eat off the floor . . . got that?

BOTH: Yes, Corporal.

WILL: I'll be across in my quarters. Report to me when you're finished. I'll come and inspect it.

(*He goes. They stand rigid for a few moments, to make sure he's really gone.*)

DOBSON: Fat bastard . . . I think he's broke my toes.

(*Sits and starts to remove his boot.*)

JOHNSTONE: But, baby . . . what about the bird . . . and why does fat man not want her to know who he is?

DOBSON: Skinny bird like that . . . get her pregnant it'll show in two weeks.

JOHNSTONE: I reckon as ugly birds go she's a prizewinner.

DOBSON: How do you reckon Fat Taff does it then – mean he can't have seen his jolly old cock for years.

JOHNSTONE: It's like touch typing, isn't it? (*He makes thrusting actions with the brush.*) In out, two, three . . . in, out, two, three.

(*They laugh.*)

DOBSON: Here . . . you reckon he ever brings her back here?

JOHNSTONE: Don't be daft . . . he doesn't want her to know who he is, he's not going to bring her home, is 'e. I know he's Welsh . . . but even a Taff can't be that daft.

DOBSON: Here . . . I'd love to find out who she is.

JOHNSTONE: What for . . . you fancy her too then?

DOBSON: Shag off . . . no . . . what's old Will's surname then?

JOHNSTONE: Surname . . . Pryce . . . (*Mimics*) Corporal Taff Will Pryce.

DOBSON: If we could find out where the dragon lives . . . we could send a little letter to the cave . . . signed Taff Will Bloody Fat Bollocks Pryce.

(*They roar with laughter.*)

47

28. INT. THE FARM KITCHEN

MARY *is made-up. She is at dresser looking for something.* SEAN *and* GRUNTER *are there drinking tea.*

SEAN: What on earth's the attraction in Ballymena?

MARY: I just want to have a look around . . . there's a few new shops.

SEAN: When did you start taking such a big interest in shops? And make-up . . . you look like one of Fossetts' clowns. (GRUNTER *sniggers. Then makes his grunt.* MARY *looks at him in disgust.*)

GRUNTER: Great ones for the shops and wasting good money, the women. That sister of mine's the same. Dresses for this, dresses for that. Then she's never out over the door to wear them. (*Grunts again.*)

MARY: (*Disgusted*) I think when I am out I'll buy you a packet of handkerchiefs and teach you to use them. (*She goes.*)

SEAN: The women can be quare and cutting when they take a mind.

GRUNTER: Thon was a right big box she put in the car as I came in.

SEAN: Doesn't like going in for dinner . . . so makes herself a pile of sandwiches. I blame that fancy pants one. Mary hasn't been the same since thon one was about the place.

GRUNTER: And Liam gubbed the soldier . . . (*Sniggers*) . . . gubbed him in the middle of the street.
(*Laughs.* SEAN *joins him.*)

29. INT. THE MAJOR 2IC'S OFFICE

MAJOR *enters with the* INTELLIGENCE OFFICER.

INTELLIGENCE OFFICER: It's all very worrying, Major. Corporal Pryce and Mary McCabe . . . Then Corporal Daniels and Liam McCabe trying to assassinate each other in the gutter. McCabe should have faced an attempted GBH charge.

MAJOR: According to the RUC report, Corporal Daniels had been making passes at McCabe's wife.

INTELLIGENCE OFFICER: We know our RUC friends like nothing better than to throw mud at soldiers. Corporal

Daniels tells a different story. According to him she was
encouraging him all night.

MAJOR: . . . Encouragement . . . Corporal Daniels . . . he's one
of the reasons we don't have a mascot.

INTELLIGENCE OFFICER: It's well known the McCabe woman
likes to flaunt herself.

(*Pause.*)

MAJOR: (*Wearily*) Have you spoken to Corporal Pryce?

INTELLIGENCE OFFICER: . . . my job is to gather and collate
information . . . not question suspects.

MAJOR: Suspects . . . Corporal Pryce? Now come on . . . I've
suspected Corporal Pryce of a few things . . . mainly that
he'd no interest in women. I'm quite relieved to discover
that my chef is normal.

INTELLIGENCE OFFICER: With all due respect, Major . . . I
don't think you're taking this matter seriously enough.

MAJOR: (*Irritated*) I take my food very seriously. (*Pause.
Thinks.*) All right . . . I'll have a word with him.

INTELLIGENCE OFFICER: Can I be present?

MAJOR: At the questioning of suspects? . . . We must have
lunch together – in case he tries to poison me.

(*Pause. They look at each other.*)

INTELLIGENCE OFFICER: It has been known.

30. EXT. BISHOP'S ROAD
The Bishop's Road overlooking Downhill beach. MARY *and* WILL
standing holding hands. They are looking down.

MARY: Well . . . do you like it?

WILL: It's magnificent . . . bloody magnificent, begging the
pardon of ladies . . . but it bloody is.

MARY: That's Donegal over there.

WILL: Donegal . . . the South?

MARY: Well the North-West . . . but the Republic.

WILL: It's close isn't it. I hadn't realized. Wouldn't be a big job
to run guns up on to that beach, would it?

MARY: I wouldn't know anything about that.

WILL: Of course not . . . I wasn't suggesting . . .

MARY: Let's go down on to the beach.
(*They clamber back into the car, laughing happily.*)

31. EXT. THE FARM

SEAN *and* GRUNTER *working on the wall. They have it almost restored.*

SEAN: Dermatitis my backside. She let it all out one night in a temper.

GRUNTER: Boyso . . . your own son.

SEAN: A lazy good for nothing get. (*Pause.*) You know I looked at her one day . . . and the way she sat, I saw more than was good for me.
(*They giggle.*)
But I thought . . . she was a fine looking woman.

GRUNTER: (*Giggling like a naughty schoolboy*) I took the odd squint or two myself . . . fine looking's right.

SEAN: She was too good for him . . . my own son . . . but she was too good for him.

GRUNTER: And him gubbed the soldier . . . that's the best of it . . . gubbed a soldier.
(*They suddenly become aware that they are surrounded by soldiers.*)

SOLDIER A: (*Prodding* GRUNTER *hard in the stomach.*) What's that, scum?

GRUNTER: Ah now wait a minute . . .
(SOLDIER A *kicks him in the privates sending him sprawling in the muck.* SEAN *stands white-faced, fists clenched. The* CORPORAL LIAM *punched is grinning at him.*)

CORPORAL DANIELS: What you hiding in the wall then, Grandad?

SEAN: Hiding . . . (*Catching*) . . . hiding . . . sure I've nothing to hide.

SOLDIER B: (*Kicking the repaired wall down*) I reckon it's rifles, Corp.

CORPORAL DANIELS: You got a sledge hammer, Grandad?

SEAN: Ah now wait . . .
(CORPORAL DANIELS *drags* GRUNTER *from a sitting*

position to his feet.)

CORPORAL DANIELS: Get me a sledge, scum . . . quickly.
(GRUNTER *hobbles away.*)
We got this report from our intelligence section . . . they
reckon there's guns hid in this wall . . . that right,
Grandad . . . eh?
(*The* SOLDIERS *laugh.*)

SEAN: (*Close to tears.*) I'm seventy-six years old . . .

SOLDIER C: Happy birthday you old bastard.
(GRUNTER *returns with a heavy sledge, hands it to* SOLDIER
A, *whom the* CORPORAL *has pointed to.* SOLDIER A *holds it by
the stock and drops it on* GRUNTER'*s foot.* GRUNTER *writhes
in pain.*)

SOLDIER A: Sorry about that, Corp . . . just slipped out of my
hand.

CORPORAL DANIELS: Could happen to the vicar.
(SOLDIER A *hands his rifle to* SOLDIER B, *and begins to
demolish the wall. Hold on* SEAN. *His face taut, grim. The thuds
of the hammer, the laughing soldiers. Tears run down his cheeks.*)

32. EXT. THE BEACH AT DOWNHILL

MARY *and* WILL *tripping through the waves. They are laughing and
holding hands.* WILL *has his trousers rolled up, he carries his shoes
and socks.* MARY *carries her shoes. They stop.* WILL *looks around
and then gazes out to sea. Pause.*

MARY: What's the matter?

WILL: I'm just thinking . . . all that power . . . and look . . .
just wild ocean as far as you can see. (*They stand and gaze
seawards.*) It's like us.

MARY: Like us?

WILL: Yes . . . the power of the feelings between us . . . not
quite knowing what's out there at the end of it all.
(*Pause.* MARY *and* WILL *look into each other's faces and kiss,
for the first time. Not for long. They break and look at each
other.*)

MARY: (*Quietly*) Oh God . . . do it again, please.
(*They kiss again, longer, deeper, lingeringly, and again.*)

WILL: Am I doing it right?

MARY: (*Looks at him.*) I don't know.

(*They laugh and embrace. They kiss. A wave comes a little higher, soaking his trousers and her skirt, but they don't appear to notice. Pull back and leave them there, specks against the massiveness around them. Hold.*)

33. INT. THE FARM KITCHEN. LATER

GRUNTER *is with* SEAN. *The kettle is boiling,* SEAN *is holding a letter in tweezers, steaming it open.* GRUNTER *has one foot in plaster.*

SEAN: What does S.W.A.L.K. mean?

GRUNTER: Damned if I know, Sean . . . S what?

(SEAN *shows him the back of the letter; there are kisses on it too.*)

SEAN: It's for Mary . . . do you know what it means?

GRUNTER: Indeed I don't . . . (*Sad.*) . . . but I know what the XXXs mean.

SEAN: Damn it, she's up to something. Out again tonight.

(*Pause.*) Are you sure this works . . . I'm near scalded.

GRUNTER: It does . . . sure many's the time I seed my ma do it on my da's letters.

SEAN: I'll find out what's going on.

(*Letter open. See Regimental crest and 'Fondest love and kisses – Will'.*)

34. INT. THE FARM KITCHEN. LATE

SEAN *sits. The car drives up. After a moment* MARY *enters.* SEAN *sits gazing into the fire.*

SEAN: You're late.

MARY: I got a puncture . . . lucky a man stopped and give me a hand.

SEAN: Was he a soldier?

MARY: What?

SEAN: (*On his feet roaring*) A soldier . . . a Brit . . . a mother-cursing whoremastering Brit . . . is that who fixed your puncture?

MARY: I don't know . . .
   (*He throws the open letter on the table, lifts a stick that has been
   propped against the table and brings it down with a crash on the
   envelope.*)
SEAN: *Swalk . . . Swalk . . .* God alone knows what that filth
   stands for . . . but there's no doubt about the filth on the
   inside . . . language you wouldn't use to a cur . . . how did
   I ever raise a daughter like you . . . a whore.
   (*As* MARY *runs to the front door he catches her across the back
   of the neck with the stick. She screams with pain, and he's on
   her, hammering her.*)

35. INT. THE FARM KITCHEN
SEAN *is on one side of the table. We see him past a* MAN *in an
anorak, the hood up, his back to us.* SEAN *hands him a piece of
paper and a pile of notes.*
SEAN: All you need to know's on that . . . so don't hang on to it
   any longer than you have to.
MAN: (*Taking both.*) Don't tell me my job. (*He goes.*)

36. INT. WILL'S ROOM
WILL *in his room. He is ready to go out . . . whistling, happy.
There is a package sitting on his chair . . . in gift paper. He lifts it.
There's a knock at the door,* WILL *opens it.*)
SOLDIER: Major . . . wants to see you right away, Corporal.
   (WILL *exits.*)

37. EXT. THE FARM YARD
SEAN *is standing gazing down his devastated lane. He smokes a
pipe. Pause.* MARY *exits farmhouse; she walks to her car carrying a
heavy case. The car is packed with her belongings. She gets in and
drives away.* SEAN *is left gazing after her.*

38. MAJOR 2IC'S OFFICE, BARRACKS
The MAJOR *is sitting behind his desk, the* INTELLIGENCE
OFFICER *to one side.* SOLDIER A *shows* WILL *into office.*

SOLDIER A: Corporal Pryce. (SOLDIER *exits*.)

MAJOR: Corporal Pryce . . . sit down.

WILL: Sir?

> (*He sits looking from one to the other. Pause.*)
> Excuse me, sir . . . I have someone waiting for me outside.

MAJOR: As from now, Corporal Pryce you are confined to barracks.

WILL: (*Dumbfounded*) Sir . . . I don't understand.

MAJOR: Mary McCabe . . . there was a rather nasty incident . . .

WILL: (*Jumping to his feet*) Is she hurt?

MAJOR: (*Firm*) Sit down, Corporal Pryce . . . sit down.
> (*Pause.* WILL *sits.*)
> Miss McCabe is fine . . . to my knowledge. You Welsh are as excitable as the Irish. (*Pause.*) Now, let me continue. There was a rather nasty incident on the McCabe farm . . . involving some of our soldiers. In the light of that . . . as a precaution, in your own interests, we're sending you home.

WILL: (*Stunned, almost in tears*) But . . . no, you can't . . . you can't, sir. (*Looking at the* INTELLIGENCE OFFICER.) You can't . . . I've committed no offence.

MAJOR: (*Irritated*) You've been bloody silly, Corporal Pryce.

INTELLIGENCE OFFICER: Calm down, Corporal . . . We can do this, as you well know.

MAJOR: You are aware of Section 69 of the Army Act 1965?

WILL: (*Quiet*) I'm aware of it, sir.

MAJOR: (*Looking at the* INTELLIGENCE OFFICER) We've been watching you for some time, Corporal. We're taking this action with great reluctance . . . but we have reason to believe in the best interests of your personal safety.

WILL: (*Visibly crumbling*) I'd like to appeal to the Commanding Officer, sir.

MAJOR: There will be no appeal, Corporal Pryce.

WILL: Mary's not involved in anything, sir . . . I'm certain of that.

MAJOR: She's involved in a romance with you . . . perhaps you're in love . . . yes. (*Pause.*) I am sorry, Corporal Pryce.

WILL: She's outside, sir . . . she's waiting for me . . .
   (*The* MAJOR *just sits. The* INTELLIGENCE OFFICER *leans
   across and whispers to the* MAJOR. *Pause. The* MAJOR *takes
   out a sheet of paper and an envelope from a drawer. He passes
   them and a pen to* WILL.)
MAJOR: You may write her a note.
   (WILL *writes.*)

39. MAIN ENTRANCE OF THE BARRACKS
The INTELLIGENCE OFFICER *emerges, with* TWO ARMED
SOLDIERS. *They walk to* MARY's *parked car. The* INTELLIGENCE
OFFICER *speaks down into her, and hands her the letter from* WILL.
*We can see the car is packed with her belongings. We hear nothing of
what is said. The* INTELLIGENCE OFFICER *and the soldiers return
to the barracks. Close on* MARY *as she reads the letter. Tears course
down her cheeks. Pause. She carefully folds the letter and places it
on the seat beside her. She starts the car up and drives off. We watch
the car out of sight.*

40. THE BEACH AT DOWNHILL. SUNSET
*Through the telescopic sight of a rifle. It searches and closes on a
solitary figure. Hold. It is* MARY. *She is gazing out to sea. She holds*
WILL's *letter in her hand. The* SNIPER *searches the beach . . .
There is no one else. Pause. The rifle is dropped and we close on*
MARY. *Hold. Then pull back to leave her solitary on the totally
deserted beach.*

41. THE FARM
Dusk gathering in. SEAN *is sitting on a pile of the debris of his
broken wall. He looks very old, and very tired . . . and profoundly
sad. Hold.*

OUT OF TUNE

Cast:

SAM	Des McAleer
ANNE	Stella McCusker
ERIC	Tyler Butterworth
TONY	Andrew Paul
SERGEANT BANDSMAN	Mike Savage
PHYLLIS	Maureen McAuley
BETTY	Susie Kelly
WALTER	James Duggan
LUCINDA	Helen Magill
DAVE	Dan Gordon
HADLEIGH	Charles Dale
WALKER	Anthony Frew
P. C. RUSSELL	Brian Hogg
SERGEANT GUARDROOM	Robert Gary
LANCE-CORPORAL	Nick McCall
SMART	James Nesbitt
KEN	Roy Heayberd
SAM'S MOTHER	Sheila McGibbon
KATIE	Tracey Lynch
KEVIN	Con Lynch
POLICEMAN	Michael Foyle

1. INT. BANDROOM. NIGHT I

ERIC *is playing his trombone. A number of instruments, music stands, sheet music, etc., lying around. Hold. He stops playing and listens, then goes to the window. He sees soldiers in full combat gear clambering into the back of a number of Land Rovers. They roar off into the night. The* SERGEANT *walks into the room.* ERIC *turns from the window, begins to play again. The* SERGEANT *stands for a moment, listening, before* ERIC *stops, realizing he's there.*

SERGEANT: I was talking to the bandmaster about you today, lad. (*Pause.*) There are two or three others we'd love to have making the request you're making. You're a musician, Maitland, you're not a soldier. You've got talent, real talent. Anyone can learn to point a rifle, to squeeze the trigger. Anyone can tramp around the streets of Belfast . . . anyone. You don't need any talent to do that. You don't even need to have much intelligence, or much imagination to do that. That's why they do it, don't you realize that? They're not bright, or imaginative, or talented. They don't do it because they've got a choice. They do it because it's all they're fit for . . . and that's it. That's all they're required to be . . . reasonably fit and healthy.

ERIC: I just feel I'm wasted, Sergeant. There's a war going on and I'm making no contribution.

SERGEANT: No contribution? Oh come on, lad. Don't dignify what's going on here by calling it a war. It's just a series of murders . . . with soldiers trying to play policemen, and policemen trying to play soldiers. Music is more important than that. You're good, son . . . you've got a gift. You could go to Neller Hall, and some day write a piece of music that will be played and remembered long after we've forgotten who was involved in this mess. That's your contribution.

ERIC: I could do that, after I've made my contribution here, Sergeant.

61

SERGEANT: I see . . . you intend to chop and change every few years, do you? Every time some thick Paddy fires a gun, you'll lay down your instrument and chase after him? (*Pause.*) Are you planning to join the RUC, lad?

ERIC: The RUC! . . . no way, Sergeant.

SERGEANT: Listen, Maitland, by the time your request is processed, assuming it is, and you do your basic training . . . this unit might be just about to leave here. Your chances of serving, as a British Soldier, on the streets of Belfast are pretty remote. You're well-intentioned, son, but misguided. (*Pause.*) Why don't you just forget it?

ERIC: I appreciate all you've said, Sergeant . . . but I'd still like to see the bandmaster.

SERGEANT: You shouldn't have written to the bandmaster . . . your request for an interview should have gone through me . . . so before we do that . . . have another good hard think, Maitland. (*Pause.*) Goodnight, lad.

ERIC: (*As the* SERGEANT *goes.*) Goodnight, Sergeant. (*Pause.*) (ERIC *plays another few bars. Stops and goes back to the window; takes out cigarettes and lights up. He gazes out of the window again. The vehicles are gone.* TONY *enters.*)

TONY: Bloody hell, I thought you'd done a bunk. How long have you been here?

ERIC: Not long . . . There's a patrol going out . . . there must be something on.

TONY: Poor sods.

ERIC: I don't know. Sometimes I think I wouldn't mind a bit of action.

TONY: You must be mad . . . that's all I can say, mate. A warm bed and a late reveille . . . that's all I ask for.

ERIC: Do you ever fancy a bit of action?

TONY: Piss off . . . action . . . What, chasing after bloody Paddies, who don't even have the guts to face you? It's not action, mate . . . it's hide and go bloody seek, if you ask me. Here, give's a drag, two's up.

(ERIC *passes him the cigarette. He sucks in deeply. Pause.*)

ERIC: I'm thinking of giving up the band.

TONY: You what . . . give up a cushy number like this?

ERIC: I've asked for a transfer to the Infantry.

TONY: What do you want to do a bloody daft thing like that for?

ERIC: I'm a man of action at heart.

TONY: A man of action!! You never stopped moaning when we were doing our basic training. You were useless.

ERIC: That was different. I didn't feel like this then.

TONY: You were a joke. The Chelsea Pensioners could have lapped you on the assault course.

ERIC: I didn't have the motivation then.

TONY: So where did the motivation suddenly come from?

ERIC: What use is music in a war?

TONY: It's in every war movie I've ever seen.

ERIC: In this war?

TONY: Ah . . . you're forgetting . . . this isn't a war . . . this is an emergency.

ERIC: What part are we playing in the defeat of the IRA? Do they think if we play Irish jigs, they might dance themselves into a state of exhaustion?

TONY: ECM . . . that's us, mate . . . ECM . . . entertainment, ceremonial, and morale. That's why we're here now . . . to restore the morale of the fighting men.

ERIC: We'd do more to restore the morale of the fighting men if we went out and fought alongside them. (*Pause.*) We fiddle while Belfast burns.

TONY: (*Laughing*) You've been reading the *Beano* again. I'm going to my pit.

(*Hold.* ERIC *looking out window.*)

2. EXT. STREET

A Police Land Rover driving along a darkened street. We hear a distant crackle of shots. The radio crackles. The vehicle takes off at speed, its siren screeching. Crossfade to a street corner. A number of Police Land Rovers are parked at different angles. There are POLICEMEN *in firing positions. There are two* POLICEMEN *lying, one dead, the other wounded, being attended to by colleagues. To one side* SAM *sits on his backside, propped up against a wall. He is in a*

*state of shock. A colleague stands watch over him; both look
dazed. The loud wail of the ambulance siren is heard. Injured*
POLICEMAN *taken to ambulance. Army vehicles begin to arrive.
The* SOLDIERS *tumble out.*

PC: (*With* SAM) What gets me most, is having to be polite to the
old whores. Some of them know who it was.

SAM: Maybe, but all of them don't. How do you decide who
knows and who doesn't?

PC: You go in hard . . . frighten the shite out of them.
Somebody'll crack.

SAM: Derry '69. It didn't work then.

PC: London . . . derry, and it could have worked, if the
politicians hadn't got cold feet. (*Pause.*) We're only going to
rough a few people up but there's one of our mates dead.

3. INT. THE BEDROOM OF A SMALL KITCHENHOUSE

SAM'S MOTHER *is sitting up in bed reading. There is a large transistor
radio, and a telephone, on the bedside locker. Hold. A shot is heard, far
away, but distinctly. She stops reading and listens intently. Pause.
There is a crackle of shots. She puts her book down and turns the radio
on. She tunes it in frantically, searching for the police frequency. It isn't
very clear, but she thinks she's found it. Out of an indistinguishable
crackle comes 'Collect a Mr Johnston and take him to Chlorine Gardens,
over'. She grunts in disgust, and tries to tune it in again. It is very
difficult. She twists the aerial, and changes the position of the radio.
There is a faint crackle. She puts her ear right down against the radio.
Pause. Switching off the radio, she scrambles out on to the side of her
bed. She picks up the telephone and dials a number. As it rings at the
other end she shows great, and rapidly increasing, impatience. Hold.*

SCENE 4. SAM'S BEDROOM

Bedside light on. ANNE *is sleeping. The phone rings, she wakes up
and lifts receiver.*

5. EXT. SAM'S HOUSE. NIGHT

A car approaches. SAM *gets out. The bedroom lights are on.* SAM
quietly approaches house and enters.

6. INT. THE LIVING ROOM OF A SEMI-DETACHED HOUSE IN A
MIDDLE-CLASS AREA OF BELFAST

SAM *enters . . . the shocked policeman seen earlier. He is in
his thirties. He carries his tunic and his RUC cap. He drops
these into a chair . . . and drops himself heavily into another
one. He sets his gun on a small table beside him and cups his
head in his hands for a moment. Pause. He sits back in the chair
. . . gazing ceilingwards. Pause. His wife,* ANNE's, *voice is heard,
off.*

ANNE: Sam . . . Sam . . . is that you Sam?
      (*He just lies there, makes no response. Pause.*)
      Sam . . .
      (*The door opens and* ANNE *enters. She just stands for a
      moment, staring at him; he doesn't even look at her.*)
      Didn't you hear me calling you?
      (*He just gazes at her.*)
      Well . . . didn't you?

SAM: Of course I heard you . . . Christ . . . have you ever tried
     not to hear you, when you're roaring?

ANNE: Why didn't you answer me? (*Pause.*) Do you think I
      enjoy lying up there, my stomach in knots, listening for you
      coming in?

SAM: No . . . I think you enjoy coming down here, to pester
     me. (*Pause.*) I've told you before . . . go to sleep.

ANNE: Oh yes, it's that simple.

SAM: If I'd the chance to sleep I'd find it easy.

ANNE: Were you near that shooting tonight?

SAM: The man next to me . . . Harry Webster . . . but we're
     not trained to put heads together again . . . so there was
     nothing I could do.

ANNE: (*Her hand to her mouth in shock and horror*) It could have
      been you. My God . . . (*Crossing herself*) and all you can say
      is 'go to sleep'.

SAM: There isn't much you could have done if it had been me, is
     there? (*Pause. Ignoring her distress.*) Somebody else got leg
     injuries. How did you know about it anyway?

ANNE: Your mother rang me . . . I was asleep.

SAM: That bloody woman . . . I've told her hundreds of times,
it's illegal to listen to us.

ANNE: You bought her the radio . . . and you showed her the
frequency.

SAM: I only did it to set her mind at rest.

ANNE: It seems a funny way to try and set her mind at rest.

SAM: Well you kept moaning about her ringing you every half-
hour, when I was on nights. I didn't know it was going to
become her hobby.

(SAM *rises and pours himself a large Scotch.*)

ANNE: Is that going to help?

SAM: I'll bet Harry Webster's wife wouldn't mind if he was
pouring himself one right now. (*Pause.*)

ANNE: Look . . . away on up to bed and I'll make you a cup of
tea.

SAM: You go to bed. I don't want tea.

ANNE: You come with me . . . please.

SAM: I'm not ready yet. I'll follow you.

ANNE: Sam . . . I don't want the children finding you in the
chair tomorrow morning.

SAM: (*Pouring himself another drink*) I'll bet Harry Webster's kids
wouldn't mind finding him in the chair in the morning.

ANNE: (*Angry*) Oh to hell with Harry Webster . . . we didn't
shoot him, so for goodness' sake stop punishing us for it.

SAM: That's lovely . . . you're a really big-hearted human being.

ANNE: You didn't even like him.

SAM: That's got nothing to do with it.

ANNE: I'm not going to have a slanging match, to waken the
children.

SAM: Well go back to bed then and give me peace.

ANNE: You'd better ring your mother . . . let her know you're
all right, before she rings here again to see if you're home.

SAM: You ring her . . . (*Sitting down with the bottle and the glass*)
I'm busy.

(*She stares at him for a moment, angry and upset. Pause. She
goes. Pause. He rises. Puts the bottle and the glass away and
follows her, turning out the light.*)

7. HARRY WEBSTER'S FUNERAL

SAM *is standing to one side as the coffin, with Harry's cap on top, is loaded into the hearse. Go quite tight on* SAM's *face. It is tight, hard, a mask . . . a reflection of his feelings of anger, bitterness, and sadness at the death of a colleague. We can hear the buzz of others around. The shuffling of the mourners. The sound of the RUC band playing the 'Funeral March'.*

8. INT. MOTHER'S ROOM

Close up on SAM's *face. Pull out and see that his face is a large close up on a television. His* MOTHER *sits watching it. Pause. She turns to the phone by her side.*

9. SAM AND ANNE'S HOUSE. THEIR BEDROOM

SAM *is dressed, ready to go out. She is on the phone.*

ANNE: Your mother's just seen you on the telly. I still think it's silly and irresponsible.

SAM: Don't moan at me . . . it isn't my fault.

ANNE: I know it's not your fault. Couldn't you complain about it?

SAM: What good would that do? . . . It's over and done with now. (*Crosses to end of bed.*)

ANNE: Maybe if someone had complained before, it wouldn't have happened today. (*Applying her lipstick*) I mean, a close-up . . . as if we haven't enough to worry about.

SAM: Oh come on . . . those who want to know about me, know about me.

ANNE: Even so, why remind them . . . why focus on you?

SAM: Because they thought I was good-looking?

ANNE: It's not funny. You'd almost think they did it on purpose.

SAM: Now you are being silly.

ANNE: Am I . . . television's full of left-wingers, sympathizers. (*He snorts.*)
Well come on . . . how many Catholics were there today?

SAM: I don't know, a few . . . more than just me . . . the Chief Constable for one.

ANNE: Huh, him . . .
> (*She continues making-up. He sits on the edge of the bed, watching her intently. She notices, in the mirror, that he's watching her, gazing at her.*)
> What is it?
> (*She addresses him through the mirror.*)

SAM: Nothing . . . just thinking how well you look.
> (*She smiles, pleased. She rises and turns towards him.*)

ANNE: Come here . . .
> (SAM *goes to her. They embrace and kiss.*)

SAM: You'll ruin your lipstick.

ANNE: Who cares . . . I can do it again.
> (*They gaze at each other, she mumbles 'Oh Sam' . . . they kiss again, deeply and passionately. Hold.*)

10. INT. THE ARMY BILLET

TONY *is dressed almost ready to go out. It is later on the evening of Harry Webster's funeral.* ERIC *enters from washroom, dressed up, a little out of date, fashion-wise.*

TONY: Get a move on . . . they'll go without us.

ERIC: So . . . we'll go in on our own.

TONY: Out on the van . . . and in on the van . . . that's the order. Come on.

ERIC: It's like being back in school.

TONY: It's a bit different. You disobey the rules at school, you get caned. Disobey the rules here, and you could end up with air-vents in the head . . . Armalite-size.

ERIC: What's this joint again?

TONY: The Stormont Hotel.

ERIC: Stormont . . . is Paisley the barman?

TONY: They say it's good . . . plenty of randy women.

ERIC: Yeah . . . now where have I heard that one before? I've yet to meet anyone who's actually had one of these randy women.

TONY: You should check in sick-bay.
> (*Both laugh.*)

ERIC: Piss off . . . not Irish pox-bags!

TONY: Come on, you'll do.

ERIC: (*As they go*) Listen . . . if we do score, we're not bandsmen.

TONY: Why not?

ERIC: Use your imagination.

TONY: I am doing . . . I'm rather proud of my instrument.
(*Laugh as they go.*)

ERIC: Randy women like a bit of excitement . . . they're looking for men of action.

TONY: Right . . . we're SAS . . . carrying out secret operations, behind enemies' backs . . . and between randy Irish legs.
(*They go laughing.*)

11. INT. LOUNGE. STORMONT HOTEL

SAM *getting drink at bar.* BETTY *and* PHYLLIS *are also standing at the bar. They move away from the bar. The* WAITER *gives* SAM *his change.* SAM *joins* ANNE *at table with their drinks.*

SAM: (*Drinking*) Cheers.

ANNE: You're so impatient.

SAM: What?

ANNE: They do serve the tables . . . if you give them time.

SAM: Well, we have it now. (*Drinking*) I needed the exercise.
(ERIC *and* TONY *enter, look around, see* PHYLLIS *and* BETTY. TONY *nudges* ERIC, *who looks uncomfortable.* TONY *nods and winks at the two women, then turns to bar.*)

BETTY: That's the first tonight. Surely to God things can only improve.

PHYLLIS: The one on the left's not too bad.

BETTY: No . . . he'd do at a pinch . . . but I don't like the one you're getting.
(*They giggle.*)

PHYLLIS: I think they're soldiers . . . either that, or they're out on parole. (*Giggles.*)

BETTY: Soldiers . . . I can smell them. It just shows you how the cinema lies. You never see runts like that in war pictures.

PHYLLIS: You do . . . but they're usually the ones who crack-up in action . . . and wet the bed. (*Giggles again.*)

BETTY: (*As* TONY *crosses to exit*) Here's one of them coming over. . . .

PHYLLIS: Ask him if he carries spare batteries for Action Man.

BETTY: (*Laughing*) You're awful . . . shut up. Right . . . I'm not with you.

(TONY *crosses the room passing their table on the way to the loo.*)

TONY: Evening, ladies.

PHYLLIS: (*Looking all round*) He's going to the loo. Ah . . . and there's me thinking he was going to speak to us.

(*They explode with laughter.* ERIC *turns to look at* BETTY *and* PHYLLIS. *They are still laughing. When they catch his eye, he quickly drops his head, embarrassed, and turns back to the bar. This only encourages them to laugh even louder.*)

12. INT. LOUNGE, A LITTLE LATER

ANNE *and* SAM *are sitting at the table.* SAM *drains his glass and hails a* WAITER.

SAM: Could I have a pint, and a wee Irish, please. Anne?

ANNE: (*Displeased*) I've barely started this one.

(*The* WAITER *goes.*)

Sam . . . I don't want to nag . . . but I'm not here to watch you getting sozzled.

SAM: I'm not going to get sozzled . . . I just needed a quick one. (*He gazes around –* TONY *passes them.*) They're not very busy, are they?

ANNE: I've never seen this place crowded . . . but then there's a dance as well, I suppose a good lot have gone through to that.

SAM: There's a Brit with a twitch. (*He glares across at* TONY *and* ERIC.)

ANNE: A twitch . . . what do you mean?

SAM: That wee wanker . . . winking across at those two women. (ERIC *and* TONY *walk to* PHYLLIS *and* BETTY.)

ANNE: How do you know they're Brits?

SAM: It's obvious . . . the dull eyes, obvious lack of intelligence . . . last decade's fashion.

ANNE: (*Irritated by his attitude*) The women seem to be enjoying it. (*Pause.*) Stop glaring at them. Anyway they're doing no harm.

SAM: Doing no harm . . . doing no good either. You bury your mates, and then have to watch these wee shites . . . the only thing they care about's getting a leg over.

ANNE: Will you stop getting all worked up . . . come on, we're out for a quiet, relaxed evening.

SAM: It gets on your nerves though. (*Pause.*) And look at the women . . . old enough to be their bloody mothers.

ANNE: Maybe that's the whole attraction . . . they're probably just homesick, and just yearn for some female companionship.

SAM: While we take the bullets in the back for them!

ANNE: Oh come on, for goodness' sake. Live and let live can't you.

SAM: Aye . . . it's a great day for that.

(WAITRESS *in. Serves the drink,* SAM *pays,* WAITRESS *exits.* WALTER *and* LUCINDA *walk into lounge, the* WAITRESS *approaches them.*)

ANNE: Isn't that Walter Moore.

SAM: (*Glances round*) Aye.

ANNE: Who's that with him?

SAM: I don't know . . . his latest girlfriend I suppose.

ANNE: My God . . . (*Leans back. Giving the girl close scrutiny,* ANNE *moves forward.*) She's young enough to be his daughter.

SAM: Maybe she is his daughter.

ANNE: He doesn't have a daughter. Myrtle and him only had the two boys. (*Pause.*) Look at him . . . slobbering all over her, it's disgusting.

SAM: Why not . . . she's a nice looking girl.

ANNE: I think Myrtle's well shot of him.

SAM: Live while you can . . . we could be burying him by

this time next week.

ANNE: (*Staring at him, angry*) You hypocrite.

SAM: What are you talking about, hypocrite?

ANNE: Well you are. You're only after giving off about those young soldiers . . . and at least they are young. What makes it different for a policeman?

SAM: I've just told you what makes it different. We're out risking our necks . . . you live while you can.

ANNE: Is that so, and is that what you get up to when I'm not around?

SAM: Don't be daft. Walter's separated.

ANNE: Of course he is, and that's the reason . . . Myrtle walked out on him, because he couldn't keep his hands off trollops like that.

SAM: What makes her a trollop? Typical married woman . . . any woman with bigger tits, a nicer bum, and a bit of life, is a trollop. She's probably a very nice girl.

ANNE: It's certainly not reflected in her taste.

SAM: Oh balls . . . just because you and Myrtle were friends. You don't know what she was like to live with, do you? Sure she'd the face gerned off herself.

ANNE: All boys together. When will you admit that there are men who are rotten . . . and putting on a policeman's uniform doesn't make them any less rotten.

SAM: And what makes you think that putting on a Brit uniform makes those wee wankers something special?

ANNE: I don't think I said they were special. Half of them are just big youngsters, they haven't even had a chance to grow up yet.

SAM: Do you know who you're talking to? I'm a cop . . . the average age in the British Army runs from eighteen to twenty-two . . .

ANNE: That's the age span, not the average . . .

SAM: Just shut up for once, and listen. Eighteen to twenty-two . . . vicious bastards. That's the age of the muggers . . . the scum who attack old women. All those vicious, animal instincts are what the British Army unleash on the streets of

Belfast . . . and now we're pushed out to take it in the neck for them.

ANNE: You're talking absolute nonsense, and you know it. Isn't that what you wanted? Didn't you always moan about what you could do, if the Brits weren't there . . . Ulsterization . . . the primacy of the RUC . . . I had that to breakfast, dinner and tea . . . now you've got that, so what are you going on about?

SAM: (*Furious*) Whose side are you on?

ANNE: We're not taking sides are we? I'm on my side . . . you're supposed to be on my side . . . and so are they . . . furthermore, you're both supposed to be on the same side.

SAM: Is that what you think? If it wasn't for us they'd pull those little wankers out . . . and the chinless wonders who command them . . . The British Army couldn't give a damn about you . . . or the rest of the innocent civilian population . . . Jasus Christ . . . we could have had the IRA wiped out, if it wasn't for them and their puppet-masters in Whitehall . . . playing games with our lives.

ANNE: I don't believe this . . . you're talking like a Protestant . . . if I didn't remember we were married in chapel, I'd put you down for a Paisleyite. Do you remember who you are?

SAM: (*Fiercely*) I'm a policeman . . . not a Catholic, not a Protestant . . . an RUC man . . . that's it . . . as far as I'm concerned it's the RUC first, always, and for ever.

ANNE: (*Angry and stunned*) Sam . . . (*Shaking her head*) . . . let's just forget it.

SAM: Never mind forget it . . . you're taking the part of those Brit whoremasters over me.

ANNE: (*Angry*) Don't be so childish.

SAM: Childish now am I . . . I'll show you how childish I am . . . (*Drinking deeply*) . . . I'll go over and spread those two wee shites all over the floor. (*Drinking.*)

ANNE: That would certainly prove the point. Listen, Sam (*Stopping him putting the glass to his mouth.*) . . . listen I

said . . . now just you calm down . . . I'm warning
you . . . just pull yourself together, otherwise I'm walking
straight out of here.
(*He holds her gaze for a moment, then relaxes, puts his glass
down. Pause.*)

SAM: Sorry. (*Gesturing towards the drink*) I'll slow down.

ANNE: Thank you. (*Smiling beyond* SAM) Oh dear, Walter has
spotted us.

(SAM *turns and waves.*)

I hope he stays where he is.

SAM: I think he's got what he wants there.

ANNE: I don't know . . . he always makes a point of flaunting
his women. The younger and better-looking they are, the
more he flaunts them. Especially to friends of Myrtle's.

SAM: Well, if he comes over, just tell him you've fallen out with
Myrtle.

ANNE: I'd love to tell him that she's living with a 22-year-old
athlete, with massive biceps.

SAM: Wait a minute . . . what do you know about biceps? (*They
laugh.*) Do you think he'd care?

ANNE: I'm quite certain he would. It would be such a blow to
his ego, to think Myrtle could get by without him.

SAM: It would be quite a strain on his imagination, to think
Myrtle could get a 22-year-old athlete . . . with or without
big biceps.

ANNE: Why . . . she's not a bad-looking woman.

SAM: Come on, she's no raving beauty.

ANNE: Well look what he's got . . . and I wouldn't call him
good-looking.

SAM: He must have something. Anyway, you're too prejudiced
against him to know whether he's good-looking or not.

ANNE: Even before I really knew him, I wouldn't have given
him a second glance.

SAM: Aye . . . but look what you have to compare him with.
Tell me what woman wouldn't be happy in your position?
(*Pause. She just smiles.*)
Another thing . . . if he's as bad as all you women say . . .

why does Myrtle want him back?

ANNE: Probably just to know she can do it . . . and then have the satisfaction of throwing him out.

(*Pause.*)

13. INT. WASHROOM OF THE TOILET

ERIC *and* TONY *are there.* TONY *is combing his hair.*

TONY: What more do you want, mate, a printed invitation?

ERIC: Why do you think that just because a woman smiles at you, she wants to jump into bed with you?

TONY: I don't think that . . . she's too old to jump . . . but I think she'll topple, playfully.

ERIC: Oh balls (*Exasperated*) they're probably married.

TONY: All the better . . . a bit of experience . . . no hanging about the gates, pleading for a little gold band.

ERIC: What about their husbands?

TONY: (*Considering*) No . . . I'm strictly hetero. (*He laughs, but* ERIC *only shows his annoyance.*) Do you know what I think, Eric . . . I think you're afraid of it. What about this 'man of action' image?

ERIC: Sex isn't action.

TONY: (*With a smug laugh*) It is the way I do it, mate. (*Looking at* ERIC) Here, you're not a screaming woofter, are you?

ERIC: (*Angry*) You just bloody watch what you're saying.

(TONY, *moving close to him, menacingly.*)

TONY: Or what . . . mate?

(*As they stand confronting each other,* SAM *enters. He stands and stares at them. They break, embarrassed.*)

SAM: (*Sneering*) I have to tell you, lads, I'm a policeman, and it's not allowed here, not even for soldiers.

(ERIC *and* TONY *look at each other, a bit alarmed at him knowing.*)

TONY: You'd better watch it, mate.

SAM: Is that a fact . . . or what, Brit?

TONY: You might just end up with a very sore head.

SAM: (*Taunting*) Is that so . . . soldier boy. Will I wait, or will you send for me?

ERIC: Come on, Tony, ignore him . . . we've better things to do.

SAM: I'd take his advice if I were you.

(*They stand glaring at each other. Someone else enters. Pause.* ERIC *and* TONY *leave.*)

14. INT. LOUNGE. STORMONT HOTEL

SAM *returning from the toilets.* WALTER *and* LUCINDA *are sitting with* ANNE.

WALTER: Sam . . . this is Lucinda. Lucy for short. Cindy for affection. Darling for all other purposes.

(*He puts an arm around her. They giggle.* SAM *shakes her hand.*)

SAM: I'm pleased to meet you. (*Sits.*)

ANNE: (*To* SAM) You're looking very pleased with yourself.

SAM: Yes . . . (*Looking across at* TONY *and* ERIC, *who are now sitting beside* BETTY *and* PHYLLIS.) I had a pleasing exchange with our Brit friends.

(ANNE *disapproving.*)

WALTER: Aren't they pathetic . . . and look at what they're chasing, eh? (*Tugging* LUCINDA.) You wouldn't see them with a classy bit like Cindy.

LUCINDA: I wouldn't be seen dead with a soldier.

ANNE: (*Sharply*) Why not? They're just ordinary fellas . . . they choose a different uniform, that's all.

(*Awkward pause.*)

WALTER: (*With a laugh*) Yes . . . well, it's all a matter of taste, isn't it? And when you look at me, you realize that Cindy has superb taste.

(*They snigger, but* ANNE *doesn't respond.*)

SAM: (*Embarrassed*) We put another good lad down today, Walter.

WALTER: (*Looks puzzled*) Oh, aye, . . . Harry. A decent man . . . one of the best. (*Pause.*) Did you know him, Anne?

ANNE: Yes. Personally I didn't like him very much.

(*Awkward pause.*)

76

WALTER: Well . . . we'd ah, . . . we'd better be getting into this dance.
(*They rise. They go, making their farewells.*)

SAM: (*Seething with anger*) Right . . . (*Draining his glass*) . . . we're going home.

ANNE: (*Regards him for a moment*) I'm not ready to go home yet.

SAM: (*Rises*) You come now . . . or you can bloody well walk.

ANNE: I'll walk.

SAM: (*Fighting to keep control*) I'm warning you . . . I'm going.

ANNE: (*Furious now herself*) Well hurry up . . . before all the nice Brits are snatched up.
(*He sits, speechless with rage, unaware he's being watched. She calmly settles herself, drains her glass and hails the* WAITRESS. *Pause.*)

15. EXT. STORMONT HOTEL
We see ERIC *with* PHYLLIS *and* TONY *with* BETTY *leaving the hotel and walking to the security hut.*

16. EXT. OUTSIDE BACK OF THE HOTEL. LATER
ERIC *has* PHYLLIS *up against a wall at the back of the hotel. He is industriously groping under her coat. She is standing gazing over his shoulder, looking totally disinterested and bored. Pause.*

PHYLLIS: (*Pushing his hand away when he gets a little too ambitious*) Cut that out.

ERIC: Come on . . . what's the matter with you?

PHYLLIS: I don't want any of that.
(*He pauses a moment and then returns to work. She stops him again.*)

ERIC: For crying out loud . . . what is wrong with you, woman?

PHYLLIS: I've told you I don't want that, so just stop it.

ERIC: (*Pausing*) So what are we doing here?

PHYLLIS: (*With a degree of contempt, looking him up and down*) I'm minding you until your friend comes back to take you home.

ERIC: (*Furious. He clutches her face with both hands.*) Now listen you . . . you little Irish whore . . .

77

(PHYLLIS *sinks her knee hard into his groin. He groans and crumples to the ground, grovelling in agony. She coolly straightens herself, steps round him, and strolls casually away. Pause.*)

17. INT. THE BILLET. NIGHT

ERIC *is lying on his bed, playing scales on his trombone.* TONY *comes in. He is dressed to go out. He stops by* ERIC's *bed. After a moment* ERIC *stops playing.*

TONY: Do you want me to ask her about another mate tonight then?

ERIC: No, don't bother.

TONY: Why not . . . you reckon that dig on the nuts has made you impotent?

ERIC: You see . . . there you go again. Even if I did go out with another one of her friends, why assume we'd jump into bed? You're never going to meet a nice girl, unless you start to respect them.

TONY: Who wants to meet a nice girl? (*Pause.*) Anyway, Eric the Honourable, she didn't give you a dig on the nuts for treating her like a nice girl, did she? It didn't happen to me, did it? No, mate . . . I'm the one who came back with a smile on my face. Your problem was a little touch of the virgin's rush. (*Sits.*)

ERIC: (*Jumping up, angry*) Who are you calling a virgin?

TONY: (*Squaring up to him*) You . . . why?

(*They glare at each other for a moment.*)

ERIC: (*Flopping back on to his bed*) Forget it.

TONY: When I was fourteen, mate I stole a fiver off my dad, and had it off with the local bicycle.

ERIC: Why did you need a fiver, if she was the local bicycle?

TONY: She charged the young ones, 'cause she didn't get much out of it. You should head down to the local red-light district . . . get it over with.

ERIC: Ah piss off. What do you take me for?

TONY: What's wrong with that? You don't make a fool of yourself that way.

ERIC: I don't make a fool of myself . . . I know what I'm doing.
(TONY *just sneers.*)
It was the drink the other night. (*Pause.*) Anyway, I didn't
really like her . . . too coarse, rough. I like nice girls.

TONY: Nice girls . . . or pretty little boys.
(ERIC *is furious.* TONY *runs away laughing, and* ERIC *chases
after him. Pause.* ERIC *returns, annoyed.* WALKER, *another
soldier, enters. He is in a dressing-gown, having returned from
having a bath. He sees* ERIC *is upset. Pauses.*)

ERIC: What are you looking at, Walker?
(WALKER *just tries to walk away.*)
Walker. . . !
(*Crossing to him, punching him on the shoulders, alternately.
Forcing him down the room.*)
I asked you what you were looking at, four-eyes? Lost your
tongue have you?
(WALKER *has the pained expression of the eternally bullied. He
makes no reply, just winces in pain as the blows become
heavier.*)

18. INT. THE FRONT ROOM OF SAM'S HOUSE
SAM'S MOTHER *is sitting.* SAM *enters.*

SAM: Mother . . . (*Comes across and kisses her.*) How are you?

MOTHER: I'm all right.

SAM: Anne'll have the tea in a minute. Are you warm enough?

MOTHER: I'm all right.
(SAM *sits, uncomfortable.*)

SAM: It's turned colder.

MOTHER: Aye, well I suppose I'd be warmer at my own fireside.
(ANNE *wheels in a trolley, with tea and biscuits, etc. She sorts
things out, and starts to serve.*)

ANNE: (*Aware of the unease. Trying to be cheerful.*) Have you two
run out of things to say already?

MOTHER: There's nobody in my street'd harm him you know.
(ANNE *and* SAM *exchange glances.*)
A son should visit his mother. God knows, I'll not be
around for ever.

ANNE: I baked that sponge for you.

MOTHER: What happens when I'm not able to come over here?

ANNE: Come on now, Mother, I collect you in the car . . .
you're able for that.

MOTHER: It's not the same. I'm sure the neighbours think he's a
right son, that never visits his mother.

ANNE: Everybody knows why he doesn't visit. You know why.

MOTHER: What happens if I'm bedridden?

ANNE: We'll cross that bridge when we come to it.
(*Pause.*)

MOTHER: (*To* SAM) Why you wanted to join that lot's a mystery
to me. Sure there was never any policemen in our family.

SAM: What about your Uncle Sean?

MOTHER: (*Glaring at him*) My Uncle Sean . . . sure thon fella
wasn't thorough. Didn't he marry a Protestant intil the
bargain?
(*Pause.* ANNE *sits.*)

SAM: Is Mick going to do your bedroom?

MOTHER: No he is not. I wouldn't let that fella near the place.
I'll never know what your sister saw in him. (*Pause.*)
No . . . I suppose the bedroom'll just have to do me my
day.

ANNE: (*Firmly*) It will . . . because Sam certainly isn't going
over to do it.

MOTHER: I didn't ask for Sam to come and do it. I've said it'll
do. It's desperate to be old and feeble, when your own
won't do for you.
(ANNE, *upset, leaves the room.*)

SAM: Is your tea all right?

MOTHER: Where's she running off to?

SAM: The phone . . . I think the phone rang.

MOTHER: Huh . . . I didn't hear no phone.
(*Pause.*)

SAM: Have you thought any more about the bungalow?

MOTHER: I'm too old to move house.

SAM: A nice pensioner's bungalow . . . I could visit you then.

MOTHER: I'm not going to give up the bits and pieces it's taken me a lifetime to gather up.

SAM: (*Pouring more tea into her cup*) Do you want more milk and sugar?

MOTHER: Sure I didn't ask for more tea.

SAM: Do you not want it?

MOTHER: I'll take it now that it's poured.

(ANNE *returns and sits.*)

Who was on the phone?

ANNE: (*Puzzled*) Pardon? (*Glancing at* SAM) Oh . . . it was a wrong number.

MOTHER: It must be a quare soft ring on the phone, I didn't hear it.

ANNE: (*Offering plate*) Did you get enough to eat?

MOTHER: I've had plenty. Would the pair of you stop fussing.

(ANNE *puts the plate down.*)

Anyone would think you were fattening me for Christmas.

(*She stretches across and takes something from the plate* ANNE *has just put down.*)

19. INT. THE NAAFI HUT AT HOLYWOOD

ERIC *is with* SOLDIER *at computer game.*

ERIC: Were you out the other night?

SOLDIER: Yeah.

ERIC: How was it?

SOLDIER: Rough.

ERIC: Did you fire?

SOLDIER: Course I fired. What do you think I am, a mug?

(*Walks to table.*)

ERIC: Who did you fire at?

SOLDIER: Who do you think I fired at? Snipers . . . there were three of the bastards. (*Pause.*) I hit one of them.

ERIC: Did you . . . did you capture him?

SOLDIER: You don't capture corpses, mate . . . and when I hit them, that's what they are.

ERIC: I didn't hear anyone was killed.

SOLDIER: So what do you know? There was an RUC man killed too.

ERIC: I knew that. Did you see the body.

SOLDIER: The copper? . . . Of course.

ERIC: No, the other one . . . the one you shot?

SOLDIER: You never see them, mate. They get them out. Spirit them away.

ERIC: How do you know he's dead then?

SOLDIER: I hit him on the bloody head, that's how.

(ERIC *looks sceptical.*)

Don't believe me, I don't care. What do you bleeding music men know? (*Rising.*) Want another one?

ERIC: Yeah . . . and a bag of nuts.

(SOLDIER *goes. Pause.* DAVE *comes from darts board. Sits down.*)

Hello, Dave, how are you?

DAVE: Ok. What's John Wayne on about?

ERIC: He's just gone to get another drink. Why do you call him John Wayne?

DAVE: He's a cowboy, that's why. What has he been telling you?

ERIC: He was just talking about being out the other night.

DAVE: Yeah, I'll bet that was good. I was out too.

ERIC: He says it was bad . . . three snipers.

DAVE: Three! More like three hundred. I got ten.

ERIC: (*As* DAVE *laughs.*) Balls to you, mate. Come on . . . what was it like?

DAVE: It was cold and boring. All the shooting was over by the time we arrived. One cop dead, another one wounded . . . but we never even saw a gunman . . . we searched the whole area . . . found nothing. I'll tell you something . . . if I could blow a trumpet I'd do it . . . To hell with this real soldiering bit, I tell you.

(SOLDIER *returns with the drink. Sits. He nods at* DAVE.)

Sergeant Major's looking for you.

SOLDIER: For me . . . what for?

DAVE: They're offering you a VC . . . choice of four colours.

SOLDIER: Piss off. Wank head.

DAVE: (*Laughs and rises*) Game of pool?

SOLDIER: Balls.

DAVE: That's right . . . and two cues . . . coming?

SOLDIER: We're talking.

DAVE: (*As he moves off*) Tall tales from a terrifying Tommy. (*Exits.*)

SOLDIER: You know, I'll have that wank head one of these days.
(*Pause. They drink.*)

20. EXT. SAM'S HOUSE
ANNE *returns by car, having driven* SAM'S MOTHER *home. She gets out and walks to front door.*

21. INT. HALL SAM'S HOUSE
ANNE *into hall. Takes off her coat and hangs it up behind door.*

22. SAM AND ANNE'S FRONT ROOM
SAM *is reading golf magazine.* ANNE *comes in.*

ANNE: That woman's getting worse.

SAM: I suppose it's her age . . . What can you expect?

ANNE: I can expect her to get a little wiser, as she gets older. Imagine wanting you round there to decorate . . . has the woman no sense at all?

SAM: She's probably right though . . . I grew up there. Who's going to harm me in my own street?

ANNE: (*Looking at him*) If old age is her excuse . . . what's yours?

SAM: I miss that wee street . . . the crack with the neighbours. (*He rises.*)

ANNE: Yes . . . there'd be some crack now . . . but I'm afraid you wouldn't hear it. You knew what you were doing, when you put on that uniform.
(*Pause.*)
Do you want another cup of tea before you go?

SAM: No thanks . . . I drink far too much tea. (*Slapping his stomach*) Got to watch my figure.
(KATIE, *their 14-year-old daughter, enters.*)

ANNE: Homework's all finished, love?

KATIE: Almost . . . I've just a bit of reading to do.

SAM: Why didn't you come down and see your granny?

KATIE: I was down, just before you came in . . . I went back up to finish my homework.

(ANNE *into hall from kitchen.*)

SAM: You can't have spent very much time with her.

ANNE: Come on, Sam, you know she's a lot to do.

SAM: It's not too much to ask. It's not as if she's going to be around for ever. (*Pause.*) Where's that other one?

ANNE: He's over in Simon's.

SAM: Great . . . he doesn't even come to see me, let alone his granny.

ANNE: Really . . . I think that's enough, Sam.

(*He looks at her, then rises and leaves the room.*)

KATIE: There, you see . . . no matter what I do he moans. I'm sick of it.

ANNE: (*Sits*) Be patient with him, love. Your granny was being rather difficult today.

KATIE: It's always the same. If it's not my granny, it's the job. He never stops.

ANNE: That's enough . . . I don't want you talking like that, just before he goes out. You can just go and fetch Kevin, please.

(KATIE *picks up the cup and goes.* ANNE *tidies up a bit . . . fussy.* SAM *re-enters. One sleeve is rolled up to the elbow.*)

22 CONT. INT. KITCHEN

SAM: Where's she just gone?

ANNE: To fetch Kevin.

SAM: Don't bother on my account.

ANNE: It's time he was in anyway.

SAM: That ballcock's away with it again. Tell them just to lift the lid and hold it. I'll have to get it fixed.

ANNE: And the leak at the kitchen tap . . . and Kevin's bedside lamp. Then there's . . .

SAM: All right . . . all right. (*Exits.*)

22 CONT. INT. HALL

ANNE: So if you ever do have any spare time, decorating your
mother's bedroom would not be top of the list.
(SAM *puts on his jacket.*)

SAM: And no sitting up. Take the phone off the hook if you like.
(SAM *kisses her cheek and goes.*)

ANNE: Just you go and let me run this place please.
(*He goes. Pause. Voices outside. Car drives away.* KATIE *and*
KEVIN *are at the gate.* KATIE *enters followed by* KEVIN.)

22 CONT. INT. KITCHEN

KEVIN: I don't know why Dad doesn't wear his uniform. Sure if
they see he's not wearing a seat belt they'll know he's a cop.
He should have another policeman with him riding
shotgun.

ANNE: That's enough . . .

KEVIN: If I was him I'd get a machine-gun. (*He makes a
machine-gun noise and rakes the room.*)

ANNE: (*Firmly*) I've told you that's enough. (*Pause.*) Up you go
and get ready for bed.

KEVIN: Can I have a glass of milk and a biscuit, please?

ANNE: Go on . . . I'll bring them up.

KEVIN: But there's no point cleaning my teeth if I'm having . . .

ANNE: (*Cutting in and shouting at him angrily*) You can get
changed and washed . . .
(*Pause.* KEVIN *to door.*)
(*Quieter, calmer.*) Just leave your teeth until you've had your
biscuit. (*Pause.*) Go on now, like a good boy.
(*Pause.* KEVIN *looks at* KATIE, *and then goes.* ANNE *stands,
fighting for self-control.* KATIE *looks at her.*)
I know . . . I'm sorry.

KATIE: It's all right. I'll get him his milk and biscuit.
(ANNE *to living room.* KATIE *gets milk from fridge, pours it.
Crosses to get biscuit, then exits.*)

22 CONT. INT. HALL
(KATIE *exits kitchen into hall.*)

KATIE: (*To* ANNE *from hall*) I'll tell him you'll be up later to kiss him goodnight. (*Pause.* KATIE *goes upstairs.*)

22 CONT. INT. LIVING ROOM
ANNE *is sitting in living room. She is crying.*

23. THE BILLET
WALKER *is seated on the bed polishing* ERIC's *boots.* ERIC *is lying on his bunk, reading an army magazine.* WALKER *approaches, timidly, holding* ERIC's *boots.* ERIC *inspects the boots. He nods, and gestures towards his locker.* WALKER *places the boots in* ERIC's *locker, and walks away.* ERIC *waits a few moments.*
ERIC: Walker . . . come here.
   (WALKER *comes and stands by the foot of the bed.*)
   (*Shouting*) Come here! They're the wrong way round. I want the toes pointing out.
   (*Pause.* WALKER *turns the boots around.*)
WALKER: Is that all?
   (ERIC *doesn't bother to reply, or even look at* WALKER. *After a moment he does look up, and scrutinizes the pathetic* WALKER, *but still says nothing. He returns to his magazine.* WALKER *stands for another few moments and then walks slowly away.*)

24. AN RUC OPERATIONS ROOM
A number of policemen sitting around. SAM *is sitting looking through some papers. Another policeman,* KEN, *enters; he gives* SAM *an unfriendly look.* SAM *looks up, but they don't speak.*
KEN: I hear they didn't find a St Christopher on Harry Webster's body. Maybe if he'd been wearing one of those he'd have been protected from all harm. (*Pause.*) I wonder was that it . . . the power of a redundant saint . . . or did they maybe know who they were shooting at?
   (SAM *rises and glares at him.*)
   Or who not to shoot at.
   (SAM *goes out.*)
   Fenian bastard.
1ST RUC MAN: (*Rising*) Maybe Harry brought it on himself . . .

talking the way you do.

KEN: What do we have here, a Fenian-lover?

1ST RUC MAN: Fenian or not, I'd rather take my chances beside him as beside you, any day. (*Goes.*)

KEN: That's the sort of bastard we've really got to watch.

2ND RUC MAN: (*Rising*) D'you know something, Ken, every time you come into a room you bring a bad smell with you. (*He just glares at* KEN *before he goes to the only remaining officer.*)

KEN: Do they know what they are?

3RD RUC MAN: Cool it, Ken . . . we're all out there together in a while. That's where the war is, not in here.

25. INT. KEVIN'S BEDROOM

ANNE *is in his bedroom.* KEVIN *is in bed reading.*

ANNE: Come on, Kevin, it's time you were asleep.

KEVIN: (*Reading*) Can I just finish this chapter? (*He kisses her.*)

ANNE: Goodnight, love . . . You did your face and teeth. (ANNE *leaves the room.*)

26. INT. HALL, SAM'S HOUSE

ANNE *comes downstairs and goes into living room.*

26 CONT. INT. LIVING ROOM

KATIE: I think I'll go up soon. I'll copy this out in bed.

ANNE: Did you get it finished then?

KATIE: Yes.

ANNE: Good . . . well?

(KATIE *looks questioningly.*)

Are you pleased with it?

KATIE: I think it's fine. Mum . . . Michael McVeigh has asked me to go to a disco on Saturday night. Can I go?

ANNE: You'll have to ask your father.

KATIE: (*Gloomy*) No need . . . I know what the answer'll be.

ANNE: Get him in a good mood.

KATIE: Huh, I'm never there when he's sleeping.

(*She exits.* ANNE *just looks at her, a little hurt.*)

27. EXT. A BELFAST STREET IN THE EARLY HOURS OF THE MORNING

A fish and chip shop. A Police Land Rover sits by the kerb opposite. A POLICEMAN *stands by the doorway, shotgun at the ready. There are a few civilians around. Pause.* SAM *emerges from the shop, carrying bags of chips.* SAM *and the* POLICEMAN *walk to the kerbside, ready to cross the road to their Land Rover. The* ARMED POLICEMAN *relaxes. He and* SAM *chat and laugh. Just as they step on to the road, three shots from an automatic weapon ring out.* SAM *is hit twice and collapses in the roadway. Panic ensues. The civilians scatter. The Land Rover is reversed to protect* SAM's *body from the front. Two other* POLICEMEN, *guns in hand, tumble from the Land Rover. The* POLICEMAN *who was covering* SAM *races back to his body. He has been running around trying to establish the gunman's position. For a moment there is an eerie silence. Everyone is frozen. Then a civilian runs to attend to* SAM. *She is a* NURSE. *Another* POLICEMAN *rushes to assist her.* SAM *is moaning, conscious. His eyes are open, dancing about in his head. Alarmed, fearful, but alive. Shocked. Not speaking. The bag of chips lies by his side, soaked in blood. The Land Rover's radio crackles. Activity resumes. One* POLICEMAN *herds all the civilians into the shop, including two who were sitting in parked cars. The* FISH-FRYER *comes towards* SAM, *carrying a glass of water. Freeze on the face of the* POLICEMAN *who was guarding* SAM. *His face is white, drained, taut. He is alert, angry, prepared for action. Ready to kill. Hold.*

28. EXT. BARRACKS

ERIC *wandering in confines of barracks.*

28 CONT. PERIMETER FENCE OF BARRACKS. NIGHT

ERIC *wandering around. Ends up gazing through fence. Sounds of city in background. A far-off siren. A Land Rover drives towards him. Stops.* ERIC *is put into vehicle by* LANCE-CORPORAL.

29. INT. GUARDROOM

ERIC *is marched in, fully dressed, by a* LANCE-CORPORAL; *an angry* GUARD SERGEANT *and another soldier,* SMART, *present.*

SERGEANT: You weren't planning to do a bunk, were you? So why were you wandering around fully dressed, in the middle of the night?

ERIC: I just couldn't sleep.

SERGEANT: I just couldn't sleep . . . Sergeant.

ERIC: I just couldn't sleep, Sergeant.

SERGEANT: Maybe if you bloody pansies did a proper job of work you'd be able to sleep, wouldn't you?

ERIC: Yes, Sergeant.

SERGEANT: If you were real soldiers you could sleep. I could sleep if I had your chance. I wouldn't be wandering around in the middle of the night, would I?

ERIC: No, Sergeant.

(SERGEANT *glares at him. Pause.*)

SERGEANT: Right, Bandsman Maitland (*Full of contempt and anger*) so you can't sleep. Well I think we can do something about that. Lance-Corporal Wilson?

LANCE-CORPORAL: Sergeant?

SERGEANT: I'm going to take our little musical friend down on to the square and see that he gets enough exercise to make him so tired, he'll be only too grateful to crawl back up into the nice bed you'll have prepared for him here.

LANCE-CORPORAL: Right, Sergeant.

SERGEANT: (*Regarding* ERIC *for a moment, barking*) Bandsman Maitland, stand easy. Atten . . . tion! As you were. You little pillock . . . you move on the command . . . not on anticipation of it . . . got it?

ERIC: Yes, Sergeant.

SERGEANT: Now . . . (*Fiercely and quickly*) Bandsman Maitland, attention. Lance-Corporal . . . take over.

LANCE-CORPORAL: Yes, Sergeant. (*He goes to behind counter.*)

SERGEANT: Bandsman Maitland, about turn . . . by the front quick march . . . left wheel, left, right, left, right. (*As* ERIC *is just outside the door*) Mark time . . . left, right, huh. (*At the door, to* SMART.) Could you sleep now, Smart?

SMART: You bet, Sergeant.

SERGEANT: Well don't lad . . . just don't.

SMART: Sergeant.

SERGEANT: (*Giving* ERIC *a dig in the back*) Quick march . . .
    left, right, left, right. (*As they move off.*) Swing those
    arms . . . swing them . . . higher . . . left, right, left,
    right . . . (*Out of hearing.*)

SMART: Poor little sod.

LANCE-CORPORAL: Serves him right . . . they get it too cushy.
    (*Pause.*) Better get that bed made up smartish, Smart.

SMART: (*Going*) Corp.

30. INT. BANDROOM

TONY *is by the window, smoking and laughing, looking out at* ERIC
being drilled. We see the SERGEANT *putting* ERIC *through gruelling
drill routines, thumping him from time to time as he gets it wrong.
Hold.*

31. INT. ANNE AND SAM'S FRONT ROOM

A POLICEMAN *sits, uncomfortable. The* TWO CHILDREN *sit, in
their night clothes, huddled together on the settee. A* NEIGHBOUR *is
there.* ANNE *enters, dressed to go to the hospital. She has the aspect
of a sleep walker. The whole scene is conducted through nods and
gestures.* ANNE *exits with the* POLICEMAN*. Pause. The two*
CHILDREN*, frightened, confused, hurt, huddle a little closer
together. Hold.*

32. INT. SAM'S MOTHER'S BEDROOM

SAM'S MOTHER *is lying sleeping, her head dropped back, her mouth
hanging open. Her open library book has fallen face-down on the
bed. The radio crackles frantically on the bedside locker. Slow fade.*

33. INT. THE BILLET

TONY *is there,* WALKER *also.* ERIC *enters. Stands.*

TONY: Oh . . . you're back . . . I saw you last night . . .
    thought the transfer'd come through. (*Smirks.*)

ERIC: They try to transfer me now I'll shoot myself.

TONY: (*With a laugh*) Not fancy the real soldiering then?

ERIC: The Band Sergeant was right. They're animals . . .
  mindless animals.
  (*Pause.* TONY *just chuckles.* ERIC *sits and starts to play. Hold
  on him playing for a moment. The* BAND SERGEANT *enters,
  listens, then moves further in.*)
SERGEANT: I've had another word about you, Maitland. As
  soon as we get back from our tour of the London Parks,
  you'll be seeing the Bandmaster. We'll get your transfer
  moving. (*Exits.*)
  (*Pause.* TONY *and* ERIC *just look at each other.*)
TONY: If I was you I'd run after him, mate.
  (*Hold on* ERIC'*s face. As we fade he is rushing towards the
  door. Hold.*)

GOING HOME

Cast:

COLETTE	Anne Hasson
MARY	Paula Hamilton
PAUL	Tony London
CAROL BROWN	Eileen Fletcher
BRIAN BROWN	David Coyle
MRS BROWN	Trudy Kelly
MR BROWN	Joe McPartland
LOUISE BROWN	Libby Smyth
JIM	Anthony Fraites
MARY'S BOYFRIEND	John Hewitt
MRS DONNELLY	Doreen Hepburn
MR DONNELLY	Louis Rolston
GERARD DONNELLY	Killian McKenna
FAMILIES OFFICER	Anthony Dutton
INTELLIGENCE OFFICER	Richard Bartlett
MAJOR 2IC	Edward Wilson
RUC POLICEMAN	Dermot Graham
SOLDIER A & I	David Calvert
SOLDIER B & 2	Paul Herriott
PRIEST	George Shane

Plus supporting artists

1. EXT. FAMILIES OFFICER'S OFFICE

2. INT. THE FAMILIES OFFICER'S OFFICE
CAPTAIN WHITE *is sitting, gazing into space. There is a knock on door. He pretends to busy himself with papers. Calls 'Come in'.*
COLETTE *enters. She is Belfast born, wife of a soldier,* CORPORAL PAUL RODGERS. *She is small, good-looking, quite bright. She walks to the desk.*
FAMILIES OFFICER: Mrs Rodgers, good to see you again. Sit down won't you. (*Gestures.*)
COLETTE: (*Sitting, she is timid, ill at ease*) Thank you.
FAMILIES OFFICER: (*He is calm, self-possessed, firm*) I've spoken at length to the Adjutant. He's spoken to your husband, Corporal Rodgers. (*Pause.*) Corporal Rodgers is quite adamant that the children should not go to Belfast with you.
COLETTE: Captain, my father's dying. He wants to see his grandchildren.
FAMILIES OFFICER: I'm very sympathetic, Mrs Rodgers. I have to say though that Corporal Rodgers is genuinely concerned about the safety of the children.
COLETTE: (*Emotional*) He couldn't care less about their safety. It's just to get back at me. It's just to spite my family.
FAMILIES OFFICER: We in our turn are concerned for the safety of Corporal Rodgers, which is linked very much to his peace of mind. Do your people know he's serving there at the moment?
(*She shakes her head.*)
We needn't go over the past . . . but we both remember the serious trouble your family gave, at the time of your marriage to Corporal Rodgers . . . and they made very serious threats against him.

COLETTE: Of course they did. They threatened me too, but he's not going to see them. They're not going to harm our children.

FAMILIES OFFICER: Experience shows that they're more than capable of doing that.

(*She glares at him.*)

Some of them. Suppose someone sees him on the streets . . . they could draw some very silly conclusions about why you're back. (*Pause.*) You are an army wife, you are fully aware of the situation. Your own safety can't be assured. He doesn't want you to go either, although he knows you must. He's concerned about you, and so are we.

COLETTE: I was very close to my father. I was his favourite, until I married Paul.

FAMILIES OFFICER: (*Pause.*) As I've said, Mrs Rodgers, we are not unsympathetic. None of us are . . . including Corporal Rodgers. It's all such a complicated business really. Look . . .

(*She glares at him.*)

Of course you must go to see your father . . . that's obvious, in the circumstances. Don't you think though, quite apart from the dangers, it's not going to be a very pleasant atmosphere for young children? (*Pause.*) For all our sakes the children have to stay here. Corporal Rodgers has made arrangements for his mother . . . to look after them while you're away.

COLETTE: (*Upset*) You're supposed to help me.

FAMILIES OFFICER: Mrs Rodgers . . .

COLETTE: You're an officer, you're supposed to have authority. You hate us, don't you? Even when we marry your bloody soldiers, you still hate us.

FAMILIES OFFICER: (*Placatory*) Really, Mrs Rodgers . . .

COLETTE: (*Rising, angry and upset*) Stuff your Mrs Rodgers. I hope the next time you go to Belfast they get you.

(*He is angry as she storms out.*)

FAMILIES OFFICER: Come back . . . Mrs Rodgers.

3. INT. DONNELLY BEDROOM. DAY TWO – AFTERNOON
GERARD *exits with tray of uneaten breakfast.* DAD *dozing.*

4. INT. HALL AND STAIRS/LIVING ROOM
GERARD *goes downstairs. Enters living room.*

5. INT. THE DONNELLY HOUSE. DAY TWO
MOTHER *sitting smoking.* GERARD, *her 20-year-old son, comes downstairs. He is carrying a tray on which is most of an uneaten tea, scrambled egg, crustless fingers of toast.*

MOTHER: (*Surveying the tray*) He hardly touched it. There's three good eggs in that. Could you not eat it?

GERARD: I'm not going to eat after him.

MOTHER: Good God . . . he is your father.

GERARD: Even so. Anyway, I've just had my breakfast.

MOTHER: Breakfast, and it near tea time. It's time you stopped lying all day. What's he doing now?

GERARD: Hang gliding from the window sill.

MOTHER: Don't be so damned funny, you.

GERARD: He's dozing. (*Turns to kitchen.*)

MOTHER: Did you read him the paper?
   (GERARD *to doorway.*)

GERARD: Ma, I hate that paper. Why don't you get the *Irish Times*?

MOTHER: What do we want with the *Irish Times*? All we want's an outline of what's going on. Not clever boys like yourself telling us why it's going on, and how to stop it.

GERARD: Anyway it's a morning paper. Why don't you read it to him in the morning?

MOTHER: He likes you reading to him. I think it's only right that you should do something for him.

GERARD: I feed him.

MOTHER: We all feed him, and he eats less for you than any of us.

GERARD: (*Sitting*) That's not my fault.

MOTHER: Of course it is. You don't show enough interest, in him or the food.

GERARD: Rubbish . . . I know . . . I'll dress as a bunny-girl
. . . do you think that would help?

MOTHER: You should be on the stage, son.

GERARD: (*Rising*) What time does the Brit-bird arrive?

MOTHER: That's enough out of you. She's your sister.

GERARD: Why should that mean more to me than it did to her?
How long is she staying?

MOTHER: Who knows?

GERARD: You do all realize that he could linger for weeks,
months even. Are we going to have her and her two
Brit-brats all that time? (*Pause.*) What's she call them
anyway?

MOTHER: I'm not sure . . . I think it's Peter and Paula.

GERARD: (*Laughing*) Peter and Paula . . . you're joking? They
sound like two budgies.

6. INT. CAROL BROWN'S HOUSE. DAY TWO – AFTERNOON

CAROL BROWN *is twenty-one, pretty, a shop assistant. She enters
from kitchen.* MRS BROWN *enters living room.*

MRS BROWN: I could have described your da when we were
going out.

CAROL: I'm sure.

MRS BROWN: Brian and Louise are coming round.

CAROL: What for?

MRS BROWN: To meet him . . . he is your brother.

CAROL: For goodness' sake. We just wanted a quiet night with
you and my da . . . not a party.

MRS BROWN: It's not a party. They're family.

CAROL: I didn't want a crowd.

MRS BROWN: Since when were two a crowd?

CAROL: That's it . . . we're not coming.

MRS BROWN: Not coming . . . you'd better come . . . I've
everything in . . . and Louise has baked.

CAROL: If he knows there's going to be a crowd he'll not come.

MRS BROWN: Will you shut up about a crowd?
(CAROL *streaks her lipstick across her face three or four times.*)

CAROL: (*Rising*) Right . . . I'm ready.

MRS BROWN: Ready . . . like that? For goodness' sake catch yourself on. (MRS BROWN *exits to kitchen.*)

7. INT. CAROUSEL AT ALDERGROVE. DAY TWO
COLETTE *arrives at carousel.* MARY *is there to meet her. There is a slight awkwardness between them.*
COLETTE: I could have walked past you. You've lost a lot of weight . . . and the hair.
MARY: It has been four years.
COLETTE: Yes. (*She almost breaks down. Blows her nose.*) Sorry.
MARY: We should have kept in touch. We should have written. I wanted to . . . once or twice . . . I'm not a letter writer.
COLETTE: No . . . nor me.
MARY: I will when you go back. (*Pause.*) I didn't mean . . .
COLETTE: Of course not. (*Pause.*) This place has changed . . . well a bit.
MARY: They're always chopping and changing this place. You get the impression that they don't know what they want. (*Pause.*) How is . . . (*Uncertain of the name.*)
COLETTE: Paul. (*Pause.*) He's fine. He didn't think it was a proper atmosphere to bring the children into.
MARY: I'd have been surprised if he'd let you bring them.
COLETTE: Would you?
MARY: Well yes . . . I wouldn't have in his position.
COLETTE: Will Dad be disappointed?
MARY: I suppose he will. Did you bring photographs of them?
COLETTE: Yes, but they're in albums, in my case.
MARY: No, not for me . . . for him and my ma.
COLETTE: So . . . what about you . . . no sign of you getting married or anything.
MARY: I haven't even enough applicants for a short list.
COLETTE: When I left Gerry McManus was making a strong claim. (*Pause.*) Well?
MARY: Gerry's in the Maze . . . ten years for armed robbery . . . and he has a wife and two children waiting for him.
COLETTE: I'm sorry.

MARY: I'm not . . . I'm seeing someone at the moment . . . just casual.

COLETTE: Do I know him?

MARY: No.

(*They get in car. Pause.*)

COLETTE: Well, tell me.

MARY: I have told you . . . it's just a casual thing. (*Pause.*) He's not marriageable.

COLETTE: Not a soldier?

MARY: No.

COLETTE: A Protestant?

MARY: No.

COLETTE: So what else is there?

MARY: Fifty-two and married with six children.

COLETTE: Holy God.

MARY: Welcome home.

(MARY *and* COLETTE *sit for a moment.*)

COLETTE: Mary? . . . Don't breathe a word of this to a living soul . . . (*Pause.*) Paul's back in Belfast. They were posted back a while ago.

(*Pause.*)

Please don't mention it at home . . . please.

8. EXT. FRONT WINDOW. DONNELLY HOUSE. INT. HALL
AND LIVING ROOM. DAY TWO – AFTERNOON

EXT. WINDOW
MOTHER *looks through curtains and then moves quickly away as car arrives with* COLETTE *and* MARY.

INT. LIVING ROOM
MOTHER *goes and sits in armchair.*

EXT. FRONT DOOR
MARY *and* COLETTE *enter the hallway.*

INT. HALL. REPEAT ENTRANCE
MARY *and* COLETTE *pass through into the living room.*

INT. LIVING ROOM

COLETTE: Hello, Mother.

>   (MOTHER *turns to* COLETTE.)

MOTHER: Where are the children?

9. INT. SMALL FRONT BEDROOM OF THE DONNELLY HOUSE.
   DAY TWO – AFTERNOON

COLETTE *sitting by her* FATHER'S *bed, two photograph albums on
her knees. Her* MOTHER *standing by the door watching her. The*
FATHER *is propped up. Frail. Breathless.*

FATHER: Wouldn't let them come. Typical English . . .
hostages. My own grandchildren.

COLETTE: (*Holds up her albums*) I've brought photographs.

>   (MOTHER *grunts in the background.*)

FATHER: Photographs? (*As she opens one*) Not now . . . What is
it you call them?

COLETTE: Peter and Paula.

FATHER: (*Giggling*) Two little Dickey Birds . . . (*Pause.*) How
long are you staying?

COLETTE: (*Uncertain*) I don't know . . .

FATHER: I'll not keep you, if you're in a hurry.

COLETTE: Dad, please . . .

FATHER: No . . . I'm ready. I can go anytime now . . . I waited
to see the children. Hostages . . . that's the English all
right.

COLETTE: Is there anything I can get you?

>   (*He just looks at her.*)

>   I mean anything here?

MOTHER: We get him anything he wants here. He's not
neglected you know.

COLETTE: I wasn't suggesting that.

MOTHER: I think we should let him sleep now.

COLETTE: (*Pause.*) I'd like to stay.

MOTHER: You'll tire him out.

COLETTE: No I won't . . . I'll just sit here. I'll not talk.

MOTHER: Suit yourself . . . if you had it to do every day you
wouldn't be so keen. (*She goes.*)

10. INT. THE BROWN HOUSE. DAY TWO – 8 PM

BRIAN, LOUISE, MR *and* MRS BROWN *are sitting waiting. They are sitting silently, anxious, with the looks of people who have been waiting longer than they anticipated. A car arrives and stops. They perk up. Pause. The car drives off. Pause.* CAROL *enters, ushers* JIM *in, as everyone stands up.*

CAROL: This is Jim.
> (*They are all frozen . . .* JIM *stands, smiling. He is coloured.*)
> (*Introducing*) Jim, this is my mum.
> (*They shake hands.* MRS BROWN *attempts to say 'Hello' . . . but no words come out. The other introductions follow. Still they all remain standing. Pause.*)
> Jim, sit down.
> (*He does. The others slowly sit . . . still stunned.*)
> (*Moving to the scullery*) Will I put on the kettle?

MRS BROWN: (*Jumping up*) I'll do it.

LOUISE: (*Also jumping up*) I'll give you a hand.

CAROL: Well you two go ahead then. (*She sits.*) Jim's a soldier.
> (MRS BROWN *and* BRIAN *just stare at her dumbly.*)
> Aren't you, Jim?

JIM: Yeah . . . I'm a soldier. (*Pause.*)

MR BROWN: We expected you to be . . .

CAROL: (*Quickly*) Dad. . . ?

MR BROWN: Earlier.

JIM: Yes . . .

CAROL: Oh . . .

MR BROWN: (*To* CAROL) What?

JIM: The taxi was late. (*Pause.*)

BRIAN: Where are you from, Jim?

JIM: Bradford.

BRIAN: I mean originally.

JIM: Bradford. I got paid off, like . . . went to London to look for work . . . tramped the streets, like. So in the end I just joined up.

MR BROWN: Are there many like you in it?
> (*Pause.* JIM *looks puzzled.*)
> Who just joined up to get off the dole?

JIM: I reckon there are some. Mind you it's not bad. I'm quite enjoying it, like.

LOUISE: (*Emerging with plates of sandwiches*) Does your friend take sugar, Carol?

JIM: Jim . . . no ta. I'm sweet enough.

LOUISE: (*A weak smile*) The tea's just coming. We'd the kettle boiled earlier. (*She stands, awkward.*)

BRIAN: Sit down, Louise.

LOUISE: I'd better fetch some more stuff. (*Goes.*)

MR BROWN: Do you like Northern Ireland then?

JIM: It's all right.

(LOUISE *re-enters with plates of sandwiches and home-made buns.* MRS BROWN *follows with tea for* JIM *and* CAROL. *They serve the others and then bring their own out.*)

MRS BROWN: Is that tea all right, Jim?

JIM: It's great ta.

MRS BROWN: Just help yourself. We don't stand on ceremony here . . . just muck in.

(*They eat. Silence.*)

MR BROWN: (*Just to break the silence*) This is a lovely bit of corned beef . . . is it fresh?

MRS BROWN: Of course it's fresh. In the name of goodness, do you think I'd serve up stale meat?

MR BROWN: No, I meant was it tinned or sliced?

MRS BROWN: (*Furious*) It's tinned . . . but I sliced it.

(*Pause.*)

MR BROWN: (*A little louder than necessary*) Do you like corned beef, Jim?

MRS BROWN: (*Over* JIM'*s 'Yes'*) You don't need to shout at him.

MR BROWN: I didn't shout. Did I shout at you, Jim?

MRS BROWN: (*As* JIM *smiles helplessly*) Of course you shouted. We're all sitting here. We all heard you.

MR BROWN: Jasus Christ, I only spoke to the bloody fella.

MRS BROWN: And you needn't start shouting at me now.

(*Pause. Another silence, tense.* JIM *and* CAROL *look at each other.*)

JIM: (*Deciding*) Look . . . Mr and Mrs Brown . . . I know I'm not what you expected, and I'm sorry if we've embarrassed you . . . but . . . (*Reaching out and taking* CAROL'*s hand.*) Carol and me, we're sort of serious.

ALL: ???

CAROL: Jim and me are getting engaged. (*Smiles.*)

11. INT. DONNELLY HOUSE. HALL, STAIRS AND LIVING ROOM. DAY THREE – MORNING

COLETTE *comes downstairs with coat.* MARY *and her* MOTHER *are sitting.*

MOTHER: Are you going out?

COLETTE: Yes . . . I'm just going into town. Just to take a look around.

MOTHER: Huh, there's nothing in there. It doesn't change much you know.

COLETTE: Still, it has been four years.

MARY: Maybe I'll come with you . . . or did you want to do it on your own?

COLETTE: No . . . I'd love you to come.
(MARY *rises.*)

MOTHER: Will yous be back for your tea?

COLETTE: Maybe we'll have it out. I'll treat you, Mary.

MOTHER: Huh, the army must be paying big wages now.

COLETTE: It'll not be terribly expensive I'm sure.

MOTHER: So yous won't be back until bedtime?

COLETTE: We'll be back before that.

MARY: I might be going out for a while later on. (*Exit for coat.*)

MOTHER: It's getting like a hotel, the comings and goings.

COLETTE: Does anyone around here have the telephone, Mum?

MOTHER: What do you want with the telephone?

COLETTE: Well, what do you think? To phone Paul . . . or to give him a number to phone me.

MOTHER: (*Rising*) Have you taken leave of your senses? Ask one of my neighbours to take phone calls from a Brit?

COLETTE: He is my husband.

MOTHER: They know that only too well. You phone him when you're in the centre of town, well away from here.

COLETTE: Do you mean I'm going to have to go into the centre of town every time I want to phone home?

MOTHER: You can do it whatever way you like. I'm telling you you can't use anybody's phone around here.

COLETTE: Honestly, half the people round here should still be living in caves.

MOTHER: Never you mind where they should be living. You married him . . . you knew what you were doing. The people round here haven't changed.

MARY: (*Re-entering, before* COLETTE *can reply*) Don't let's have all this now.

COLETTE: (*Angry*) I suppose you'd rather I'd been like our Theresa . . . got pregnant and married a good Catholic boy . . . who batters the head off her, every time he has a couple of drinks.

MOTHER: At least he is a Catholic, and an Irish one. He'd know what the inside of a chapel was like.

COLETTE: Only from memory, and not half as well as he'd know what the inside of a pub was like.

MARY: Colette . . . I'm going.

MOTHER: He'd make ten of that one you've married.

COLETTE: I think I'd have married anybody to get away from you.

MOTHER: You did.

MARY: (*Screaming*) Colette . . .
(*Pause. They look at her.*)
Will you both shut up?

MOTHER: You stop screaming and your father lying up there dying.

MARY: That's it, isn't it? He's lying up there dying no matter who he is, or what he is. That's the way we'll all go . . . no matter who we are, or what we are.
(*They lapse into silence. Pause.*)

COLETTE: I'm sorry, Mum . . .

MOTHER: (*Fiercely*) About what?
(COLETTE *just looks at her. Pause.* COLETTE *and* MARY *go.*)

12. EXT. CENTRAL BELFAST. DAY THREE

COLETTE *and* MARY *just wandering around central Belfast.*
COLETTE *taking in everything. Looking in shop windows, just
absorbing the atmosphere. At one point she just stops dead, and lets
people mill around her. Drinking it all in . . . until* MARY *jerks her
along, laughing. A* POLICEMAN *is standing.* COLETTE *stops with
him.*

COLETTE: Excuse me, Officer . . . could you tell me how to get
　　to Great Victoria Street please?
　　(MARY*???*)

POLICEMAN: Of course, love . . . (*Using his hands*) . . . go back
　　up here. Do you see the City Hall at the top? . . . Turn
　　right . . . go down to the bottom, you'll see the Tech and
　　Inst. just facing you, turn left and it's straight on.

COLETTE: Thank you, Officer.

POLICEMAN: Anytime, love.

MARY: (*As they walk on. Furious.*) What the hell are you playing
　　at?

COLETTE: I just wanted to hear him talk, that's all.

MARY: That's all . . . have you no bloody sense?
　　(COLETTE*???*) You never know who sees you in this town.
　　It's bad enough you being married to a soldier . . . now
　　stopping in the town to talk to a policeman!

COLETTE: Sorry, I never thought.

MARY: Well start thinking, will you? Think . . . I am in Belfast
　　now . . . everyone here is mad . . .
　　(COLETTE *laughs.*)
　　And I'm not joking.
　　(COLETTE *stops laughing. They walk on a little. They look at
　　each other, both laugh and cling on to each other.*)

13. INT. DONNELLY HOUSE. HALL, STAIRS AND LIVING
ROOM. DAY THREE – LUNCHTIME

MOTHER *comes downstairs with tray.* GERARD *sitting, just up; his
dishes are sitting around him.* MOTHER *enters with tea tray. Most of
the meal eaten. Takes it to the table. Returns. Sits.*

GERARD: Well, did he eat it?

MOTHER: Most of it.

GERARD: You must have held his nose and shovelled it down.

MOTHER: It just needs a bit of patience.

GERARD: Did you read him the paper?

MOTHER: He prefers you to do that.

GERARD: Ma, I've told you . . . I hate that paper. For goodness' sake.

MOTHER: He's sinking you know. I can see it. It's as if he's just waited for her to come home.

GERARD: Where is she anyway?

MOTHER: Down the town . . . strutting around like Lady Muck. Taking her and Mary in for tea, if you don't mind.

GERARD: What is he, a general?

MOTHER: That's what I said . . . where do they get the money?

GERARD: She spends a lot of time with my da.

MOTHER: Oh aye . . . he'll do that. I run after him, until the very last. Then he coaxes her back, they kiss and make up and I'm left.

GERARD: Here, Ma, I think you're jealous.

MOTHER: I'm hurt, not jealous. We agreed she'd never set foot in this house again. Huh, if it was me up there dying, she wouldn't have been allowed back in.

GERARD: You wouldn't have asked for her though, would you?

MOTHER: Whether I'd asked or not . . . he wouldn't have let her near the place.

GERARD: I suppose when you're dying you see things differently.

MOTHER: (*Tight*) I won't. She caused a lot of hurt and heartache in this family. Then she throws up to me about our Theresa's man.

GERARD: That bastard.

MOTHER: Bastard or not, that's not for her to say. At least he's one of our own. I'll not let Miss High and Mighty put her Englishman above one of our own. (*Pause.*) They're talking you know.

(GERARD???)

The whole place's talking. I can see them, standing in knots

in hallways, at corners, in the shops. When I go in or get
near them, conversation stops . . . and it takes them all
their time to say 'hello'.

GERARD: I'm getting a bit of banter in the Club.

MOTHER: A bit of banter . . . we'll be lucky if we get away with
just a bit of banter. I wish she'd just pack up and go away
home to hell out of this.

14. INT. A BARRACK ROOM. DAY THREE

JIM *is tidying himself up. Singing to himself,* 'She loves you yeah,
yeah, yeah'. *Just a few words a few times. After a moment he
becomes aware that* CORPORAL RODGERS, PAUL, COLETTE's
husband, is standing watching him. CORPORAL RODGERS *looks
very unhappy.*

PAUL: Are you going to marry her?

JIM: Corp?

PAUL: Don't.
    (*Pause.*)

JIM: Are you all right, like, Corporal Rodgers?

PAUL: My wife's here . . .
    (JIM?) . . . in Belfast.

JIM: Very nice . . . will I meet her then?

PAUL: She's over to see her family . . . even I won't see her.
    She's . . . well, you know what she is.

JIM: I'm sorry . . . that's tough, like, Corp.

PAUL: If you are planning to marry her . . . don't do it until
    you're out of the army and then get out of this country.
    (*Pause.*) Every time I'm out I'll be looking for her.

JIM: Why don't you go sick?

PAUL: Yeah, marriage fatigue . . . but they don't recognize it.

JIM: Nerves . . . tell them they've gone. You can't afford to be
    out there thinking about your missus, and whether you're
    going to bump into her. It's dangerous, like.

PAUL: For me, or yourself?

JIM: For you . . . for me . . . for all of us. I'm serious,
    Corp . . .

PAUL: Go on, Younger . . . piss off . . . don't keep your little

Colleen waiting.

JIM: This one's not a Colleen . . . reckons's she's British.

PAUL: One of them.

(*They take their leave of each other.* JIM *goes. A* SOLDIER *enters.*)

SOLDIER: There's a call for you, Corporal.

15. EXT.

COLETTE *in a telephone kiosk.* MARY *standing outside.* PAUL *is on a telephone in the barracks. She dials. Pause.*

COLETTE: Paul . . . it's me.

PAUL: Surprise, surprise. I was beginning to think you didn't care.

COLETTE: Don't be silly, of course I care.

PAUL: Yeah, about who?

COLETTE: For goodness' sake, Paul, he's my father.

PAUL: Why didn't you phone when you arrived?

COLETTE: None of the phones near hand are working, and I can't use any of the neighbours'.

PAUL: Why not?

COLETTE: Oh come on, you know why.

PAUL: Yeah, because you're with them and I don't count.

COLETTE: Paul please . . .

(*He hangs up.*)

Paul . . . Paul! (*Pause.*)

(COLETTE *emerges from the telephone kiosk.* MARY *realizes something is wrong, that she's upset. She says nothing. They walk off together.*)

16. INT. THE BROWNS' HOUSE. DAY THREE

MRS BROWN *sitting.* MR BROWN *enters. He has been out for a few drinks, but isn't 'drunk'. He is dressed up. Removes his good cap and jacket. Sits.*

MR BROWN: Is she out?

MRS BROWN: No . . . she's upstairs getting ready.

MR BROWN: Did you tell her?

MRS BROWN: No . . . not yet.

MR BROWN: I'll tell her then.

MRS BROWN: Be careful.

MR BROWN: Careful what?

MRS BROWN: Don't upset her.

MR BROWN: I'll tell her . . . if it upsets her too bad.

MRS BROWN: She does love him you know.

MR BROWN: Don't talk crap . . . love!

MRS BROWN: It's her choice . . . (*Pause.*) I mean it's her life.

MR BROWN: Didn't even tell us . . . didn't warn us. The lying wee bitch.

MRS BROWN: What lies?

MR BROWN: What lies do you think? She said she couldn't describe him, didn't she? She couldn't describe him! Winkie Bell was able to describe him to me . . . 'Who's the Cadbury's Bourneville your daughter's got?' Marvellous, isn't it? (*Pause.*) I've to drink in this town you know.

MRS BROWN: What did you do?

MR BROWN: Do . . . it was Winkie Bell . . . I smiled and bought him a drink.

MRS BROWN: You did what? Why didn't you slap his kisser for him?

MR BROWN: Winkie Bell! Me slap Winkie Bell? You're going to be the mother-in-law of a Black Fenian . . . do you want to be a widow as well? Winkie's one of the hardest men in this town.

MRS BROWN: Hard man! Sure his sister married that half-wit who exposed himself to the Lord Mayor's wife.

MR BROWN: He's a half-wit 'cause Winkie has him bate stupid. He's a hard man I'm telling you. A Cadbury's Bourneville . . . thank God he sees the funny side of it.

MRS BROWN: Can you hear yourself? You're talking like a big frightened youngster.

(*As* CAROL *comes downstairs.*)

You tell Winkie Bell to mind his own damned business. Our daughter'll choose whoever she likes.

CAROL: (*Enters*) Thank you, Mum. What's all this about Winkie Bell?

MR BROWN: Never you mind all that . . . I want to talk to you.

CAROL: (*Pause*) Well hurry up, I'm going up.

MR BROWN: (*Looking at* MRS BROWN) Your ma and me aren't happy.

CAROL: (*She looks from one to the other and pretends not to understand*) Oh, Dad . . . you're not divorcing, are you?

MR BROWN: There's nothing to joke about, girl. You've made us a laughing stock.

CAROL: (*Angry*) I haven't made you any such thing.

MR BROWN: (*Angry too*) Haven't you . . . it's just a bloody triple disaster that's all, a soldier, a nigger, and a Fenian.

CAROL: (*Going close to him*) Jim . . . that's the only thing I ever want to hear you call him . . . Jim.

MR BROWN: (*Leaping up, furious*) Jungle bloody Jim . . .
(CAROL *kicks him hard on the shin. He squeals in pain. Instinctively he slaps her face, sending her back across the room, crying.* MRS BROWN *gives him a two-fisted thump on the chest that sends him crashing back into his chair.*)

MRS BROWN: Don't you ever lift your hand to that wee girl . . .
(*Grabbing him by the hair*) don't you ever lay a finger on her again, or God forgive me but I'll swing for you.
(*He doesn't retaliate, because he immediately regretted hitting* CAROL. CAROL *pulls her* MOTHER *off.*)

CAROL: (*Near hysterical*) Mummy, Mummy, don't . . . don't . . .

MR BROWN: (*Pulling up his trouser leg*) She kicked me, look . . . she kicked me.

MRS BROWN: (*With a frightening fury*) Don't you ever lift your hand to her again.
(CAROL *clings on to her and they lapse into silence. Pause.*)
You go on now, love . . . fix your make-up and away you go on and see Jim. Go on. (*At* MR BROWN) If Winkie Bell or anybody else remarks on it, I'll give them their answer.
(MR BROWN *refuses to meet her gaze.*)

17. INT. 'TRUFFLES'. DAY THREE
In Donegall Square West. COLETTE *and* MARY *are sitting, sipping*

tea. They haven't spoken since the telephone call. MARY *is just watching* COLETTE.

COLETTE: People here hate me for being married to him. He hates me for being related to people here. I don't know who I am any more, where I belong.

MARY: I don't hate you . . . I never hated you.

COLETTE: No . . . you stayed neutral, I think that was even worse. (*Pause.*) Sorry.

MARY: I had to go on living here . . . with them.

COLETTE: I know . . . I'm being unfair. (*Pause.*) It's not working, Mary. (*Pause.*) I blame them in a way. They hated him so much . . . they were so anti-him . . . I think I tried to compensate. I don't think there was ever enough love there for marriage.

MARY: You have the children . . . your youngest's only a matter of months.

COLETTE: Yes . . . the classic mistake . . . reconciliation pregnancies. We had separated . . . nearly a year apart. (*Pause.*) If I'd brought the children with me, I don't think I'd go back. He realized that . . . I think that's the real reason why he wouldn't let them come with me.

MARY: That means he wants you back.

(COLETTE *looks at her.*)

Colette . . . whatever your future is, it's not here. Wherever you belong it's not here . . . not any more. You can't come back to this place.

COLETTE: (*Pause.*) No, I suppose not.

18. INT. THE BEDROOM OF THE DONNELLY HOUSE. DAY THREE – EVENING

GERARD *is folding the paper.*

GERARD: (*Disgusted*) That's it, Da.

FATHER: Times has changed. I remember the times there was twice as many.

GERARD: It's a bit morbid.

FATHER: Not at all . . . it's natural . . . death.

GERARD: Death might be . . . but reading them all out of the paper isn't.

FATHER: I knew Peter Maguire. Many's the haircut old Peter
give me. He was a barber . . . a proper man's barber . . .
not one of these girly hairdressers you get nowadays. Read
me out that verse his daughter wrote again.

GERARD: Ach, Da . . . it was sick.

FATHER: Would you do what you're asked to do . . . and less of
your oul comments.

(GERARD *reluctantly turns to the obituary column again.*)

GERARD: (*Searching*) 'I remember your last word
the last breath you took.
I'll remember your going
When the whole world just shook.
I'll never forget you darling
    Daddy my own,
I'll remember you always until
    I'm called home.'

FATHER: I'd like a poem.

(GERARD *looks at him in disgust, but his* FATHER *is lying
quietly, his eyes closed. Pause. He stands. Suddenly moved, he
touches his* FATHER'*s forehead. Pause. As* GERARD *goes.*)

FATHER: (*His eyes still closed.*) Thanks, Son.

19. INT. SMALL TELEVISION LOUNGE IN THE BARRACKS.
NIGHT THREE

JIM *and* CAROL *snogging. The door opens, a* SOLDIER *enters. They
spring apart. The* SOLDIER *excuses himself and leaves. They sit.
Pause.*)

JIM: You shouldn't have moved. They can't see me in the dark.

CAROL: They can see the whites of your eyes.

JIM: My eyes are closed when I'm kissing. (*Pause.*) I could try
for a weekend pass and we could go away somewhere.

CAROL: Where?

JIM: Anywhere . . . just somewhere we can get a bit of time
together, and a bit of privacy.

CAROL: Jim, I don't think you understand this place. They
probably wouldn't even let us into a hotel together . . .

especially in the country.

JIM: What about Bangor? We've been there together.

CAROL: We didn't try to spend the night in a hotel together. People here are primitive. They don't understand.

JIM: We could go to London.

CAROL: Are you mad? I couldn't afford it.

JIM: What's money?

CAROL: It's what we haven't got enough of . . . and what we're going to need a lot of to get married. (*Pause*.) We are getting married, aren't we?

JIM: Of course we are. Why do you ask a daft question like that?

CAROL: Sometimes I think you're a chancer.

JIM: What do you mean by that?

CAROL: Well, you say things and I'm not sure if you really think about them.

JIM: You mean you think I'm an idiot?
(*She refutes this*.)
Great . . . a nigger . . . a Fenian . . . and an idiot.

CAROL: Oh shit . . .

JIM: And a shit.
(*She protests, he grabs her. They giggle and caress. She breaks away*.)

CAROL: When do you go up there anyway?

JIM: Where?

CAROL: Girdwood.

JIM: Tomorrow.

CAROL: To do what?

JIM: Foot patrols . . . searches . . . whatever. General security duties . . . and we're on standby the whole time.

CAROL: I think it's daft. Why stick you up there for five weeks . . . and not let you out? I don't know why you joined the Army anyway.

JIM: Well if I hadn't we wouldn't even be sitting here talking about it, would we?

CAROL: Oh Jim . . . I just want to get married, and just settle down and be ordinary people.

JIM: We're going to.

CAROL: When? It's going to take ages to save up. I think you
should leave the Army.

JIM: (*Kissing her*) You talk too much.

CAROL: Stop . . . I'm serious.

JIM: So am I . . . about you. (*Lunging at her.*)

CAROL: Stop it . . . we need to talk.

JIM: Later . . .

CAROL: (*Pushing him back*) No . . . now.

JIM: For Christ's sake . . . we're not going to see each other for
five weeks . . . we can talk later.

CAROL: (*Irritated*) In five weeks?

JIM: Look . . . what are we going to do for the rest of our lives,
if we talk about everything now?

CAROL: (*Pause. Laughs.*) You fool . . . come here.
(CAROL *and* JIM *embrace and are getting into it when the door
opens and a* SOLDIER *enters.*)

SOLDIER: Sorry . . . (*Going to switch on the TV.*) I just want to
see the football.
(*Pause.* JIM *and* CAROL *look at each other.*)

20. INT. THE SECOND-IN-COMMAND'S OFFICE. DAY FOUR –
MORNING
The MAJOR *is in his office. The* INTELLIGENCE OFFICER *is with
him.*

INTELLIGENCE OFFICER: I'm not suggesting Private Younger
himself constitutes a security risk . . . just the situation.
There aren't many Blacks in Northern Ireland. He's
conspicuous. People realize he's a soldier.

MAJOR: I can't confine one of my soldiers to barracks . . .
because of his colour.

INTELLIGENCE OFFICER: I still feel it's an unacceptable risk.
Talk to him. Explain the situation to him. And let's hope
he's bright enough to see it for himself.

MAJOR: Do you mean he'll confine himself to barracks?

INTELLIGENCE OFFICER: I'd hardly think it's a serious
romance, would you?

MAJOR: I don't know . . . I wasn't even aware there was a romance at all. (*Realizing.*) I see what you mean . . . well it does happen.

INTELLIGENCE OFFICER: I'm spending an increasing amount of my time on this sort of thing.

MAJOR: Young soldiers chase women . . . always have. It's healthy . . . we'd have more to worry about if they chased each other. Thank goodness its not the Navy. Anyway, I'll talk to Private Younger. What about this Colette Rodgers case?

INTELLIGENCE OFFICER: Yes . . . I've handed that one over to the RUC, their pigeon really. Rather sad, actually.

MAJOR: There was nothing on the Donnelly family.

INTELLIGENCE OFFICER: Not a thing. They live in a strong Republican area . . . they're probably sympathetic, but not active . . . none of them – as far as we know!

MAJOR: (*Drily*) How much further can we go?
(*Pause.*)

INTELLIGENCE OFFICER: What about Corporal Rodgers?

MAJOR: We were going to restrict him to barrack duties until this business is all over . . . but he came and asked to be allowed to carry on as usual.

INTELLIGENCE OFFICER: Do you think that's wise?

MAJOR: He's an excellent NCO, I think it's wise to trust him, yes.
(*The* INTELLIGENCE OFFICER *just gives him a quizzical look.*)

21. INT. DONNELLY HOUSE. BEDROOM. DAY FOUR – NIGHT
COLETTE *with her* FATHER. *His eyes are closed. He appears to be asleep.* (*Pause.*)

FATHER: Are you happy, Colette?
(COLETTE *startled, as his eyes open.*)

COLETTE: I thought you were asleep. (*Pause.*) No . . . I'm not happy, not particularly.

FATHER: We've lost all those years . . . grandchildren I'll never see . . . they'll grow up to hate me.

(*Pause.* COLETTE *rises and sits beside him.*)

COLETTE: I'm angry with you . . . Dad, especially now. There's no time for either of us. You'll be . . . (*Realizing*) . . . I'm sorry. (*She rises.*)

FATHER: Dead. Say it. I'll be dead soon. (*Dry laugh.*) Don't try to keep it a secret from me . . . I was the first to know.

COLETTE: Mum hates me. When you die the whole place dies for me. I'm frightened, Dad . . . I don't know what's going to happen to me.

FATHER: Is he bad to you?

COLETTE: Dad please . . . his name's Paul . . . please, just once.

FATHER: (*Pause.*) Is, Paul, bad to you?

COLETTE: No, not really. We're bad to each other I suppose. There's just a kind of wall between us. He's nothing to me . . . that's the problem.

FATHER: Do you know, it must be about twenty years since me and your mother kissed . . . or held each other . . . or touched as if we meant it. Something kept us together, though . . . habit . . . the romance, the love, it goes you know. Even now we can't get it back . . . not even for this last wee while . . . but there's still something . . . she's my woman, my wife . . . she'll be my widow . . . (*Pause.*)

COLETTE: Would you not be pleased if I left him?

FATHER: No . . . not unless he was being bad to you . . . beating you or something.

COLETTE: He's never done anything like that.

FATHER: Suppose I wrote him a letter? I don't feel guilty, Colette . . . I can't say I feel guilty. If it happened again I'd probably do it again. I didn't ask you to come over here to beg for forgiveness . . . do you understand that?

COLETTE: Yes.

FATHER: Your mother thinks I have. (*Pause.*) You were always my favourite, Colette . . . I don't really know what that means . . . I loved you all . . . but it was just wee things when you were growing up. They kept coming into my

head . . . that's why I wanted you back. That's why I
wanted to see the children . . . do they look like you?

COLETTE: Yes . . . everybody says so, Dad. I've brought
photographs.

FATHER: No . . . I remember you well, so I know. (*Pause.*) Be
patient with your mother, love . . . ignore her, I mean what
she says. You see, she's jealous.

(COLETTE *looks questioningly at him.*)

She thinks I'm going to apologize, that you're going to
forgive me, and then she'll get all the blame.

COLETTE: She was the worst . . .

FATHER: No . . . she was the most honest. I didn't always agree
with her . . . yet I let her have her way. We're unique
round here you know. Not one of our family's involved . . .
not one. We're Republicans . . . always have been . . . but
no connection of mine's ever taken a life for any cause. So
when you did that we were all under suspicion. You put us
all at risk you see. I'm not blaming you . . . but don't you
blame us. We did what we thought we had to do. (*Pause.*)
We could have writ . . . answered your letters, but we
didn't.

COLETTE: I love you, Dad.

FATHER: Love me! . . . Jasus, I should hope so.

(*She gets tearful.*)

Don't . . . no gerning . . . anybody cries in this room I tell
them to get out.

COLETTE: Are you frightened, Dad?

FATHER: Frightened . . . no I'm not frightened. I've got over
that. You realize it's happening and there's not a damn
thing you can do about it. I'm a bit curious. I can't imagine
just being nothing. I often wonder if you maybe live on,
inside your own head. Do you know, in the past couple of
weeks I've remembered things I forgot years ago.

(*Pause. They look at each other, the absurdity makes them
laugh.*)

See what you can do about it, love . . . your own thing.
Don't blame him . . . (*Pause.*) . . . don't blame Paul for

not being Superman . . . just see if you can work it out.
For Christ's sake take a good look at us all before you go,
see what this place has done to us, and don't entertain any
thoughts of coming back to it. Do you hear me?
(*She smiles and nods her head.*)
Right . . . you'll have to excuse me now . . . I need to do a
pee.
(*She goes quietly, closing the door. He gazes at the door for a
moment, then he stretches under the bed, and brings up his
urinal bottle.*)

22. INT. THE DONNELLY SITTING ROOM. DAY FOUR –
NIGHT
MOTHER *is sitting.* COLETTE *comes downstairs. She has been
crying. Her* MOTHER *just looks up at her. Hold. They gaze at each
other.* COLETTE *sits, blows her nose. She sits back, gazing at the
fire. Her* FATHER *has a bout of coughing. She looks ceilingwards.
Her* MOTHER *gazes at her.* COLETTE *drops her gaze as the coughing
stops. They catch each other's eyes. Hold.*

23. INT. BARRACK ROOM. DAY FOUR – NIGHT
PAUL, *his gear packed, leaving his room. He is going to do a stint in
Girdwood. He leaves the room. Pause. He returns. Goes to his
locker. He removes a small, oval-framed photograph of* COLETTE;
*glances at it, considers, then putting it in his pocket, locks the locker
and leaves.*

24. A PARKED CAR. NIGHT FOUR – DARK
MARY *is sitting with her man. He is in his fifties, balding, with a
tiny beard, neat appearance.*
MAN: I've booked for the rugby international in Dublin next
month.
MARY: I don't like rugby.
MAN: No, not for the match . . . I'll go with the lads . . . I've
booked for the hotel.
MARY: A dirty weekend?
MAN: What's wrong with you tonight? You're edgy.

MARY: I'm pregnant, I think.

MAN: What? (*Nervous laugh*) Don't talk rubbish, you're on the pill.

MARY: You're so virile I don't think the pill's strong enough for your sperm.

MAN: What is this?

MARY: It's true . . . you've produced a super-sperm. You could stand in West Berlin and impregnate women in East Berlin.

MAN: What is this?

MARY: You're repeating yourself. (*Pause.*) We're going to Dublin . . . me, you, and a crowd of your crude, rude, loud . . . mates. You'll get so pissed you'll compete with their dirty jokes by telling them about us. I'll be groped and flaunted . . . offered for hire. I've just realized what it is I don't like about you.
(*The* MAN *looks puzzled.*)
You're a bastard.

MAN: (*Starting the car, muttering*) I don't know what this is all about.

MARY: Stop the car.

MAN: Why?

MARY: Turn it off.
(*Pause. He does so.*)
Are you going to leave your wife?

MAN: I've six children.

MARY: Six and a half.

MAN: What . . . (*Angry*) . . . now don't start all that again.

MARY: I am pregnant.

MAN: You're not pregnant . . . you're on the effing pill . . . you can't be pregnant.

MARY: Maybe it's not yours.

MAN: What do you mean? If you're pregnant of course it's mine. Have you been messing about?

MARY: Have you been sleeping with your wife? (*Pause.*) Have you?

MAN: Of course I've been sleeping with my wife. I'm married. (*Pause.*) Ach come on . . . what do you expect? We've six kids. They'd know something was wrong if we didn't sleep together. (*Pause.*) She would guess . . . (*Pause.*) Mary, I don't understand.

MARY: Take me home please.

MAN: I'm taking you nowhere until you tell me what this is all about.

MARY: There's two policemen over there . . . (*Winding down the window.*) . . . now if you don't start this car and take me home I'm going to start screaming.

(*He hesitates a moment, then starts the car and drives off.*)

25. EXT. ANTRIM ROAD AREA OF BELFAST. NIGHT FOUR
An army road block on Antrim Road. The soldiers are all blacked up. BRIAN *comes along and is stopped.* PAUL RODGERS *moves up to question him and check his licence.* JIM *is to the side. He recognizes* BRIAN. *When* PAUL *moves around to the back of the car,* JIM *goes and whispers to him.*

PAUL: (*Going and pulling the driver's door open*) Right, out of the car . . . hands on the roof, legs apart . . . move!
(BRIAN, *ashen-faced, scrambles out of the car and does so. He is sprawled across the car.* PAUL *kicks feet apart. Pause.*)

JIM: (*Close to his ear*) How's that lovely little sister of yours, man?
(JIM *roars with laughter* . . . PAUL *joins in.* BRIAN *for a few seconds doesn't know whether to laugh or cry.*)

BRIAN: (*A squeal*) Jim . . . (*Stronger*) . . . Jim . . . it's you . . . Jasus . . . you gave me a fright. I didn't recognize you . . . I mean . . . (*Looking at the other black faces*)

JIM: (*Laughing*) Did you think you'd been stopped by Zulus?

26. INT. THE DONNELLY HOUSE. HALL AND STAIRS. DAY FIVE – AFTERNOON
The PRIEST *is on the stairs.*

27. INT. THE DONNELLY LIVING ROOM
COLETTE *is sitting gazing into the fire. Pause.* PRIEST *comes downstairs.* PRIEST *enters.*

PRIEST: Hello, Colette.

COLETTE: Hello, Father.

PRIEST: (*Sitting*) Would you like to pray with me for your father?

COLETTE: (*Shaking her head*) No, the only thing I want is for him to live, and we both know that is impossibe.

PRIEST: Nothing is impossible with the Lord, Colette.

COLETTE: Please, Father, give me credit for some common sense. He's dying . . . there's going to be no miracle.

PRIEST: (*Irritated*) Are there any Christians at all in England, Colette? (*Pause.*) The number of young people who go to that Godless country and lose their faith is disturbing. Why do you think that is then?

COLETTE: (*Looking straight at him*) I think it's because there are too many Irish people over there, Father.

PRIEST: I confirmed you.

COLETTE: As what?

PRIEST: Why such hostility, Colette?

COLETTE: Why such dishonesty, Father?
(*The* PRIEST *looks questioningly.*)
God has abandoned my father. (*Sits back.*)

PRIEST: Don't talk rubbish, child.

COLETTE: Child! I'm no child. (*Pause.*) I'm sorry. He's dying, we both know that. I don't want him to die, and I'm sure he doesn't want to die . . . now you might think God knows best . . . but I don't happen to agree with him . . . so please . . .

PRIEST: Your husband couldn't come with you?
(*She just glares at him.*)
Of course not. Are the children well?

COLETTE: Fine, thank you.

PRIEST: A boy and a girl I'm told . . . very nice. I don't suppose you're finding people around here very friendly, are you?

COLETTE: I prefer it that way . . . the silent hostility is honest.

PRIEST: That's become a great word with you, Colette. Are you being honest with them? Didn't you realize that in

marrying a British soldier, in times like these, you were
making a statement? It's not good enough to say you were
in love. Your people assumed you loved them . . . so in
doing that you were rejecting them . . . throwing them over
for one of the enemy.

(*She glares at him.*)

I'm a man of God, Colette . . . a man of peace . . . but I
have watched my people suffering at the hands of the
British Army.

COLETTE: Of course British soldiers don't suffer like the rest of
us. They don't hurt and bleed. English parents don't really
love their children, so they don't suffer when their children
are murdered and maimed.

PRIEST: This is our country. They are an army of occupation.

COLETTE: Do you know, Father . . . the last conversation we
had was what finally decided me that I had to get out of this
place. I'm grateful to you again . . . you've confirmed for
me that I can never return.

PRIEST: Just for funerals. Just to watch people who loved
you . . . people you hurt . . . slipping unhappily away.

COLETTE: I think you're evil, Father. You're supposed to teach
people to live in peace . . . to forgive . . . to love their
fellow men.

PRIEST: I am an Irish Patriot. The English I can forgive, and
live with quite peaceably . . . with them in their country,
and me in mine. Being a Christian is not incompatable with
being a nationalist. You just don't realize the enormity of
your betrayal.

COLETTE: It's wrong to teach people to hate.

PRIEST: Hate. We don't hate the English . . . we merely love
Ireland and the Irish.

COLETTE: What about the Protestants then? They love Ireland.
This part of it especially. They're Irish. What about the
RUC men, and the UDR men, your . . . patriots . . .
murder?

PRIEST: They are in league with our enemies. They too have
betrayed us.

COLETTE: What a convenient philosophy. Everyone who doesn't agree with you has betrayed you, is an enemy . . . so you can butcher them, or condone their being butchered, without conscience. You can't gloss over your bigotry with nationalism.

PRIEST: That's what living with the English does for you. You distort . . . you distort the very language. An Irishman who fights for his country is a murderer . . . a terrorist. An Englishman who goes to the Falklands . . . the Falklands! . . . and fights, is a hero. I suppose your husband was there?

COLETTE: So what were the Irish troops doing in the Middle East . . . apart from murdering each other?

PRIEST: I suppose I should have realized . . . when you went ahead and married your Englishman, your bullying Brit . . . that you're beyond reason. (*Pause. He is angry. He rises.*) I suppose I'd better be off.

COLETTE: (*As he hesitates*) You'd better.
(*Pause.*)

27 CONT. HALL
He goes. Pause. MOTHER *comes slowly, wearily down the stairs.*
Pause.

27 CONT. INT. DONNELLY LIVING ROOM
MOTHER *enters living room.*
MOTHER: Is that Father McKenna just away now?
(COLETTE *nods.*)
He's a lovely man. You two must have had a great chat.
(*She is pleased.*)
(COLETTE *just looks at her, across a widening gulf.*)

28. INT. THE BROWN HOUSE. DAY FIVE – EVENING
CAROL *is sitting with her* MOTHER *and* FATHER. BRIAN *comes in.*
They all exchange greetings.
BRIAN: Well, Carol . . . how's Jungle Jim?
(*She glares fiercely at him.*)

MRS BROWN: For goodness' sake don't start her.

BRIAN: What's wrong . . . it's not all off, is it?

MRS BROWN: He hasn't bothered since he moved up the Antrim Road.

(CAROL, *upset*. BRIAN, *grinning*.)

CAROL: Are you sick, Brian? I mean what's so funny about that?

MR BROWN: Leave her be, Brian.

BRIAN: Don't worry, Carol . . . he still loves you.

CAROL: Piss off.

MRS BROWN: Brian . . . ?

BRIAN: Serious . . . I'm serious. He still loves you, I know.

(CAROL, *upset, getting up and making for the stairs*.)

He told me.

(CAROL *looks puzzled*.)

He sent his regards. He even said he would definitely try and write.

CAROL: What are you playing at?

BRIAN: Right . . . listen in. Last night. I went up to Glengormley to look at a car. Coming home . . . There's a road block . . . the Brits. I'm stopped, searched, hand over the licence . . . next thing . . . Christ, I near jumped through the roof . . . there's this big black face grinning in at me . . . Jungle Jim himself.

(CAROL, *leaping on him in delight*.)

CAROL: Oh, Brian, I love you. What did he say . . . tell me what he said?

BRIAN: He said . . . (*Putting on an English accent*) How's Carol, like . . . tell her I haven't forgot her, like. Tell her I'll write as soon as I can, like. That was it.

(CAROL *bursts into tears and goes to her mother*. BRIAN *and* MR BROWN *look at each other, puzzled*. BRIAN *shrugs*.)

MR BROWN: (*Throwing his eyes ceilingwards*) Bloody women. (*He shakes his head*.)

29. INT. DONNELLY HOUSE. DAY FIVE – EVENING

COLETTE *is sitting writing a letter*. GERARD *comes in. Pauses*.

MARY *in kitchen*. COLETTE *speaks, but he doesn't reply – obviously resentful. He's drink taken.*

GERARD: (*As* MARY *enters from kitchen, with two cups, puts them on table*.) Writing a love letter to the Brit? Darling Bastard . . . (GERARD *moves*.)

MARY: (*Pushing him violently*) Shut up, Gerard. (*She is in a highly agitated state*.)

GERARD: Who do you think you're pushing?

MARY: Just shut up and leave her alone.

COLETTE: It's all right, Mary.

GERARD: I've got a message for you, Brit-Bird. They want you out.

MARY: How many pints did it take to give them the courage to make that threat.

GERARD: I'm warning you.

COLETTE: They know why I'm here, they know when I'll go.

GERARD: They're not prepared to wait.

MARY: Tell them to send one of their heroes to bump him off then . . . that's about their level.

(*He goes towards the stairs*.)

Or . . . are you going to do it yourself . . . promotion?

(*He goes towards her, furious, as if to strike her. She stands her ground*.)

COLETTE: (*Rises sharply*) Gerard!

(*He stops, regards her,* COLETTE, *then goes upstairs. Pause*.)

I take it there's something going on?

MARY: I know . . . I've been acting strange lately, withdrawal symptoms.

(COLETTE *looks questioningly at her*.)

Yes, I've finished it.

COLETTE: Why did you?

MARY: Dad . . . in a way. I don't suppose there ever was any future for us. If there was I suddenly began to see him as Dad . . . dying . . . possibly; leaving me with his six children . . . or one of our own. Leaving me anyway. I can't bear it. You've left. Dad's about to . . . I can't bear it. All the time you're growing up, it seems to take for ever, nothing changes. The same old faces are around seemingly for hundreds of years . . . then suddenly they go . . . one after another . . . and you're alone. I don't want to be alone, Colette. I just see the future as a big mouth . . . I hear it as an echoing howl. You're lucky.

COLETTE: Me . . . lucky?

MARY: Lucky . . . lucky. When this absurd thing is over you've got somewhere to go. You've got someone to go to. You've got children. If I discover I can't have children I'll kill myself. (*Pause.*) Do you think I'm mad?

COLETTE: (*Looking at her, smiling*) Yes, I think you're nuts. (COLETTE *rises, crosses to living room, crumpling up her letter and throwing it in the fire.*)
That's it . . . I've got to be mad.
(*They look at each other and laugh.*)

MARY: I'm going to go back with you.

COLETTE: What . . . (*She rises*) to England?

MARY: God . . . put like that I'm not so sure . . . to your place . . . just for a holiday . . . a week, maybe two. If I look around and like it . . . well? Can I?

COLETTE: (*Going and embracing her*) Oh yes . . . yes . . . yes. (*They are clutching each other, half-giggling, half-crying as* MOTHER *comes downstairs. They look at her, her at them. Pause.*)

MOTHER: Your father's dead. (*Hold.*)

30. INT. BEDROOM, DONNELLY HOUSE. DAY FIVE – EVENING
MOTHER *by bedside – holding* FATHER's *hand. Places it across his chest. Crosses herself. Covers him with sheet. Exits.*

31. EXT. TELEPHONE KIOSKS BY THE SIDE OF THE CITY HALL. DAY SIX
CAROL *is checking her change, selecting coins. Looks around. A kiosk door opens and* COLETTE *emerges from it – looking happy. She holds the door open for* CAROL.

CAROL: Thank you . . . you wouldn't happen to have a couple of ten-pees, would you? (*As* COLETTE *looks.*) Just in case I don't have enough.

COLETTE: (*Smiling*) I know the feeling. I've three.

CAROL: (*Checking her change*) I'll just . . . wait . . . oh no, I thought that was a five. Never mind, two should be fine.

COLETTE: Take the three . . . go on.

(*She presses the three on* CAROL *and takes the change for two.* CAROL *thanks* COLETTE.)

I hope you need them all.

(*They smile and part.*)

32. INT. A SMALL BUNK-ROOM IN GIRDWOOD BARRACKS. DAY SIX

Two SOLDIERS *are sitting playing cards with* PAUL. JIM *enters, reading a letter.*

FIRST SOLDIER: Are you in, Jim?

JIM: No, not me, mate.

SECOND SOLDIER: Don't you see he's got a love letter to read? (*They laugh.*)

All those 'phone calls and letters . . . there's going to be some fun when you get back to Holywood.

JIM: You bet. (*Clambers on to his bunk and sprawls out reading the letter.*) You bet.

(*When he finishes the letter he places it across his face. Pause. The soldiers look at* JIM *and smile.*)

PAUL: There you have it, lads . . . the real definition of love . . . in black and white.

(*They laugh, including* JIM. *He folds the letter and puts it in his breast pocket, contented. Hold.*)

33. INT. THE BEDROOM OF THE DONNELLY HOUSE. DAY SEVEN

The bed is empty, and neatly made up. MOTHER's *nightdress now lies across it.* GERARD *is helping her to fold up* FATHER's *clothes and put them neatly into boxes. She is dressed in black. Hold.*

34. INT. COLETTE'S LIVING ROOM. DAY SEVEN – EVENING

MARY *crosses from hall to living room and sits on floor.* COLETTE *is out at the front door, saying goodbye to her mother-in-law. Pause.*

The noise of a car driving away. COLETTE *comes into the room.*

COLETTE: Is she asleep?

MARY: She fell asleep before I'd finished the story. Has she gone then?

COLETTE: I think you reading the story was the final straw.

MARY: I don't think she liked me.

COLETTE: You'll survive I'm sure. She isn't the worst in the world. She's good to the children.

(*Pause.* MARY *and* COLETTE *sit, lost in private thoughts – but both quite happy, contented.*)

MARY: You'll never go home again, will you?

COLETTE: I am home.

ATLALEMENTO

ATTACHMENTS

Cast:

MAJOR	Nigel Gregory
ROBERT	John Wheatley
PETE	Jonathan Morris
SMICKS	Richard Tolan
SOLDIER 1	Simon Adams
SOLDIER 2	Paul Codman
NCO	John Laing
RUC INSPECTOR	Denys Hawthorne
RUC SERGEANT	Oliver Maguire
IRISH DRUNK	Paddy Joyce
GRANNY BRENNAN	Leila Webster
LIAM	Noel Magee
EUGENE	Sam McNulty
HOSPITAL SISTER	Kate Kelly
NURSE	Grainne McCann
ALICE	Carmel McSharry
BEN	Joe Brady
DOROTHY	Linda Wray
CHRIS	Nick Maloney
SAMANTHA	Heather McIlwaine
GRANNY	Catherine Gibson
MAVIS	Annette Ekblom
LUCY	Shirin Taylor
TOM	John Altman
DORA (WO)	Rosaleen Pelan

1. AN ARMY PRE-NORTHERN IRELAND TRAINING CAMP

*Belfast streets have been recreated to give a feeling of authenticity.
From an audience point of view this should appear to be an actual
Belfast street scene. There are two or three 'civilians' around. An
army foot patrol enters the street. Cautious, alert, focus on* ROBERT, *then* PETE, *then* SMICKS. *They look very tense and nervous. They
progress for about a hundred yards. Suddenly a shot rings out. The
bullet strikes the wall just behind* ROBERT's *head. The soldiers drop
into firing positions, hunkered.* ROBERT *is the last to go down. The
'civilians' get off the street quickly. Pause. On signals from the* NCO
*the soldiers begin to move forward in short, sharp runs. A voice
booms out over a loudhailer.*

VOICE: All right, Corporal . . . bring your section in.
> (*The soldiers begin to move back down the street, relaxed,
> laughing, chatting.* ROBERT, PETE *and* SMICKS *are together.
> The civilians fall in behind the soldiers.*)

PETE: You didn't move . . . if he'd had a second go you were
gone.

ROBERT: I know . . . I was expecting it the whole time, but I
never thought it would be at me.

SMICKS: You were all right, Robert . . . I'd the firing point
covered . . . I'd have dropped him before he got another
one off.

PETE: Chancer . . . you hadn't a clue where it came from.

SMICKS: You'll see . . . it'll all be on film . . . I'll be the first
soldier to get a medal before I even get to Northern Ireland.
(*Hold.*)

2. EXT. ENGLISH ARMY BARRACKS

*We see the soldiers who had been part of the pre-Northern Ireland
training exercise return to their camp in England. They pass the
regimental flag, drive up to the top camp and park in the car park
beside their barracks.*

3. INT. A LECTURE HALL

Some hours later. We see it from the platform, from the point of view of the RUC OFFICER, *who has been lecturing. Pick out* ROBERT, PETE, SMICKS. PETE *is dozing.* ROBERT *nudges him. He stirs. The* RUC OFFICER *appears to be staring straight at him.*

RUC OFFICER: As I said (*Shuffling his notes*) . . . as I was saying . . . (*Pause.*) . . . As I've said . . . cooperation between ourselves and the army is vital. (*Pause.*) We need to be united to defeat terrorism. There have been unfortunate incidents in the past, as I'm sure everyone is aware . . . but those days are behind us now. There is now mutual respect and cooperation right across the board. We're anxious for that to continue . . . and that's one of the reasons why we're here today. (*Pause.*) I'm sure with this regiment that process will continue and we look forward to meeting you again in Belfast, and working in harmony with you. (*Pause.*) Thank you.

MAJOR: Right . . . are there any questions?

PETE: (*Keen to give the impression that he was listening*) Who would you say are the greatest threat . . . the Catholics, or the Protestants?

RUC OFFICER: (*Rising, with the weariness of one who has to repeat himself*) As we've already pointed out . . . we prefer to use specific labels for terrorist organizations . . . IRA, INLA, UVF, UDA. We don't refer to them as Protestants or Catholics. As far as the RUC's concerned they're all of them a threat . . . an equal threat to law and order and a stable society.

PETE: But the IRA have killed more soldiers, haven't they?

RUC OFFICER: The IRA and the INLA have killed more soldiers, UDR men, and policemen. They do at the moment pose the biggest military threat. (*Sits.*)
(PETE *rises.*)

PETE: (*Trying to goad*) Do you think the RUC is trusted by the Catholics? (*He sits.*)
(*Uncomfortable pause. The two army officers on the platform are now taking a keener interest in the questioner. A few giggles*

at the policeman's discomfort.)

RUC OFFICER: We feel we have the trust of the vast majority of the civilian population. (*Pause.*)

PETE: (*As the* RUC OFFICER *sits*) Are there any Catholics in the RUC?

RUC MAN: (*Glancing round at his colleague*) My colleague is a Catholic . . . as he pointed out, to those who were awake. (*Pause*).

MAJOR: Well done . . . that chap at the end was obviously very interested.

(*The* RUC OFFICER *looks at his mate, then glares at the* MAJOR.)

RUC OFFICER: That . . . chap . . . spent the entire lecture fast asleep . . . as did a lot of the others.

MAJOR: (*Embarrassed*) They have had a very busy morning. (*Awkward pause – rise.*) Now men . . . we're extremely grateful to our RUC colleagues for their interesting and illuminating talks. I hope you took it all in. Tomorrow you're off on a week's leave . . . and then you're on the streets of Belfast for real. (*Pause.*) Remember all you've learnt here. Remember all you've been told . . . and remember, above all, it is for real. We can't call you in and re-run it if you make mistakes there. (*Pause.*) Good luck. Enjoy your leave . . . and I'll see you in Belfast.

(*The soldiers come to their feet as the platform party prepare to leave.*)

ROBERT: Pete's our secret weapon . . . they're going to let him infiltrate the IRA . . . as a sleeper.

PETE: I wasn't the only one you know. Before I dropped off, I could see the Major's head dropping on to his chest.

SMICKS: It is a bit silly though. They knacker us in the morning . . . give us a big lunch . . . and then expect us to stay awake during hours of boring lectures in the afternoon.

ROBERT: I thought a lot of what they had to say was interesting enough.

PETE: Piss off.

SMICKS: That's just because they're Paddies like you.

ROBERT: Sneer if you like . . . at least they know what it's like.

PETE: Now who hasn't been listening . . . it's because of their incompetence and biasedness that it's as bad as it is.

ROBERT: Hold on a minute . . .

SMICKS: Listen to Robert now, Pete . . . after all, his granny's an expert on the whole situation.

ROBERT: (*Angry*) Stuff you . . . (*Putting on his beret.*) . . . I'm going to the cookhouse.
(*Goes. The other two laugh and follow him. Hold.*)

4. INT. ROOM OF THE RUC MEN

The TWO RUC MEN *in their room. The speaker at the lecture,* JOHN WILSON, *is getting dressed to go out.* PAT DOHERTY *is leafing through a book.*

PAT: Who is it tonight?

JOHN: (*Beside table*) Same as last night. (*Straightening his tie*) This is the back-breaker . . . the last night.

PAT: I think I'll turn in early . . . is this book any good?

JOHN: (*Going to wardrobe*) It's rubbish . . . another ex-para having a wank over the Ulster crisis. You know, the sad thing is . . . I think they believe half them things themselves.

PAT: I suppose it makes them an easy few bob.

JOHN: (*Going to the bed*) If they want to write fairy tales they should start them with 'once upon a time'. That clown's got a real John Wayne complex . . . and he's redesigned the geography of Belfast. No wonder they were never where we needed them.

PAT: I thought all you Prods loved the paras?

JOHN: A shower of frigging cowboys. I reckon every tour the paras did trebled recruitment to the IRA . . . and the UDA. They'd do their damage, then skip off to play cowboys somewhere else and the wee terrorists they've created take their revenge by picking off us and the UDR.

PAT: If we were armed and trained the way they are . . . and as unaccountable for our actions . . . it would be over in a fortnight.

JOHN: A fortnight . . . why would you take your time?

(*They laugh. Pause.* JOHN *goes to dressing table.*)

Look . . . why don't you get ready? I'll give her a ring, and tell her to bring a friend.

PAT: Not at all . . . I've been married too long . . . I wouldn't know where to begin with a woman now.

JOHN: You're not married any longer than me.

PAT: (*Looking at him*) No . . . you run on. I'm a bit tired.

JOHN: (*Going to wardrobe for jacket*) Tomorrow you're back in Belfast . . . why not have a good time while you can?

PAT: I'm having a good time . . . being away from one woman. I'm not going to spoil it by taking up with another. (*Pause.*) That's not the way I have a good time. (*Pause.*) Does she know you're married?

JOHN: I'm a widower . . . lost my wife and two children in a terrorist bombing . . . joined the RUC to protect others from the same fate.

PAT: Ah, come on, John . . . for goodness' sake . . . how can you say things like that?

JOHN: Because she doesn't want to hop into bed with a middle-aged RUC man . . . a career cop, with two children, a boring wife, and a big mortgage. She wants an adventure with a superman . . . then she can kid herself that it was something special.

PAT: I don't think it's right . . . I mean, what's going on back there . . . you're tempting providence.

JOHN: Christ . . . you know I'm no bigot, but if you're a typical Catholic . . . thank goodness there aren't more of you in the force.

PAT: Why are you doing this . . . to impress her? To prove something to yourself?

JOHN: Spare me the psychology.

PAT: You're a sad man, John.

JOHN: Crap . . . read your book. (*The words have hit home.*) Suppose we both get it in the neck next week?

PAT: We're both dead . . . and I'll not feel I missed anything because I didn't jump into bed with some loose English woman.

JOHN: (*Annoyed*) Is that your objection . . . that she's an English woman?

PAT: My objection is that you feel you have to do this . . . you feel you have to do this when you're away from home, to prove you're a man . . . to maintain your manly image of yourself.

(JOHN *is angry. He regards him for a moment.*)

JOHN: I'm going.

(*Pause.* PAT *doesn't look at him.* JOHN *goes. When he's gone* PAT *regards the closed door. Hold.*)

5. INT. THE BARRACKS

PETE *coming in from washroom.* ROBERT *writing a letter.* ROBERT *is in bed.* PETE *sits on top of his bed, next to* ROBERT'S.

PETE: Honest . . . who are you writing to now?

ROBERT: Lucy.

PETE: What the hell for, we're going home tomorrow.

ROBERT: So what? She might get it before I see her.

PETE: I don't know what you have to say all the time . . . I hate writing letters.

ROBERT: I like getting them . . . and if you want to get them you have to write them.

PETE: Did you hear on the news tonight . . . about those UDR men?

(ROBERT *just looks at him.*)

You know what I think?

(ROBERT *looks questioningly.*)

I think all the bloody Irish are daft.

ROBERT: Yeah . . . well no British soldier's won Mastermind yet.

PETE: Whose side are you on? I thought living over here had civilized you.

ROBERT: Living with the likes of you? You must be joking.

PETE: Right (PETE *jumps off his bed.*) . . . bloody traitor.

(*He tilts* ROBERT's *bed up.*)

ROBERT: Hey . . . put it down . . . stop you daft bugger.

PETE: A daft bugger am I?

(*He tips* ROBERT *on to the floor amidst much shouting and laughter.*)

SPUD: (*From another bed*) Why don't you two grow up? I'm trying to get some kip.

PETE: Go flush your head down the loo.

SPUD: (*Coming up to confront* PETE) I'll put your head through that wall.

PETE: Come on then.

ROBERT: All right you two . . . knock it off.

SPUD: (*Furious*) I'm trying to sleep.

ROBERT: All right . . . sorry . . . now go back to bed.

PETE: Don't crawl, mate . . . come on, let's see you put my head through the wall.

(ROBERT *steps between them as they seem about to start throwing punches.*)

ROBERT: Knock it off . . . both of you. We'll only get into trouble. Come on . . . we're going home tomorrow.

(*Pause.* SPUD *goes back to his bed, mumbling.*)

PETE: If I ever do a foot patrol with that creep he'd better watch his back.

ROBERT: (*Angry*) That's not funny.

PETE: It's not meant to be . . . (*Angry too, shouting at the other soldier*) Wanker.

(PETE *throws himself on his bed and turns his back on* ROBERT. *Hold.*)

6. INT. HUT
Extras: soldiers from Scene 5 going for breakfast. SMICKS *in longshot.*

7. INT. THE BARRACKS
ROBERT *and* PETE *sitting, packed ready for inspection.*

PETE: That's class . . . you haven't even arrived and they've organized your going-away party.

ROBERT: Dorothy said my mum was going to have one. (*Pause.*) There isn't that much time, we'll only be there for a week. I wish I hadn't mentioned going home.

PETE: Get away. I want to see Mavis.

ROBERT: Anyway – you're invited.

PETE: No thanks – I don't want to bump into your mum and be blamed for talking you into it . . . no thanks, mate. Hey wait a minute . . . I'll be able to show off Mavis's engagement ring.

ROBERT: It's not going to be a big party . . . just the family . . . you and Mavis . . . maybe one or two others.

PETE: Why don't we have a double engagement?

ROBERT: Give over . . . I don't want to get engaged.

PETE: Why not? You don't have to marry her.

ROBERT: Rubbish . . . so what's the point of getting engaged?

PETE: Keep her there . . . keep other blokes away, till you've made up your mind.

(SMICKS *enters waving his travel pass in the air.*)

SMICKS: . . . Oh mama . . . Belfast here I come. (*Kissing the pass for the first three words*) . . . realization . . . elation . . . fornication . . . (*Gloomy*) transportation . . . alienation . . . devastation.

PETE: Do you swallow the sodding dictionary whole . . . or do you chew it?

SMICKS: Dictionary . . . dictionary! Has the man no soul! You should be stretched on the ground and shat upon by the whole battalion . . . oh soulless soldier. I'm a poet . . . you shouldn't be here, Pete . . . you should join the army.

PETE: No way . . . join the army, maybe be sent to Northern Ireland . . . get my balls blown off.

ROBERT: He's getting engaged you know . . . he'll need to look after his equipment.

PETE: Piss off, cretin.

SMICKS: Here, I heard the Sergeant Major talking about you falling asleep yesterday, and then holding us all up by asking questions. It's battalion gossip. There's now a battalion 'Ask the RUC a silly question' competition.

ROBERT: You have to admire the cheek though . . . he fell asleep in the lecture before that one.

SMICKS: He should have had more consideration for those of us who were unfortunate enough to stay awake. I can see it all now . . . there we'll be in the middle of this war . . . the Belfast sky ablaze with tracer and flares . . . and through it all petrified Pete . . . sleepwalking.

PETE: You can piss off and all, Smicks. (*Pause.*) Anyway . . . I couldn't listen to policemen talking on principle . . . the family would never forgive me. We're the dregs of the English prisons remember. There I was happily serving my six life-sentences for raping nuns and eating uncooked orphans . . . in they come and shove me into this show.

SMICKS: Your name's gone down in the book . . . offending our RUC colleagues.

PETE: Colleagues . . . they should demob the whole lot and let us get on with the job ourselves.

SMICKS: My dear chap, you haven't been listening to anything this week, have you? They are actually running the show now. Ulsterization is now a fact of life. Talk about your life in their hands . . . bloody stroll on.

ROBERT: Had you stayed even half awake . . .

SMICKS: Like the rest of us.

ROBERT: . . . you would now know that the well-being of that rather delightful little butt of yours could depend on decisions by a creature the like of which lulled you into slumbers yesterday.

SMICKS: I suppose if the 'B' stands for 'boring' . . . he was one of the original B Specials.

ROBERT: At least the second one was funny.

SMICKS: Yes . . . but what was he supposed to be? What worries me is that those two are probably the best talkers they have.

PETE: I couldn't understand half of what they were saying. (*Pause.*)

SMICKS: Enough of this . . . to the cookhouse, then some tidying up for the kit inspection.

PETE: What kit inspection?

SMICKS: It doesn't affect you, Pete . . . it's just for the real soldiers.

8. INT. THE LIVING ROOM OF THE MILLIGAN HOUSE IN
LIVERPOOL

ALICE *is sitting in living room.* DOROTHY *and* SAMANTHA *enter
with shopping. They have been out shopping and just dropped in to
see* ALICE.

DOROTHY: What's wrong with you? You look a bit down.

ALICE: I'd a letter from Robert this morning, he's signed on
again.

DOROTHY: Oh . . . I thought he was going to come home and
settle down with Lucy. He must really like the life . . . my
Chris hated it.

SAMANTHA: I thought Daddy liked the army.

ALICE: They're going to Northern Ireland, Belfast.

DOROTHY: What sort of a silly wee bugger is he?

SAMANTHA: You said wee.

DOROTHY: (*Shooting* SAMANTHA *a fierce look*) I mean are we
all supposed to fall down impressed?

ALICE: You congratulate yourself on getting your children out
of that mess . . . then he goes and walks back into it
deliberately.

SAMANTHA: Can't you stop him going?

ALICE: There's no way we can stop him. (*She goes to the scullery
for sweets.*)

DOROTHY: How do you know? If you tell them we come from
Belfast . . . that there are still relatives there, it might work.
Tell them that me and Chris had to leave because of threats.

SAMANTHA: What threats?

DOROTHY: (*Fiercely*) Will you stop butting in. (*Pause.*) Why
don't you get Dad to talk to your local MP. Get him to tell
them you've relatives over there who're involved in the
UVF. That'll stop it.

ALICE: I don't think any of our ones are involved in anything.

SAMANTHA: Great-granny says so.

ALICE: Your great-granny lives in a wee world of her own, don't
heed her.

DOROTHY: Has he actually committed himself? Is he not just
talking about it?

ALICE: He's signed and all . . . he's doing special training for it. That's where he wrote the letter from . . . according to him he loves it. He can't wait to go.

DOROTHY: Typical, he was always a selfish wee brat. You and Dad spoilt him and Granny's filled his head with a load of romantic oul nonsense. (*Glaring at* SAMANTHA *as she appears about to pull her up on saying 'oul'.*) I've told you. (*Pause.*) You'd think he'd have learnt from Chris and me.

ALICE: Your dad and me were just sitting here talking about him the other night . . . saying how lucky he was that they hadn't been sent there during his service, now this.

DOROTHY: Sometimes I think our Robert deserves a good shaking. He's just trying to show off if you ask me . . . I wouldn't be surprised the whole thing isn't a big show to impress that Lucy one.

ALICE: If he'd even told us beforehand . . . we could have advised him. I've enough to contend with, without the worry of him twenty-four hours a day and he'll be there for eighteen months to two years.

SAMANTHA: Will he not marry Lucy now?

(DOROTHY *glares at her. Glum.*)

I wanted to be a bridesmaid. (*Hold.*)

9. EXT. RAILWAY STATION

ROBERT, PETE, SMICKS *and* SOLDIER *in a railway station.*

ROBERT *and* PETE *about to go off.*

ROBERT: Right . . . we'll see you two in a week.

SMICKS: In good old Belfast.

ROBERT: Are you making your own way over?

SMICKS: Oh . . . I forgot . . . embarkation.

PETE: Watch where you're putting your weapons . . . don't come back with herpes.

SMICKS: (*Shaking his head in mock disgust*) You do meet some crude types of chaps in today's army.

SOLDIER: (*Drunkenly*) You'll get the herbies . . . up in Liverpool . . . all them sailors.

(*They just gaze at him, as he stands with a silly grin on his face. Hold.*)

10. BOTTOM OF STEPS TO ENTRANCE TO RAILWAY STATION
ROBERT *and* SMICKS *are there. They are in civilian clothes.*
DRUNK, *an elderly man, comes in. He sees* ROBERT *and* SMICKS *and starts to sing, 'When Irish Eyes Are Smiling'. They smile at him quite tolerantly. It becomes a performance.* PETE *approaches down steps.* PETE *is quite drunk.*

PETE: You all right, Paddy, then?

DRUNK: Who're you calling Paddy? I'm no bloody Paddy. Neither then . . . nor nigh. British to the backbone . . . Belfast, and a true blue. (*He starts to sing again, this time 'Irish' becomes 'Ulster'.*)

PETE: (*Loud and nasty*) Belfast's a shit heap . . . bloody animals.

ROBERT: We're going to Belfast . . .

DRUNK: (*To them aggressively*) Soldiers . . . (*Salutes.*) . . . Royal Irish Rifles . . . (*Laughs.*) . . . What am I talking about? (*Laughs.*) Royal . . . Ulster . . . Rifles . . . best bloody regiment in the whole British bloody army . . . we won most of the friggin' wars for them.

PETE: Crap . . . Royal Ulster shit heaps . . .

DRUNK: Hey now . . . (*Throwing off his coat*) . . . proper bloody order . . . honour of the regiment.

ROBERT: Come on now . . . steady on, Grandad . . .

DRUNK: Granda . . . Granda? G'on you cheeky wee shite . . . (*He lands a haymaker on* ROBERT *sending him sprawling.*) . . . honour of the regiment.

(PETE *knocks him to the ground.* ROBERT *pulls* PETE *off.*)

ROBERT: Leave him, you bloody fool.

(*Hold.*)

11. EXT. MILLIGAN HOUSE
ROBERT *approaching the house.* ALICE *is waiting at the door, watching him approach. They embrace and pass inside.*

12. INT. MILLIGAN HOUSE: GRANNY'S ROOM; HALL AND
KITCHEN

ROBERT *and* ALICE *come down hall.*

GRANNY: Robert, step back there and let me have a look at you.
　　(ROBERT *does so.*)
　　You're filling out . . . you favour our side of the family,
　　doesn't he, Alice?
　　(ALICE *just gives a weak smile.*)
　　There'll be less oul nonsense out of their heads when you
　　get over there.

ALICE: Do you want anything, Mother?

GRANNY: I wouldn't refuse a sip of tea.

ALICE: What about you, Robert?

ROBERT: I'll have one with Granny.

GRANNY: (*As* ALICE *rises*) That's one thing about Belfast . . .
　　you'll get a decent cup of tea.

ALICE: The tea here's always been decent enough.

GRANNY: In here granted . . . that's because we're Belfast born
　　and bred. But sure these English . . . a good strong cup of
　　tea would kill them. Sure the stuff that Chris fella makes
　　has barely the strength to fall out of the pot. I wish to God I
　　was going with you, son. You'll have to go and see your
　　relations.

ALICE: Mother!

GRANNY: Mother what?

ROBERT: (*Cutting in*) We'll not really be allowed much time for
　　visiting.

GRANNY: What are you saying? Surely to goodness in two years
　　you'll get a day or two to visit your own people?

ALICE: I don't want him visiting anybody over there. (*Sits.*)

GRANNY: (*With a snort of contempt*) Huh . . . I think you should
　　write a letter to the army. Maybe they'll let you go over
　　there with him, and tuck him in at night.

ALICE: It was a slap in the face.

ROBERT: Come on, Mum. I'm a soldier . . . it's just another
　　place to go.

ALICE: Your father and me left Belfast to give you a chance to grow up in a normal place. (*Pause*) Why did you do it? Even Dorothy can't understand it. You'd done your bit of soldiering . . . what are you trying to prove?

ROBERT: Mum . . . I've been trained for action . . . that's really what it's all about. In Germany we just played soldiers . . . it wasn't real.

ALICE: Real . . . there's nothing very real after you're dead.

GRANNY: What about all those UDR men, and the RUC? Their wives and mothers worry about them . . . but they have to live there . . . somebody has to do it.

ALICE: My son doesn't . . . I didn't rear you to see you blown to pieces, or shot down like a dog in a Belfast gutter. (*She rises.*)

ROBERT: You don't understand . . . I want to go to Belfast . . . I want to see it, to live in it. You remember it . . . you know it, I don't.

ALICE: What about us . . . did you think about us at all?

ROBERT: Mum, when I go out to see Lucy . . . the dangers of being killed just crossing the roads to her place are far greater than any dangers I'll face in Belfast.

ALICE: Your sister was right. She said you were just trying to act the big man. Well I just hope you realize how selfish you are . . . and what you're putting me and your father through. Goodness knows we'd enough to go through when Dorothy and Chris were there with that child. (*Pause.*) I wouldn't be surprised Lucy encouraged you in this.

ROBERT: No she didn't . . . you did.
(ALICE *just gazes at him.*)
The fact that I was born there . . . that I have relatives over there . . . still living through it. I'm not a hero, Mum . . . but I am a man . . . I've got to live my own life.

ALICE: I see plenty of lads your age round here . . . they're not rushing out to join the army . . . and if they did they'd have enough sense not to want to go over there.
(*Pause.*)

ROBERT: Lucy had nothing to do with my decision. Besides, Lucy's just a friend.

ALICE: Just a friend! . . . What does that mean?

ROBERT: It means I don't see Lucy being around for the rest of my life.

ALICE: Has she dropped you?

ROBERT: Mum . . . (*Crosses to sit.*) . . . will you stop it?

ALICE: I hope you're not going to be messing about with girls over there. Good God is that the next of it . . . are you going to end up getting some girl or other . . . maybe a Catholic . . . into trouble? (*Pause.*) I thought you and Lucy were serious . . . I thought you were going to come out, come back here and get a proper job . . . settle down. I thought your time in the army had settled you.

ROBERT: Even if I had come out, I doubt if I'd have come back here . . . I mean there aren't many jobs anywhere . . . but especially here. Don't look at me like that . . . I want to decide for myself.

13. INT. LUCY'S FLAT. DAY THREE

LUCY, PETE, MAVIS, *and* ROBERT *are there*. PETE *and* MAVIS *have been out purchasing the engagement ring, and have come to show it off. It is quite an elaborate one.* MAVIS *looks a little bemused by the speed of it all.*

PETE: Don't hang about, mate . . . that's my advice. You're going off to a war you know. (*Looking at* MAVIS, *giving her playful prod.*) . . . and women don't hang about.

ROBERT: Don't come out with any of that old war nonsense when you come round to our house.

PETE: (*Self-absorbed*) Just keep your good suit pressed . . . you never know when I'll decide to finish the job.

MAVIS: Not until you come back from Belfast.

PETE: (*Slightly put out*) That's probably two years!

LUCY: You'll be home on leave in between, won't you?

ROBERT: Of course we will.

PETE: Right . . . we're going . . . I haven't been up to see my mum yet. (*Grabbing* MAVIS's *hand.*) Show her this.

13 CONT. INT. HALL

MAVIS *looks less than thrilled at the prospect. They go, saying their goodbyes at the door.)*

13 CONT. LIVING ROOM

ROBERT *and* LUCY *come in laughing.*

LUCY: I got the impression Mavis hasn't quite realized what's hit her.

ROBERT: You're right. This just came out of the blue . . . suddenly he was writing asking her to get engaged. I think he'd be prepared to get married tomorrow.

LUCY: She showed me the letter . . . It was full of things about soldiers shot dead with engagement rings in their pockets. I'd call it blackmail. (*Pause.*) Does he have other girls when he's away?

ROBERT: Who?

LUCY: Oh let me think . . . How many have we been talking about? Pete!

ROBERT: I don't know.

LUCY: I'm sure . . . you're probably with him.

ROBERT: Do you and Mavis have other blokes?

LUCY: You know I don't go out with Mavis.

ROBERT: I'd like to go to bed.

LUCY: Would you? So, do I jump up and down?

ROBERT: (*Rising and embracing her*) Whatever turns you on. (*Hold.*)

14. EXT. PARK

GRANNY: I'm going to miss these walks after tomorrow.

ROBERT: Doesn't Mum take you out?

GRANNY: Not often enough . . . or far enough. Then if there's a spit of rain about the place it's a great excuse. Samantha used to, but sure that Dorothy one has that wee girl slaving away at home all the time. (*Pause.*) You mind now and go and see your Uncle Billy . . . he'll be delighted to see you.

ROBERT: All right, Granny, I've told you, if I'm allowed to.

GRANNY: Allowed to! Who's going to tell you you're not

allowed to? Don't listen to your mother . . . she was always afraid of her own shadow. As for that Dorothy one . . . that one's getting terrible notions about herself . . . acting the grand lady.

ROBERT: Not Mum, or Dorothy . . . the Army . . . we can't just wander around Belfast you know.

GRANNY: Isn't he your own flesh and blood? Do they think now that people in Belfast don't have relatives? You go and see him . . . get me all the news.

ROBERT: We're supposed to be neutral.

GRANNY: Neutral my eye. Aren't you the British Army? Isn't your Uncle Billy a true blue Protestant? I'm telling you, don't listen to your ma . . . there's no loyaller road in the United Kingdom than the Shankill Road. You'll be treated like a hero up there . . . especially when they know you're Minnie Morton's grandson.

ROBERT: We'll see, Granny . . . I'll do my best.

GRANNY: Now don't let me down, son . . . my family's been loyal for generations. Wasn't your great granda one of the original UVF men . . . didn't he leave his two legs on the Somme for the British Army?

ROBERT: It's a different UVF now . . . they're terrorists now.

GRANNY: Terrorists? . . . Wee lumps of Protestant lads terrorists? . . . In the name of God . . . is it the British Army you're in at all?

ROBERT: Anyway . . . let's get on with this walk.

15. INT. THE LIVING ROOM OF MAVIS'S FLAT

We hear the sounds of someone in the kitchen. MAVIS *is dressed and made up. She appears restless and on edge. She is flicking through the pages of a women's magazine, but without a great deal of interest. She keeps glancing at her watch, and looking towards the kitchen. At last she throws the magazine aside and sits. She mouths 'hurry up', exasperated. She inspects her fingernails. Doing this she becomes interested in her engagement ring. She starts to finger it. As she does so, she looks towards the kitchen, a slight smirk on her face.*

Switch to the kitchen of the flat. TOM, *a civilian mate of* PETE'S *and* ROBERT's, *is standing waiting for the electric kettle to boil. He has been fixing it, and stands balancing a screwdriver in his hand. It comes to the boil and then switches off. He smiles, pleased with himself, then he turns towards the living room. As he enters the living room,* MAVIS *rises. They stand looking at each other, smiling.*

16. INT. THE MILLIGAN LIVING ROOM

ALICE *is sitting as* BEN *enters from work. Her eyes are red from crying. He looks at her, and is annoyed.*

BEN: For God's sake, Alice . . . are you at that again?

ALICE: I'll get you a cup of coffee.

> (*He shakes his head, wearily. Starts to remove his coat. Removes his shoes and puts on slippers.*)

BEN: Where's Robert?

ALICE: He took Mother out for a walk.

BEN: He'll look daft, pushing an old woman round the streets.

ALICE: He'd look even more daft giving her a piggy-back.
(*Pause.*) We'll have our dinner as soon as they get back.

BEN: I suppose she's filling his head with more oul nonsense.
(*Pause.*) What time's this party?

ALICE: Party . . . a wake I'd call it.

BEN: In the name of Jasus, woman . . .

ALICE: There's no need for that language. (*Pause.*) Parties are supposed to be when you're celebrating . . . a fat lot we have to celebrate.

BEN: (*Gazing at her, angry*) Holy Jasus, woman . . . you organized the damned thing. (*Throws towel.*)

ALICE: Stop shouting . . . and I've warned you before about that language. We might be glad of Jesus before this is all over.
(*He gives up.*)
I did it for him . . . because I thought it's what he would have wanted.

BEN: Why didn't you ask him what he wanted?

ALICE: It's like everything I do . . . nobody ever appreciates anything. (*After a brief pause.*) Any other man would have hounded his local MP. Not you . . . oh no . . . too much trouble for you. I'll not let you forget that if anything

happens to him. (*Pause.*) We've only got the one son . . .
but anybody'd think it was one too many for you.

BEN: (*Hurt and furious*) Would you shut up, woman, and let me
sip this coffee in peace . . . will you?

(ALICE, *also furious, rises and grabs the coffee, throws it into
the hearth. He rises instinctively.*)

ALICE: No I'll not shut up. If it's peace you want get your son
out of the Army.

(ROBERT *and* GRANNY *have come in.* ALICE *and* BEN *stand,
foolishly.*)

GRANNY: (*Taking stock*) You'll find Belfast quiet after this.

17. INT. MAVIS'S FLAT. DAY FOUR

MAVIS *and* TOM *are kissing on the sofa.*

MAVIS: Behave yourself . . .

TOM: We could have done it.

MAVIS: No . . . stop. (*She breaks away and stands.*) Please . . . it
isn't right.

TOM: Right! . . . Balls to right. It's what we both want.

MAVIS: It's not . . . it's not really what I want . . .

TOM: Listen . . . (*Rising.*) I'm getting sick of all this. You make
up your mind . . . do you want me or not? (*Grabbing her.*)
You needn't think you're just going to use me when he's
away, and then drop me.

MAVIS: He lives here . . . we're engaged. (*Displays ring.*)

TOM: All right . . . I'll go.

MAVIS: No . . . Tom . . . be patient. We just have to be
careful. (*Starts to caress him.*) After tomorrow he's away for
two years. (*They kiss.*)

(PETE *enters. They jump apart.*)

PETE: Tom . . . surprise, surprise . . . I thought I was to see
you down the pub?

TOM: Yes . . . well . . . I was ah . . . (*Showing his
screwdriver.*) . . . I was fixing the kettle for Mavis.

MAVIS: (*Hurried*) It's great to get it fixed.

PETE: Great . . . great . . . I always thought Tom was the one
who could keep you on the boil while I'm away.

TOM: Yeah . . . well look . . . see you at Robert's party then.

(TOM *moves to* PETE – *he stops him.*)

PETE: Don't rush away . . . have a beer . . . (*As* TOM *protests.*)
Mavis . . . get Tom and me a beer . . . there's a good girl.

MAVIS: What did your last slave die from?

PETE: Galloping VD . . . (*With a grin at* TOM.) . . . she caught
it from a passing electrician. In fact . . . funny
coincidence . . . he'd come to mend the electric kettle.

MAVIS: (*Nervous*) Ha bloody ha. (*She goes.*)

PETE: Sit down, mate.

(*Pause. They sit. They pour their own beer.* TOM *has sat on
armchair.* MAVIS *enters and sits next to* PETE.)

Your hair, Tom.

(TOM *looks puzzled.*)

Needs combing . . . passionate things these electric kettles.

MAVIS: Pete . . . don't be so ignorant. Tom came to fix the
kettle for us.

PETE: For us? . . . For you. After all . . . I'll have the good old
cookhouse over in Belfast. You're the one'll need the kettle.
(*Pause.*) But thanks anyway, Tom.

TOM: Best of luck over there . . . Mavis told me they were
making you go.

(PETE *just glares at him.*)

At least it seems a bit quieter over there now.

(PETE *enjoys their discomfort.*)

At least if it was the coons, you'd know your enemy.

PETE: It's hard to know your enemy anywhere . . . isn't it?

(MAVIS *and* TOM *just glance at each other.* PETE *explodes. He
throws his glass across the room, and jumps up.*)

Get out . . . get out, you bastard.

(TOM *rises, frightened.* PETE *punches him on the face, and
kicks him to the floor.*)

MAVIS: Pete . . . stop it . . . Pete . . .

(TOM, *bleeding, scrambling to his feet, terrified.*)

TOM: I'm going . . . I'm . . .

(PETE *lunges at him. Hits him again.* TOM *grabs on and
they both tumble to the floor.* MAVIS *is hysterical. She*

runs to bedroom.)

18. INT. MAVIS'S FLAT. DAY FOUR
Kitchen – high stool. MAVIS *is bathing* PETE's *face. There is a cut on his cheek.*

PETE: At least the training did some good . . . I beat him.

MAVIS: You hit him three times before he knew the fight had started.

PETE: Are you taking his part? . . . Aaagh!

MAVIS: Sit still will you. I don't know . . . it's some reward for a person who comes in to do you a favour.

PETE: Trying to screw you's no favour to me.

MAVIS: Don't be so crude . . . you're not in the barracks now. Not only do you throw the glass . . . but then you go and lie on it.

PETE: He pushed me. Listen . . . aaagh . . . go easy will you?

MAVIS: You should stay still. I don't know what you're going to be like if you're badly wounded in Belfast.

PETE: There'd better be none of that carry-on when I'm away.

MAVIS: That goes both ways.

PETE: I'll not get the chance to do anything . . . besides . . . the women over there never bother with soldiers.

MAVIS: Not half. You remember you're engaged too. (*Pause.*) Poor Tom . . . he's going to look a sight at this party tonight.

PETE: I don't want you even looking at him tonight.

MAVIS: Don't be silly . . .

PETE: (*Grabbing her wrist*) I'm not being silly . . . you just remember whose ring you're wearing.

MAVIS: Get off, you're hurting me.

PETE: I'm warning you.

MAVIS: I bloody hear you . . . and you're bloody hurting me. (*She pulls away.*)

PETE: I catch you making eyes at him tonight and it's you I'll dig.

MAVIS: Oh is it . . . you don't own me, you know.

PETE: You're wearing my ring . . . it's as good as.

MAVIS: Oh is it . . . ? (*Working the ring off*) . . . If that's the case you can take it back.

PETE: Put that ring on . . . put it on.

MAVIS: You stop bullying . . . I'm sick of you bullying me. How do I know what you'll be up to when you're away?

PETE: I'm up to soldiering . . . risking my life . . . that's what I'm up to. I need to keep alert to stay alive . . . not be wondering all the time what you and him's up to.

MAVIS: (*Guilty, putting the ring back on*) I'm sorry, love . . . you'll take care, won't you? I'm going to be so worried.

PETE: Maybe you want me killed . . . out of the way . . . then you'd have a free hand.

MAVIS: (*Putting her arms around him*) Of course I don't, please don't say that. It's just . . . I've known Tom as long as you . . . I mean this engagement's a sudden thing.

PETE: (*Pushing her arm off*) You mean you might want him?

MAVIS: No . . .

PETE: I've warned you . . . just look at him tonight and you're both dead.

(*She sticks a small plaster on the cut, pushing it on hard, so that he winces and glares at her.*)

19. INT. THE MILLIGAN HOUSE

They are having dinner. There is a tense silence.

GRANNY: I suppose you're all saving yourselves for the party.

ALICE: Would you like anything more, Mother?

GRANNY: I'd like a bit of friendly conversation . . . if that's not asking too much. (*Pause.*) You're gerning about him going away . . . now he's here and you'll not talk to him.

BEN: Mother . . . let's just finish our dinner quietly.

GRANNY: (*To* ROBERT) You'd have been better taking that girlfriend of yours away to Spain for the week, son.

ALICE: Mother . . . time enough for holidays together when they're married.

GRANNY: The young ones nowadays don't worry about things like that.

ALICE: Well they should . . . no wonder the world's in the mess it's in today.

GRANNY: (*Looking at* ALICE) Huh . . . maybe if I'd spent a
week away with your father before I married him, I'd have
had more sense.

BEN: What time are you off then tomorrow, Robert?

ROBERT: I've to be at the docks by ten hundred hours.

GRANNY: Ten hundred, what time of the day's that?

ROBERT: Ten o'clock in the morning.

ALICE: Dorothy and Chris'll be here soon . . . They're bringing
sandwiches and stuff with them.

GRANNY: Huh . . . tuna fish, or salmon . . . I think them two's
got webbed feet. Them's another two you want to ignore,
son. She married an Englishman and suddenly got above
herself. She wants to remember he was only a soldier, and
her pregnant to him at sixteen.

ALICE: Mother, please.

GRANNY: I'd love to know why she's giving herself airs and
graces.

ROBERT: I should go in a minute, and go round for Lucy.

BEN: You'll be stationed in Holywood barracks?
(ROBERT *nods.*)
(*With a look to* ALICE.) Well it's quiet enough out there.

ALICE: (*Glaring at* BEN) Maybe they'll let you do your patrols
inside the barracks.

ROBERT: A couple of RUC men lectured us at the camp.
They're in charge of security. We do very little on the
streets now.

BEN: (*Clutching at straws*) Yes, I saw something about that . . .
I'm sure they're well able to look after things.

GRANNY: Sure it's because they couldn't look after things that
the army was sent in in the first place.
(*Pause.*)

ALICE: I don't see how they can expect the army to be there for
ever.

GRANNY: They'll stay for as long as they're needed . . . I've
never heard so much fuss in my life about a full-grown man
going off to do what he wants to do.

BEN: Come on, Mother . . . be fair . . . we thought Robert was

finished with the army . . . (*Pause.*) . . . it was a bit of a
shock, that's all.
(*Pause.*)

ROBERT: Well . . . I'll get on over to Lucy . . . I'll get back by
eight . . . or shortly after.
(*Silence. He goes. Pause.*)

BEN: He's our only son, Mother.

GRANNY: I'm not your mother. My only son's in Belfast . . .
and you're telling Robert not to even call on him.
(BEN *and* ALICE *just look at each other.*)
No matter what age you get . . . an only son's an only son.
(*Hold.*)

20. INT. LUCY'S FLAT. DAY FOUR

ROBERT *and* LUCY *in bed together. They have just made love. They
lie together a moment, silently.*

LUCY: Aren't you frightened yourself . . . even a bit?

ROBERT: No.

LUCY: My hero.

ROBERT: Don't you start. We've been trained for this. All
right . . . I don't want to die . . . or leave my two legs in
Ardoyne or wherever.

LUCY: Stop . . . don't even talk about it.

ROBERT: The thing is, the more frightened I am the more likely
it is to happen. You need a certain amount of fear, but just
enough to keep you sharp.

LUCY: I hope your mum isn't going to go all weepy tonight . . .
it's so embarrassing . . . and then start asking me to coax
you.

ROBERT: She'll soon need hospital treatment for exhausted tear
ducts.

LUCY: Be patient with her tonight, love.

ROBERT: I'll try . . . I wish I hadn't come home at all . . . I
should have just written from Belfast.

LUCY: Great . . . thanks a lot.

ROBERT: You know what I mean . . . we could have had a
holiday together.

LUCY: Your mum's suspicious enough of me without that.

ROBERT: Pete doesn't bother . . . just calls in and says hello.

LUCY: He lives with Mavis . . . you had your chance. (*Pause.*) I wish we could spend the night together.

ROBERT: At least we've done it.

LUCY: Spending the night together isn't just about that. (*Pause.*) Will we survive this?

(ROBERT *looks questioningly.*) You being two years away?

ROBERT: Let's wait and see.

(LUCY *looks uncertain.*)

Of course we will.

LUCY: Pete's trying to make sure of Mavis.

ROBERT: It won't work . . . what's the point? I've taken one oath of allegiance, that's enough.

LUCY: You will write?

ROBERT: Haven't I always?

LUCY: (*Lightly*) Do you expect me just to hang about?

ROBERT: (*Shrugs*) Just play it as it comes.

(LUCY *glares at him.*)

All I ask is that you're honest with me.

LUCY: I want you to ask me to wait, and I will. (*Pause. She pouts.*) I suppose you'll meet some nice young girl in Ireland, and I'll be forgotten about. A return to the tribe.

ROBERT: Oh shut up. Do you know . . . the one thing I'd really like to forget all about tonight is Northern Ireland.

LUCY: And me . . . you didn't discuss staying in the Army with me.

ROBERT: What was there to discuss? It was my decision, I made it.

LUCY: If you feel you've outgrown me, Robert, I'd prefer you to tell me.

ROBERT: I don't feel I've outgrown you.

(SHE *looks at him and her look says that she fears he has. Hold.*)

21. INT. THE MILLIGAN HOUSE

GRANNY, ALICE, BEN, DOROTHY, CHRIS *and* SAMANTHA *are there.*

DOROTHY: We'd better all try and be a bit more cheerful when the party starts.

CHRIS: A few beer'll see to that.

DOROTHY: You just take it easy . . . and no arguments. No playing the old soldier.

GRANNY: I hope you got Guinness for me?

ALICE: I've already said so, Mother . . . don't keep on.

GRANNY: (*To* DOROTHY *and* CHRIS) What's in the sandwiches?

CHRIS: Nice fresh tuna, Grandma.

GRANNY: (*Drily*) Lovely.

SAMANTHA: Are we going to have any music?

DOROTHY: (*Giving her a fierce look*) It would answer you better to think more about your school work, and less about pop music.

(SAMANTHA *goes to the window.*)

GRANNY: Leave the child alone.

DOROTHY: You should see her homework book. It's nothing to be proud of.

GRANNY: (*Nodding at* CHRIS) Well you and him aren't very bright, so you can't expect her to be.

ALICE: (*Down*) It should have been his demob party.

CHRIS: So where is our hero then?

ALICE: Gone to collect Lucy.

BEN: Let's all have a drink now.

ALICE: We'll wait for Robert. The party's for him . . . not an excuse for you to drink.

(*They all lapse into silence. Hold.*)

22. INT. THE PARTY

ROBERT, LUCY, PETE, MAVIS, TOM *and* DORA *have joined the others. Some are eating sandwiches and drinking.* TOM's *face is badly marked. He keeps glancing across at* MAVIS, *who keeps glancing back, when* PETE's *not watching. There is no music and it is not a party-like atmosphere.*

CHRIS: (*To* DOROTHY) Another drink, love?

DOROTHY: Not for me . . . and I think it's time you stopped . . . anybody'd think you'd never seen drink before.

CHRIS: It's supposed to be a party, Dot.

DOROTHY: Don't call me Dot . . . are you too drunk even to pronounce my name properly?

22 CONT. HALLWAY

ALICE, *slightly tipsy.* SAMANTHA *passing around with sandwiches.*

22 CONT. KITCHEN

ALICE: (*Tearful*) Look at him. This time next week he'll be creeping about the streets . . . like one of the black and white minstrels . . . trying to stay alive. Why did he do a thing like that on me, Dorothy?

SAMANTHA: I'm Samantha, Granny.

ALICE: (*Glaring at her*) Are you going to start contradicting me now too?

SAMANTHA: Would you like a sandwich?

ALICE: Tuna fish! Your da has no imagination . . . why couldn't we have had a nice bit of cheese for a change?

(SAMANTHA *to living room. Cut to* TOM *crossing to* ROBERT *and* LUCY. DORA, *rather timid, tags behind him, just grinning at people.* MAVIS *and* PETE *are close by.*)

22 CONT. HALL

TOM: Well, Robert . . . going for the real action this time?

ROBERT: Tom . . . it looks as if you've beaten me to it.

TOM: (*Gently touching his bruised face*) Somebody landed a few before I was ready.

ROBERT: (*Knowing, grinning*) They certainly did land.

LUCY: Doesn't it hurt, Tom?

TOM: (*Glancing at* PETE) I'll get my own back, Lucy . . . never fear . . . (*Louder*) . . . and I'll not be skinning my knuckles when I'm doing it either.

(ROBERT *has nothing to say to* TOM. *Cut to* BEN *with* GRANNY. *She has a glass of Guinness in one hand and a bottle in the other, topping herself up.*)

22 CONT. FRONT ROOM

BEN: You all right, Mother?

GRANNY: He put onions in that tuna . . . onions repeat on me. Alice seems a bit the worse for wear.

BEN: I told her to go easy . . . you know she's no drinker. Next thing she'll be sick.

GRANNY: (*Screwing up her face*) I hope she didn't have any of that oul fish.

BEN: Not much life for a party.

GRANNY: You need music for a party . . . especially for the young ones.

BEN: If Alice gets any more to drink she'll be singing the funeral march.

GRANNY: I didn't know there were words to that.

(PETE *and* MAVIS *cross right to left. Cut to* ALICE *and* LUCY. ALICE *rather maudlin.*)

22 CONT. KITCHEN

ALICE: He'll be killed you know. You'll be left a widow, and my life'll be ruined. Why didn't you coax him like I asked you?

LUCY: He'd already signed, Mrs Milligan.

ALICE: Already signed! Signed his own death warrant. I never wanted him to join the Army in the first place, never mind Northern Ireland. It's no life for a young man from a good, loving home. It teaches them to be aggressive. (*Pause.*) Will you marry him?

LUCY: He hasn't actually asked me.

ALICE: You should have got him to ask you. Men are like that. You have to put the words into their mouths, and let them think that they thought of it by themselves. You young ones are great for jumping in and out of bed . . . thinking yous know it all . . . and yous know nothing at all.

22 CONT. KITCHEN

Cut to DOROTHY *and* PETE. CHRIS *is standing with them, but only half listening, looking around him, drinking.*

DOROTHY: I'm from there, but I've no time for any of them. I met my Chris when he was serving there. Pull the troops out and let them get on with it, that's my view.

PETE: Yeah . . .

(*Straining to keep an eye on* MAVIS, *who is talking to* ROBERT. *But* TOM *is also lurking close to her, which affects* PETE's *mood.*)

. . . well we're just there to do a job. Keep your head down and get on with it's my motto.

DOROTHY: But why? Why should young men like you and Robert risk life and limb, to keep two lots of sectarian bigots from each other's throats?

PETE: They're not all sectarian bigots . . . not the whole population.

DOROTHY: (*Sneering*) All the ones I know are . . . Savages.

PETE: We keep the peace and protect the innocent. It's up to the politicians to sort it out.

DOROTHY: (*As* CHRIS *begins to pay more attention*) The politicians . . . Irish politicians? Have you seen them . . . have you heard them?

PETE: Look . . . it's a simple thing for the soldiers . . . I don't understand anything about Irish politics . . . so I just concentrate on the little bit I do understand . . . soldiering.

CHRIS: Huh, I can see they do a good job of brainwashing you lot.

PETE: You know nothing about it.

CHRIS: I was there, son, before you, when it was really a heavy scene.

DOROTHY: And he stayed on and worked as a prison officer for years. We know all about it.

CHRIS: And I know all about the Army. Northern Ireland's our Vietnam . . . none of us wanted to be there.

PETE: I could have left the Army, so could Robert. We signed on again to do this tour in Northern Ireland.

CHRIS: What's your IQ?

DOROTHY: We all know why Robert's doing it . . . it's just to get back at the rest of us . . . to impress that Lucy one.

CHRIS: Full of romantic shit about his Irish background.

PETE: The majority of the people of Northern Ireland want to remain British . . . until that changes we have to be there and support them.

DOROTHY: But they're not British.

CHRIS: That's the propaganda of some chinless wonder . . . right-wing rubbish.

PETE: (*To* DOROTHY) What are you then?

DOROTHY: I'm British . . . married to an Englishman . . . I've fully accepted the responsibilities of being British . . . the Protestants haven't.

CHRIS: It's typical isn't it? Right-wing political expediency, translated by chinless wonders to thick Toms who just . . .

PETE: (*Grabbing* CHRIS, *loud, angry*) Who are you calling a thick Tom?

CHRIS: (*Nervous, embarrassed by the attention of all the others*) All I'm saying . . .

PETE: I heard what you said . . .

DOROTHY: How dare you? . . . Take your hands off him.

22 CONT. FRONT ROOM

ROBERT: What's up?

(MAVIS *pulls* PETE *off* CHRIS.)

DOROTHY: (*Indignant*) Nothing's up, Robert . . . we were just discussing Northern Ireland with your friend, and he became abusive.

GRANNY: (*To* SAMANTHA) Huh . . . sure they left Northern Ireland with their tails between their legs.

BEN: That's enough now . . . no fighting . . . this is a party. (*As he sweeps the room he gazes right into* DORA's *silly grin*.) Listen, why don't we have some music . . . eh? . . . I'm sure there's something on.

(*He goes and starts to fiddle with the radio. Picks up a news item.*)

ANNOUNCER: A British soldier has been shot dead in Belfast tonight. A second soldier has been seriously wounded. (*All stunned*.)

This follows a day of sporadic violence in the city. From
Belfast –
(ROBERT *switches off the radio.* ALICE *crosses to face* BEN,
cold with fury.)
ALICE: What dance would you do to that?
(ROBERT *embraces her and leads her away. Hold.*)

23. INT. THE MILLIGANS. BREAKFAST TIME

ROBERT *and his father are sitting.*
BEN: Why didn't you lie on? There'll not be many opportunities
for that now.
ROBERT: I'd rather be up. (*Pause.*) Does Mum not rise with you?
BEN: She's usually up by this . . . but she was up a couple of
times during the night . . . sick. It's her own fault . . . she
never could hold her drink.
ROBERT: It wasn't a very successful party.
BEN: Would you rather we hadn't bothered?
ROBERT: I appreciate why.
(*They keep looking at each other – not saying things both of
them want to say.*)
BEN: If only I'd left that bloody radio alone.
ROBERT: Most of the other soldiers are coming home safe.
BEN: I'm sure his people thought he was coming too. His last
few days . . . so near . . .
ROBERT: Dad . . . I know you don't understand. (*Pause.*) The
army's changed me . . . it's changed the way I look at
things . . . the person I am. You were all expecting me to
come home and be the person I was . . . but that person's
gone.
BEN: You could have stayed in London . . . got a job.
ROBERT: Tom last night . . . people like Tom . . . mates . . .
I'd nothing to say to him. My mates are in the army . . .
that's one of the reasons we stayed.
BEN: Would you have rejoined if it hadn't been Northern
Ireland?
ROBERT: You think I joined the army just for something to do.
That's what people think . . . they think we all join up just

to get off the dole . . . do they think we're all morons who can't do anything else? Dad . . . I'm a soldier because I want to be a soldier . . . I believe in what I'm doing.

BEN: I'd better be going. (*Rising. Awkward.*) You know, it's not just because of your mum . . . I mean . . .

ROBERT: I know what you mean . . . and I appreciate it. I want to go to Belfast because . . . I want to see if it means anything to me.

BEN: Aye . . . well (*Pause.*) your granny's going to miss her walks.
(*He has himself together, ready to go. Hesitates.* ROBERT *stands. They are both awkward.*)

ROBERT: I'll see you sometime.

BEN: (*Offering his hand*) All the best, son. (*Pause.*) Write to your mother . . .

23 CONT. HALL
Their handshake becomes a warm embrace. Pause. ALICE *enters. They break away, embarrassed. Hold.*

24. EXT. A RAILWAY STATION
PETE *and* ROBERT *having a cup of tea.* SMICKS *arrives.*

SMICKS: Hey up . . . the hairstyles, or lack of them . . . the manly bearing . . . would I be right in assuming you two fine looking young men are soldiers?

PETE: After the temporary sanity of civvy street . . . back to wankers like this.

SMICKS: Good leave, lads? Lots of it . . . and lots of times?

ROBERT: Training for the real thing.

SMICKS: What of all the lovely girlfriends . . . wedding all arranged, Pete?

PETE: We want it to be a really funny affair . . . so you'll be best man.

SMICKS: You try to tell jokes . . . I use humour . . . subtle difference.

ROBERT: Heard a couple of lads caught it in Belfast last night.

SMICKS: Wasn't that just the encouragement my mum needed

for the long goodbye . . . moist cheeks, declarations of undying love. I never knew she was so fond of me!

ROBERT: My long goodbye started the day I got home.

SMICKS: But your mother's Irish . . . she's got all the right emotional equipment. Pity the poor traditional English mum.

PETE: Time we moved . . . ten-to.

SMICKS: We've loads of time. What about a proper drink?

ROBERT: Proper drink's easier to come by in the army than this . . . I'm going to have another coffee.

PETE: Mixing it . . . I'll try one . . . I'd enough drink last night. (*Rising.*) What about you, Smicks?

SMICKS: Coffee! What did I do to deserve two mates like you? (*Hold.*)

25. EXT. THE BARRACKS
Four-tonner and two jeeps arriving.

26. INT. TOP OF STAIRS. BARRACKS
SMICKS: See the board? Kit inspection at 0900 hours tomorrow morning.

PETE: Bloody hell . . . my stuff's all over the shop.

SMICKS: Well you'd better get the shop tidied, scruffy little man.

ROBERT: We're out tonight and all.

SMICKS: Bit of action straight off . . . this is the life.

PETE: They might let us get settled in. Out tonight and kit inspection first thing in the morning . . . bit bloody much I'd say.

SMICKS: Well, who's fault is that? You could have been a civilian now . . . well almost.

26 CONT. INT. BILLET
They enter billet.
PETE: I don't want to be a civilian . . . I just want a bit of time to settle, that's all.

ROBERT: I'm starving . . . I can smell food.

SMICKS: It smells like food now . . . it'll look like food when we get it . . . but that doesn't mean it will taste like food.

PETE: How come you've your bed made and everything tidy, Smicks?

SMICKS: No affairs of the heart . . . I got on with it . . . no long lying letters to girls. I'm natural . . . officer material. If I was at headquarters things in this army would go right.

ROBERT: Apply for a commission then.

SMICKS: I'm not going to chase after them . . . if they can't spot natural talent, then screw them.

ROBERT: (*Suddenly*) Hey . . .
> (*They look at him.*)
I'm in Belfast . . . I was born here.

SMICKS: It's Holywood actually.

27. INT. A ROOM IN THE BARRACKS
MAJOR *addressing a platoon of soldiers.* LIEUTENANT *and* SERGEANT *are on platform.* PETE, ROBERT *and* SMICKS *are among the soldiers.*

MAJOR: Right, lads . . . this is our first one, so let's get everybody back safe. Keep your eyes and ears open . . . watch out for each other . . . don't lose touch. (*Pause.*)
There may be kids about . . . ignore them. They might be innocent enough . . . but take no chances . . . None of the frustrated nursery school teacher bit.
(*Laughter.*)
They may be being used to set you up. Now these people know we're new . . . so hitting one or two of us now is bad for our morale . . . don't let it happen. (*Pause.*)
Remember . . . a couple of hours and you'll have survived your first bit of action in Northern Ireland. (*Pause.*)
Right . . . good luck.

28. EXT. BARRACKS
PETE, ROBERT *and* SMICKS – *ready to board transport. They are blacked up.*

PETE: I feel like a minority.
SMICKS: Give us a verse of 'Mammy'.
ROBERT: At least it's not too cold. We don't need thermals.
PETE: I'm cold . . . I'm shivering.
SMICKS: Nerves . . . you're frightened.
PETE: Go wank a grasshopper, cretin. (*Pause.*) Just think . . .
　　in an hour or so we could be shooting these things for real.
SMICKS: Just you remember your own team colours if we are.
ROBERT: Come on . . . what's the hold-up?
PETE: Maybe the CO's negotiating with the terrorists . . .
　　(*Mimicking*) 'Your house or ours, old chap'.
　　(*Silence.*)
SMICKS: What are they trying to do to us?
ROBERT: What about, 'Why are we waiting'?
PETE: It's cold now all right.
　　(*Hold.*)

29. INT. LIVING ROOM. GRANNY BRENNAN'S HOUSE
The living room of a house in Belfast. Two young men are there –
LIAM *and* EUGENE. *They are kitted out for a motorcycle. They are
just putting on their helmets.* GRANNY BRENNAN *enters from
upstairs, holding a bundle.* LIAM *leaves first. She passes the bundle
to* EUGENE. *He opens it, and removes a revolver, checks it and
then pushes it into his pocket. We can now hear the motorcycle
revving up.* EUGENE *goes out quickly. Pause. The motorcycle roars
away. Hold.*

29. CONT. EXT. BACK OF HOUSE
Motorbike roars off.

29. CONT. EXT. GRANNY BRENNAN'S HOUSE
Motorbike with LIAM *and* EUGENE *going down alleyway.*

30. EXT. A WEST BELFAST HOUSING ESTATE. DAY
A foot patrol moving through a West Belfast housing estate.
ROBERT, PETE *and* SMICKS *are members of it.* SMICKS *is last
man. They are cautious, alert. When they reach a corner they sprint*

to cover again. SMICKS *walks backwards, covering their rear. There is a* CHILD *playing at a corner.* SMICKS *stops to talk to her. We hear the motorcycle in the distance.* SMICKS *stiffens, looks towards the motorcycle, watches it approach – alert. It passes and he returns his attention to the* CHILD. *The motorcycle has turned and comes back towards* SMICKS *at speed. The* CHILD *runs away. There is a tremendous roar as the motorcycle draws level with* SMICKS. *The pillion passenger,* EUGENE, *raises his arm –* SMICKS *falls and the motorcycle roars away. As the others race back to* SMICKS, *children and others appear between the soldiers and departing motorcycle. Hold.*

31. INT. GRANNY BRENNAN'S HOUSE

LIAM *slumps into a chair.* GRANNY BRENNAN *enters with tea.*

LIAM: A flesh wound . . . point blank range, and all you can manage is a flesh wound.

EUGENE: You were too damned quick . . . I didn't even get a chance to put a second one in him.

LIAM: You fired three shots . . . must have missed the frigger twice.

GRANNY: Drink your tea like good lads, and don't be arguing. Sure you'll maybe do better the next time.

LIAM: They'll probably not give us a next time . . . three shots . . . and all he gets is a flesh wound.

GRANNY: God's good . . . maybe the oul bugger'll die of lead poisoning anyway.

EUGENE: You got that gun away anyway, Granny?

GRANNY: Two minutes after you put it into my hand. Theresa took it in the pram.

LIAM: Huh, if they did catch you they wouldn't know what to charge you with. It certainly couldn't be attempted murder.

EUGENE: All right . . . if you're so good, you do the hit the next time.

LIAM: If I'd known how bad you were I'd have run over the frigger. You'd better turn this place over or I'll have you knee-capped. I'll get on to the Press. (*He exits.*)

GRANNY BRENNAN: What's he talking about – turn this place
    over?
EUGENE: So it looks like the Brits have searched it – so you can
    claim compensation!
    (GRANNY BRENNAN *just looks blankly at him.*)

32. INT. A ROOM IN A POLICE STATION
JOHN *and* PAT *are studying a map and report.*
JOHN: I wish we'd got this a couple of days ago.
PAT: Might have saved a shooting?
JOHN: (*Thoughtful*) Granny Brennan. I'd love to put that oul
    bitch well away. She's a twisted bitter old woman.
    (*Thinking.*) If she's just serving tea to terrorists she'll walk
    out of court laughing at us. We've got to get her this
    time . . . something concrete. She's the sort'll walk out of
    hell making the devil feel bad.
PAT: Do you mean you want us to fit her up?
JOHN: I'll pretend I didn't hear that. (*Pause.*) Anyway . . . you
    know how long it takes a new unit to get over the notion
    that these people are human? They'll not believe Granny
    Brennan's anything but a sweet, harmless old lady.
PAT: Surely after the shooting . . .
JOHN: No . . . you're overlooking the arrogance of the average
    Brit officer. They'll excuse the natives at first . . . put it
    down to the incompetence of the other unit. Well . . . we'll
    set up a brief and hope for the best.
    (*Hold.*)

33. INT. MUSGRAVE PARK HOSPITAL
The military wing of Musgrave Park Hospital. SMICKS *is propped
up in bed. His upper arm and shoulder are heavily bandaged.* PETE
and ROBERT *are visiting him.*
PETE: He must have been blind to miss you from that range.
SMICKS: He didn't miss did he? He wrecked my arm.
ROBERT: I think you just fell with fright, sprained it.
SMICKS: You saw the blood . . . they took a bullet out. I think
    I'll have it mounted in a glass case.

PETE: There's a big redhead up there I'd like to get mounted.

ROBERT: Get off . . . she's a sister . . . she wouldn't waste her time on you.

SMICKS: Hands off . . . she's mine.

PETE: You wouldn't be much good to her with only one arm. Boy . . . she's got a lovely ass. (*Pinching some of the grapes they've brought.*) I suppose crumpet like that's only interested in ones with pips on their shoulders?

SMICKS: She's got pips of her own.

PETE: I can see them. Cor . . . I think the army has them specially built for this place.

ROBERT: How long are you going to be in here?

SMICKS: Don't know . . . a week . . . it depends.

ROBERT: Will you get some home leave?

SMICKS: No . . . I'll probably get light duties for a while.

PETE: Jammy bugger . . . you probably set the whole thing up yourself . . . they couldn't have missed from that range if they were serious.

(*Hold.*)

34. INT. POLICE STATION

A room in a police station. INSPECTOR JOHN WILSON *is sitting with the* MAJOR. *A large pile of papers sits between them.* JOHN *is leafing through them.*

JOHN: After the war here in the nineteen-twenties most of the rebels wrote books . . . (*Dropping pages.*) . . . I'm not surprised.

MAJOR: Should we worry? . . . It's all pure fabrication. No sensible person's going to believe that disciplined British soldiers were responsible for wanton, criminal damage, are they?

JOHN: Major, you're dealing with people who make up whatever they want to believe. They're prepared to believe that British soldiers would eat their children . . . Now that the fools have granted her bail . . . the press boys have taken her up there and photographed her in the ruins of her home . . . our case is in ruins . . . she'll walk out of that

court free as a bird . . . and . . . the oul whore will
probably get a claim for damages.

MAJOR: You'll excuse me, Inspector . . . but do I detect some
kind of accusation in your tone? I got my men out of there
fast . . . to prevent a full-scale riot. My men . . . and some
of your chaps . . . were at risk.

JOHN: My chaps are at risk every day, Major. The fact that they
didn't have time to get that oul bitch to sign a statement
that the house wasn't damaged puts them at further risk. It
was a police operation, Major. (*Pause.*) You see, the
mistakes you make in your first days here will hang around
your neck until you leave.

MAJOR: (*Stiff*) I regret that you think we made a mess of
things . . . I was quite proud of my chaps . . . they were
totally new to the situation . . . and there was a lot of
provocation. (*Pause.*) Some of your chaps were rather
abusive to the locals . . . I did think that was increasing the
risks for all of us.

JOHN: Well I'm not going to put swear-boxes in the backs of
Land Rovers.

MAJOR: Well, let's hope we have both learnt something from the
event. Next time we might get it right.
(*Hold.*)

35. INT. THE HOSPITAL WARD

SMICKS *is in bed. The auburn-haired* SISTER *is at the bedside.*

SISTER: You'll be out early next week.

SMICKS: Ah . . . I wanted to stay with you for a bit longer.
(*She pushes a thermometer into his mouth. She checks his pulse.
Goes and takes his chart-records. Removes the thermometer and
checks it.*)

SISTER: Yes . . . I think you're going to live.

SMICKS: Not without you I'm not.

SISTER: Do you know, I think you soldiers must have a
phrasebook. I have never heard an original sentence from
one of you.

SMICKS: I'm just an incurable romantic . . . all soldiers are.

SISTER: Have you had a bowel movement today?
> (SMICKS *is embarrassed. She smiles.*)

SMICKS: Yeah . . . early this morning.

SISTER: Good . . . (*Just as she's about to leave.*) Oh, by the way . . . if your friends come in tonight . . . remind them that they are soldiers . . . and that we do have military rank . . . will you do that?

SMICKS: Yes, Sister.
> (*She nods and goes. Hold.*)

36. INT. THE BARRACKS

ROBERT *and* PETE *on their respective beds,* PETE *writing a letter,* ROBERT *reading one.*

ROBERT: Here . . . what on earth have you been telling Mavis?

PETE: What do you mean?

ROBERT: (*Indicating his letter*) My mum . . . she's going daft . . . now she thinks it's so bad they're censoring the news. Will you leave it out?

PETE: I'll tell Mavis not to say anything to your mum.

ROBERT: Just tell her the truth . . . that Smicks got a small flesh wound . . . not that we took it in turns to give blood to keep him alive . . . and what's this rubbish about two of our blokes being held prisoner by the IRA?

PETE: It's all right for you, mate . . . I've a rival to keep at bay. If she thought I was lying here playing with myself most of the time . . . Guilt, that's what you need to keep a woman faithful. (*Pause. Writes a little more.*) Here . . . I think I'll take the plunge with Smicks's nurse tonight. He is bound to get out soon . . . it could be my last chance.

ROBERT: I don't believe you . . . if you stayed faithful, then you might be able to trust Mavis a bit more. Anyway . . . I've warned you, that sister will chew you up . . . put you on a charge for insubordination . . . She's an officer you know.

PETE: Rubbish . . . she's a woman first . . . you just watch me, mate . . . you might learn something . . .
> (*Hold.*)

INVITATION TO A PARTY

Cast:

MARION	Lise Ann McLaughlin
MATTHEW BAXTER	David Bannerman
LES HYND	George Rossi
JOHN	Ray Burdis
SERGEANT BELL	Sean Caffrey
JOHN CLARKE	Jon Croft
DORIS GIBSON	Delia Paton
JANET BAXTER	Bridget McCann
MATTHEW'S FATHER	Frank Duncan
CAROL	Hilary Reynolds
DENISE	Jill Doyle
MAJOR	Peter Hutchinson
POLICEMAN	Kevin Moore
JOE	Derek Lord
PETER	Colum Gallivan
1ST SOLDIER	Kevin Doyle
2ND SOLDIER	Joe McGrath
MARK	Robert Farquhar
WAITRESS IN CHIP SHOP	Bridget Erin Bates

1. INT. MARION'S FLAT. MORNING

A small cluttered bedsit. The alarm clock rings. MARION *stretches over and switches it off. She lies facing the ceiling. Close on her. Hold. We see what she is thinking. The little bedroom of a small kitchen house.* MARION *and* MARK *enter. They are just married. Both in suits, wearing buttonholes, confetti in their hair.* MARK *is carrying a suitcase, which he puts on the bed. He removes his jacket and throws that on the bed. Grabs hold of her, they laugh and kiss passionately. Gaze lovingly at each other, break. She opens the suitcase and removes nightclothes, etc. He removes a cigarette packet from his jacket. It contains one half-smoked cigarette. He lights it, screws up the packet and throws it away. He speaks to her as he puts on his jacket again. Pause after he leaves.*

    Close on MARION *as she is. She is upset. As she closes her eyes tight there is the loud bang of a shot. We see* MARK *lying on the street. He is bleeding from the chest. Two* SOLDIERS *stand over him. They are Scots. They gaze down at him. In his left hand is a packet of cigarettes. Hold.*

    Back on MARION. *Pause. She gets out of bed, crosses to the small cooker, puts on the teapot. Lies against the wall, gazing aimlessly into space.*

2. INT. THE LIVING ROOM OF A SMALL FLAT

It is a part of the same flat in which the bedsit is. It is spotlessly clean. Everything neat and in order, an unlived in appearance. On a sideboard are two photographs. One is of MARION *and* MARK *on their engagement. Her proudly displaying her ring for the camera. The other of them on their wedding day. Her in her bridal gown, rather than the 'going away' suit. Hold.*

    The door opens. MARION *enters. She stops just inside the door and rests against it. She gazes around the room, speaks the name 'Mark' aloud, not so much a shout that anyone should hear. After a few moments she moves from the door, and goes to the door of the bedroom.*

She opens the door slowly, and stands gazing in. Again she speaks the name 'Mark'. Hold. Out on MARION's *back. Her framed in the bedroom door.*

3. INT. AN OFFICE AT ARMY HEADQUARTERS IN LISBURN
There are three male clerks busy at their desks. LES *and* JOHN *are good friends,* MATTHEW, *a Scot, has only recently arrived.*

LES: You're dealing with the transport, are you, Jock?

MATTHEW: Yes . . . my name's Matthew.

LES: What? Oh . . . yeah . . . You don't like being called Jock?

MATTHEW: I prefer not to be.

LES: Fine . . . (*To* JOHN) John, it's Matthew.

JOHN: A pity . . . remember that picture with Lawrence Harvey? He always called Ronald Fraser Jock . . . Sounded great.

LES: If the man prefers Matthew . . . ours is just to do or . . . etc.

JOHN: Of course . . . we have been trained to serve, and serve we shall.

LES: You should come out with us some night, Matthew, on the town.

JOHN: All good Scots love their oats . . . and this is certainly the place for it.

MATTHEW: I'm a married man.

JOHN: Most of these are married women. You got quarters then?

MATTHEW: No . . . my wife teaches.

LES: Oh . . . not trying to live on a corporal's pay then . . . lucky old you.

JOHN: What's she called then, your missus?

MATTHEW: Janet.

JOHN: Got any kids?

MATTHEW: Two . . . one of each, two and eighteen months.

JOHN: Two and eighteen months . . .

MATTHEW: What? Two and eight months.

JOHN: Eighteen you said.

LES: Right . . . eighteen months, I heard it clearly.

MATTHEW: Sorry, my mistake.

LES: Still . . . variety is the spice of life . . . so they say.

JOHN: And if the little lady is happily teaching back in Bonnie
     Scotland . . . who's to know, and what harm?

MATTHEW: I'm to know.

LES: A moral Scot . . . and a soldier . . . what is this man's army
     coming to?
     (*Hold.*)

4. INT. FLAT. MORNING

*The flat. MARION is in the bedroom. The bed is neatly made up. It
has never been slept in. A nightdress is on one side of it, a pair of
pyjamas on the other side. The pyjamas are still in their cellophane
wrapper. On the table are the same two photographs. Between them is
a third, the photograph of MARK's grave. The grave is still covered in
wreaths. Hold.*

*There is the whistling scream as a kettle comes to the boil. She moves
through to the kitchen and switches it off. She sets out two cups, but
only puts coffee into one of them. She takes milk from the fridge. There
is nothing else in it, just the milk. The kitchen is spotless. Everything is
new and shiny and unused. She pours her own coffee, and takes out a
biscuit from her bag. As she sits she stares at the empty cup lost in her
thoughts. Hold.*

5. INT. THE OFFICE

JOHN: You know . . . I wonder do the senile old bastards who
     plan these transfers have any idea of the havoc they create
     in our lives?

LES: Some senile old general in the bath, surveying his wrinkled
     old willie . . . he's more on his withered brain than our
     welfare.

MATTHEW: That soldier who was killed last night . . . what
     happens about him?

JOHN: Well . . . if his people are Christian, they bury him.

MATTHEW: (*Angry*) I don't think it's funny.

LES: We don't talk about death in here, Matthew . . . an
     agreement we have.

JOHN: We're strictly the non-fatal branch of the machine . . .

keep it outside the door.

MATTHEW: Was he married?

JOHN: We don't talk.

MATTHEW: (*Thumping his desk*) Was he married?

LES: With two children . . . two and eight months . . . wife a
   school teacher.

MATTHEW: (*Angrily confronting* LES) Do you think that's funny?

LES: That's what it is . . . kill one, kill us all. (*Pause.*) We think
   about it . . . that's all, quiet thoughts.

JOHN: I think we should have a brew. (*He goes.*)

LES: Don't mind us, Matthew . . . we've our own way . . .
   (*Pause.*) He was a married man . . . from Coventry . . . not
   only leaving here at the weekend, but due to leave the whole
   show soon. (*Pause.*) We go out a lot . . . all the time. Mix
   with the natives . . . you meet them, they're generally
   friendly . . . the women especially . . . hating them just
   doesn't work . . . when you boil it all down they're only
   bloody Irish. They can't help it.

6. INT. THE KITCHEN OF THE FLAT

MARION *has just finished her coffee. She rises and rinses her cup and
spoon. Tidies them away, plus the other, unused cup. Drains the
kettle. Returns the place to its museum state. She goes into the
bathroom. It is in the same state as the rest of the place. She gazes at
herself in the mirror, instinctively touching her hair. Everything in the
bathroom, and it is fully stocked, is new and unused. She returns to the
sitting room. She takes a number of newspapers out of the sideboard
and sits down with them on the settee. They all carry reproductions of
her wedding photograph, and large headlines: 'Horror for Honeymoon
Couple'. 'Tragedy for Belfast Girl, a Wife and Widow in one Day'.
'Tragedy of Young Honeymooners'. She has these spread out, so that
she can see all three headlines and just sits looking at them. Hold.*

7. INT. THE OFFICE

LES, JOHN *and* MATTHEW *at their tea break.*

MATTHEW: One plate broken, according to the official report.

LES: You can forget that . . . they'll have done it over

themselves . . . get the press in and then hit us with a bill for hundreds of pounds.

MATTHEW: But if the officer in charge, plus the police, have signed they've no case.

LES: Just wait and see . . . that's all I'll say.

JOHN: I'd love to go on one of those searches . . . I'd give them something to claim for. It makes you sick. You drop that cup and they'll take it out of your pay . . . no defence. Anybody who can make an enemy of the British Government has a friend for life.

MATTHEW: They arrested the old woman . . .

LES: Yeah . . . seventy-eight the old bitch is . . . and still a bloody terrorist! I'd have shot her. She provides a safe house . . . probably stores arms and then gets rid of them after a hit.

MATTHEW: If she stored arms they'd have found them, they didn't.

JOHN: You must be a Celtic supporter, Matthew . . . you seem to have a natural empathy with the Republicans.

MATTHEW: I find it hard to believe that a woman of that age is involved.

LES: Wise up . . . they're in it at all ages . . . I think after a while the porridge accumulates round your brain.

MATTHEW: Just because we're in the army doesn't mean we've got to endorse every single action.

(*They just smirk.*)

There are thugs in the army you know. I'm a Scot and proud of being a Scot . . . but that doesn't mean I think every Scot's a saint.

LES: I don't think any Scot's a saint . . . a contradiction in terms that would be.

JOHN: It's all relative, Matthew . . . I would go along with you, if we were dealing with normally decent, law abiding people . . . but we're not. You read some of the reports we get in here. All right . . . some soldiers do step out of line . . . but they're often disciplined for it . . . who disciplines the terrorists?

MATTHEW: But they're not all like that . . . you've said so yourself.

JOHN: I know what I've said . . . but I'm talking about the actual terrorists and their supporters . . . stroll bloody on. (SERGEANT BELL *enters. He is from Northern Ireland.*)

SERGEANT BELL: Corporal Hynd . . . have you got that house-search report ready yet?

LES: Yes, Sergeant . . . (*He rummages through his papers and extracts the report.*) We'll probably throw them a few pounds in the end . . . (*Handing over the report.*) . . . that's what I think, Sergeant.

SERGEANT BELL: You're not paid to think, Corporal Hynd. (*Glancing through the report.*) They've gone to town on this one. They must have virtually demolished it after we left . . . and the papers and television have it. (*Pause. Looking at* MATTHEW.) Settling in all right, Corporal Baxter?

MATTHEW: Yes thank you, Sergeant.

SERGEANT BELL: Right, good . . . (*Going*) . . . carry on.

LES: (*Mimicking*) 'Carry on' . . . he thinks he's a bloody general.

8. INT. THE STAFFROOM OF A SMALL PRIMARY SCHOOL IN RURAL SCOTLAND

JANET BAXTER *is in the staff room.* DORIS GIBSON *is also there, and the headmaster,* JOHN CLARKE.

JOHN: Any further word from Matthew, Janet?

JANET: He phoned first thing this morning. There's a letter on the way. I don't know how long it takes to get from Ireland.

DORIS: It must be a terrible worry to you, dear.

JANET: No, not really . . . he's in a very safe area. I mean he's a clerk, he's never out on the streets.

DORIS: It appears to be getting nasty over there again. That poor lad last week . . . and him almost finished with the army.

JANET: Matthew was telling me about that. He was a young married man.

JOHN: It's a terrible situation. A firm hand . . . that's what's needed.

DORIS: Take our army out; let them get on with it.

JOHN: Now, Doris, I don't think we can just run away from these situations . . . we do have our responsibilities over there. (*Pause.*)

DORIS: Does Matthew like it, Janet?

JANET: He misses the family, but that's only to be expected. He says it's very quiet most of the time.

DORIS: Well it's certainly not quiet at the moment . . . anything but.

JANET: He says the people are very nice.

DORIS: Sure the animals in the jungle are very nice . . . so long as you only have to look at them . . . but you can't trust them.

JOHN: Do the children miss him, Janet?

JANET: They're quite used to him being away now. It's the few days just after he goes back . . . they're the worst for all of us.

DORIS: I have to say I blame the government. Sure, what opportunities are there for people around here?

JOHN: Do you think many join up just to get off the dole, Janet?

JANET: I'm sure some do . . . but surely working on the fishing boats, or the oil rigs is even more dangerous than being a soldier over there. (JANET *doesn't want to have this conversation at all.*)

DORIS: Drowning's a clean way . . . compared to a sniper's bullet in the back.

JOHN: Oil's not such a clean way. (*He sniggers, but the two women just look at him.*)

DORIS: I read in the *Sunday Times*, they're using dum-dum bullets over there now.

JOHN: Are they really . . . they're a terrible thing. I remember my father . . .

JANET: (*At a rush*) Could we maybe just drop the whole conversation . . . please. (*Pause.*) I'm sorry. (*They sit for a moment in silence.*)

DORIS: One of our Madge's colleagues lost a brother over there. They closed the school on the day of the funeral. (JANET *gets up and hurriedly leaves.*)

JOHN: It's obviously more of a worry than she lets on.

DORIS: I don't think he should be there at all . . . risking all that, and her left to bring up the children. They join up in these things you know, and they never consider the risks.

JOHN: Did they close the school for the whole day?

9. INT. THE OFFICE
They are packing up for the day.

MATTHEW: Is it just for a few drinks?

JOHN: Of course.

MATTHEW: I'm not interested in chasing after any women you know.

LES: We're not going to tie you to a bed or anything.

MATTHEW: I'll maybe come for an hour. I'll check and see if there's anything worth while on the telly first.

JOHN: (*Looking at* LES) No wonder Scotch women . . .

MATTHEW: Scots women.

JOHN: . . . Look so dour . . . how do you all survive the excitement up there?

LES: It's all those kilts . . . it keeps everything cool.

MATTHEW: So you two think you lead full, exciting lives . . . Come on, waken up. You spend your lives chasing after women . . . usually other men's wives . . . I'd like to think there's more to life than that.

LES: Yeah . . . like what?

MATTHEW: Is this the way you behave at home? I can't really see you two being any different anywhere . . . drink and sex.

JOHN: Listen to this, Les . . . they don't have sex in Scotland.

LES: He'd better believe it . . . look around the average army camp . . . there's a right bit of hanky-panky goes on . . . when the cat's away . . .

MATTHEW: What are you implying?

LES: I'm just saying . . . (*Realizing* MATTHEW's *anger.*) . . . Oh forget it.

MATTHEW: (*Furious*) Are you making suggestions about my wife?

JOHN: Wrap it up, Jock . . . a one-man bloody moral crusade.

MATTHEW: Maybe that sort of behaviour's typical of English women . . .

JOHN: Oh piss off . . . You mean to tell me Scotch . . . or . . .
Scots . . . women never play around? No divorces for
adultery in Scotland?

MATTHEW: I'm talking about my wife.

LES: All right, so talk about your bleeding wife . . . bore us all to
death.

(SERGEANT BELL *enters*.)

SERGEANT BELL: Corporal Baxter . . . have you been listening
to rumours?

MATTHEW: (*Puzzled*) Sergeant?

SERGEANT BELL: I thought maybe you'd heard a rumour about
this place being sound-proofed. Well it isn't . . . and I can
hear your Scots roar all over the place.

MATTHEW: Sorry, Sergeant. (*Pause*.)

SERGEANT BELL: Corporal Hynd . . . I'd like the full transport
allocation report first thing in the morning.

LES: Yes, Sergeant.

SERGEANT BELL: (*As he goes to the door*) I don't know why it
wasn't ready this afternoon. (*Goes*.)

MATTHEW: I didn't think I was shouting.

JOHN: Excitable Celt git . . . aren't you? Let's get out of here.

10. EXT. THE STREET

A Land Rover parked by the side of the road. Two SOLDIERS
standing. One nudges the other and draws his attention to MARION,
walking towards them. As she is almost level with them one steps out.

FIRST SOLDIER: Excuse me, love . . . could I have a look inside
your bag?

(*She opens her bag. She doesn't appear friendly. The* SOLDIER
rummages around it.)

Could you tell me where you're going?

MARION: I'm on my way home from work.

FIRST SOLDIER: Oh yeah . . . all finished up for the day. Free
this evening are you?

(MARION *just looks at him.*)

Where do you work then?

MARION: In a chemist shop.

FIRST SOLDIER: (*Looking at his mate and sniggering*) That's
    handy . . . Maybe I'll start going there for my aftershave.
    (*She doesn't respond.*)
    Do you sell aftershave then?
MARION: If you don't mind I'm in a hurry.
FIRST SOLDIER: You got a date then have you?
MARION: Something like that.
FIRST SOLDIER: (*Grinning at his mate*) If it was me, sweetheart, it
    would be like nothing else in the world.
MARION: Please . . . can I go?
FIRST SOLDIER: No rush . . . I'm sure he'll wait for you. (*He
    doesn't realize how upset she is.*) You got any means of
    identification then?
    (*She starts to cry slightly. His mate draws his attention to it.*)
    Here . . . you all right, love? What's the matter?
MARION: (*Trying to maintain control*) I'd like to go please.
FIRST SOLDIER: Of course . . . look love . . . no offence
    intended . . .
    (*She glares fiercely at him and walks away.*)
    Here, what you reckon to that then?
SECOND SOLDIER: Her time of the month I reckon.
    (*They stand gazing after her.*)

11. INT. MATTHEW'S AND JANET'S LIVING ROOM
The living room of MATTHEW *and* JANET'S *house in Scotland. The
children are in bed. She is ironing their clothes. She keeps watching the
clock and from that her gaze goes to the telephone. Hold. The
telephone rings. She goes to it.*
JANET: Hello.
MATTHEW: Janet?
JANET: Hello, darling.
MATTHEW: How are things?
JANET: Fine . . . just fine. The children are in bed . . . I'm just
    doing a little bit of ironing. How are you?
MATTHEW: Great. (*Pause.*) I'm thinking of going out tonight.
    You don't mind, do you?
JANET: Mind? Why should I mind?

MATTHEW: You know I've told you about Les and John. They're always at me to go out. It's been a heavy sort of a day, so I thought I'd just go and have a few drinks with them.

JANET: That's good . . . you need to get out a bit . . . Just be careful where you're going over there.

MATTHEW: Oh I will, don't worry. They go out all the time . . . every night almost.

JANET: Well I've a little bit of news for you . . . Nicky has another tooth through.
(*He responds.*)
I noticed it tonight when I was feeding her . . . so there's something for you to celebrate.

MATTHEW: That's great. Was Dad over?

JANET: No, he's coming tomorrow to do a wee bit in the garden. I'll make him his dinner. He said he'd maybe tile the bathroom this weekend.

MATTHEW: Great . . . don't let him overdo it mind . . . He doesn't know when to stop sometimes.
(*Go out on* MATTHEW'*s line – leaving them talking.*)
I had a long chat with Sergeant Bell today . . .

12. INT. MARION'S FLAT.
MARION *has the newspapers out again. There is an envelope on the table, addressed to 'Mark'. Hold. She opens the envelope – it contains an anniversary card. She crosses and puts it on the sideboard. It says, 'Happy first anniversary, darling'. She looks at it for a long moment. We see her from behind – the card beyond her. Her shoulders begin to heave – she is crying softly. Hold. Suddenly she grabs the card and tears it to pieces, dropping the pieces on the floor.*
Pause. MARION *stops crying. She looks around. She starts to put the photographs away in drawers – doing the same with the ones in the bedroom, also removing the pyjamas from the bed. She puts the newspapers away, then gets down on her hands and knees and begins to lift the pieces of the card. When she is kneeling, the pieces of card cradled in her hands, she starts to sob softly again. Hold on her for a moment.*

13. INT. THE BARRACK ROOM

MATTHEW *and* LES *dressed to go out.*

MATTHEW: Can we trust local taxis?

LES: This is a reliable firm.

MATTHEW: There seem to be some very grey areas of security.

(LES *just looks at him, slightly irritated by his fussiness.*)

LES: Did you ring your missus?

MATTHEW: Yes, all's well there.

LES: Did you tell her you love her?

MATTHEW: She knows that anyway. I told her I was going out.
She seemed quite pleased.

LES: You must spend an absolute fortune on the phone. What do
you talk about . . . I mean every night?

MATTHEW: Don't be silly, we've lots to talk about. I tell her
about what I've been up to all day.

LES: Oh dead exciting . . . she must find telly dull after that.

MATTHEW: She tells me about her day . . . how the children are.
We live in a small village, so there's the local gossip.

(LES *just shakes his head.*)

I tell her about you two.

LES: Us! . . . Stroll on. Do you tell her about our conquests, eh?

MATTHEW: I don't think she'd be very interested in that.

LES: I can't see that there's much to say about us then.

MATTHEW: Then there's Sergeant Bell . . .

LES: Oh Christ . . . lay off, Jock . . . it bores me just to think
about it. You phone her all the time. You write as well . . .
so do you write the same things down?

MATTHEW: Do you not write to anyone, or phone them?

LES: Yeah . . . hello, love, what about getting the old knickers
off tonight. (*Pause.*) Here . . . you do know about the
Official Secrets Act . . . I mean you could get into a lot of
trouble . . . telling her the Sergeant takes sugar in his
tea . . . and refuses to issue toilet rolls, if he thinks we're
using it too fast? You never know, Jock . . . maybe after
tonight you'll have something really exciting to tell her.

MATTHEW: You're right . . . I might tell her I've split your skull
for always calling me Jock.

LES: Lay off . . . I like it. It suits you. (*Pause.*) What is keeping
    that man?

MATTHEW: Do you think you'll ever get married?

LES: Married! . . . I prefer to let other men keep the cow, and I
    just drink the milk.

14. INT. MARION'S FLAT

MARION *has attempted to give it a lived in look. She emerges from the
bathroom, made-up. She takes a check around the rooms – all the
photographs have been removed, her nightdress is crumpled, the bed
just slightly rumpled. She puts on her coat and takes a long look
around before she leaves. Hold for a moment on the empty flat.*

15. INT. A PUB

MATTHEW *and* JOHN *are sitting.* LES *is at the bar, getting their
drinks.* MATTHEW *is glancing all around looking rather ill at ease.*

JOHN: Relax will you. You've ruined all my illusions about the
    Scots.

MATTHEW: Good. I don't find most people's views of the typical
    Scot very flattering.

JOHN: I was thinking of the fierce warrior image.

MATTHEW: There seem to be a lot of female couples in here.

JOHN: They're all lesbians.
    (*He laughs at* MATTHEW'*s expression.*)

MATTHEW: Are you serious, though?

JOHN: Well known fact. That's why so many Irish men are
    drunks . . . frustration.
    (LES *returns and sets down two drinks.*)

MATTHEW: Bollocks. (*Realizing* LES *thinks he's talking to him.*)
    Sorry . . . I wasn't talking to you. (*Taking a drink*) Cheers.
    (LES *returns to the bar for his own drink.*)
    What sort of reputation does this pub have?

JOHN: Bad . . .
    (*As* LES *returns*)
    . . . It's a soldiers' pub.

MATTHEW: Isn't that dangerous . . . doesn't it invite attacks?

JOHN: Life's dangerous.

LES: (*Raising his glass*) Here's to the new tooth.
(*They drink.*)

JOHN: (*Glancing at* MATTHEW) It may be the only thing we get a chance to drink to tonight.

MATTHEW: That's all we're supposed to be here for.

LES: (*Looking around*) Plenty of crumpet around anyway.

MATTHEW: Is this your usual place?

JOHN: We start here . . . then see what happens . . . we like to move around.

MATTHEW: Do you ever go into Belfast?

JOHN: No . . . no need . . . we usually manage to get all we want here.
(*Cut to a little later. More empty glasses on the table.*)

MATTHEW: So, is this it? You just sit here swilling this stuff, then wander back to camp and piss it all away. (*With a laugh.*) Is this the high living you tell me I've been missing?

JOHN: It's early yet, mate . . . it beats watching telly back there.

MATTHEW: You can go to the club . . . you don't have to come out here.

LES: Yes . . . sit groping some randy WRAC all night . . . Do me a favour.

MATTHEW: You seem fond enough of groping them during the day.

JOHN: The whole point, mate . . . we can do that during the day . . . at night you want something different.
(MATTHEW *just sniggers.*)

LES: Even if we just get out for an hour . . . away from that place, mix with ordinary people . . . it keeps you sane. Your wife probably thinks we lead a very exciting, dangerous life.

MATTHEW: She does not . . . I tell her about the sort of life we lead . . . that it's boring most of the time.

JOHN: You can't tell them that, mate . . . my mum thinks I spend every day dodging bullets . . . you try telling them any different, they just won't believe you.

MATTHEW: Do you try to tell them anything different?
(LES *and* JOHN *just smile.* LES *nudges* JOHN, *the three of them gaze at* CAROL *and* DENISE, *two attractive girls. They cross*

194

from the bar and sit opposite the three. They are nurses, in their
twenties. Fade up on CAROL and DENISE.)

CAROL: I've never been here before . . . have you?

DENISE: A couple of times. Most of them are soldiers.

CAROL: Yes, you feel a draught as soon as you come in, they have
you stripped before you reach a seat.

DENISE: Don't look now, but I think we're being sized up.
(*They do look, pretending not to. Smiles and nods are exchanged.
The girls giggle, and giggle virtually every time they speak.*)

CAROL: There's nothing on there . . . three of them.

DENISE: One-and-a-half each. Which one will we split?

CAROL: Never mind which one . . . which way will we split him?

DENISE: You can pick them out a mile away, can't you?

CAROL: It's their tall manly bearing . . . can you picture those
three let loose on the streets?

DENISE: Maybe they're medical orderlies . . . we'll have lots to
talk about.

CAROL: God no . . . I want a man of action . . . one capable of
handling a weapon.
(*They almost choke laughing.*)
I didn't mean that way . . . you've got a filthy mind.

DENISE: Stop tittering . . . they think they've got us weak at the
knees.

CAROL: They're discussing tactics . . . I think we're in for a
killing here.
(*The girls huddle and giggle. Fade up on the lads.*)

LES: What are we tonight?

JOHN: (*With a glance at* MATTHEW) Together.

MATTHEW: Don't let me get in the way.

JOHN: We'd better make a move before they're snatched up . . .
I think we've got competition across the way . . . and they're
doing better on numbers.

LES: Don't panic . . . we're in the home straight. (*Pause.*) Play
men of action . . . secret mission routine.

MATTHEW: Why tell lies?
(*They both look at him.*)

JOHN: Have you ever known a woman to get excited about the

dangers you face changing a typewriter ribbon? (*Pause.*) It's
a pity they don't have a mate . . . just for company,
Matthew . . . it makes things easier. (*Pause.*) What do you
reckon they are?

LES: They're women . . . that's enough for me.

JOHN: If they're civil servants we'll have lots to talk about.

LES: See any wedding rings?

MATTHEW: No . . . you're lucky.

JOHN: Over here the married ones are the best . . . easier . . .
looking for adventure. Have we been wounded this
week?

LES: No . . . I don't like that . . . I'm always afraid of getting
nurses.

JOHN: Mate shot dead beside us? Or a couple blown up?

LES: Blown up . . . on a landmine. Wiping the bits of your best
friend off your face is great for sympathy. (*Pause.*) Do you
think we maybe risked our lives to drag a couple to safety?

JOHN: Absolutely . . . Didn't the bullets from the ambush kick
mud into my eyes.
(*They giggle.*)

MATTHEW: They're quite attractive.
(*Pause. They both look at him.*)

JOHN: I think we might have to draw lots on this one yet.

MATTHEW: No, no . . . I'm just saying . . . You can look at the
menu without tasting the food.

LES: Not with my imagination you can't mate. (*Drinking*) Do you
know, Matthew . . . you're not just Scottish . . . you're
almost human as well. (*Finishing his drink*) Right . . . will I
invite them over?

JOHN: (*Drinking*) Go get 'em, tiger.

16. EXT. A STREET IN LISBURN

MARION *is walking along. She has a distracted look about her. She
stops to look into shop windows, but has the appearance of someone
not taking in what they are looking at. Men passing her stop and look
back. She ignores them. She stops at a window. In it she sees* MARK
putting on his coat. Hold. She drops her head. When she looks again,

it is MARK *in the street in a puddle of his own blood. Hold. She walks slowly on.*

17. INT. THE PUB

The girls have now moved over to the lads' table. As we come in on them they are all laughing, but MATTHEW *with much less enthusiasm than the others, he does seem to be quite enjoying it, though.* LES *and* JOHN *would like him to leave. Hold.*

MATTHEW: (*Finishing his drink*) Listen, lads . . . I think I'll head back to camp.

LES: (*Obviously pleased*) Not at all . . . you're all right, mate.
(JOHN *fires* LES *a fierce glance, seen by* MATTHEW.)

DENISE: Don't let us chase you . . . I love your accent.

CAROL: We'll be going soon anyway . . . we're on our way out.

JOHN: (*Displeased*) Your way out?

LES: (*Mock serious*) Dying . . . didn't you tell him, Carol?
(*Laughter.*)

MATTHEW: I've a few things I want to clear up . . . I'm tired too.
(JOHN *and* LES *just look at each other. Pause.*)

JOHN: Matthew takes the CO a cup of hot drinking chocolate every night.

LES: Yes . . . mustn't be late with that. He also reads him a bedtime story.

MATTHEW: (*Rising*) Yes . . . well . . . (*Awkward.*)

CAROL: Ah . . . it's a pity you have to go . . . If we'd known we could have brought another friend with us.

LES: Listen . . . why don't we arrange that for some other night?

MATTHEW: It's all right . . . (*Despite his earlier statements, he is obviously enjoying the warmth of the company.*)

DENISE: We'll bring Bridie . . .
(*The girls double up at this, infecting* LES *and* JOHN, *and making* MATTHEW *feel even more awkward.*)

JOHN: She sounds like a real goer.
(*The girls are incapable of any response.* MATTHEW *is aware that the joke's at his expense now.*)

MATTHEW: It was nice meeting you anyway.

(*He offers his hand to both of them. They try to take the handshake seriously and not laugh, but it was clearly not the response they were expecting.*)

(*To* LES *and* JOHN) I'll see you two later.

CAROL: (*Putting a hand on* JOHN's *arm*) Much, much later. (*Laughter.* MATTHEW *goes off. Silence at the table.* LES *and* JOHN *feel guilty. They are torn between wanting the girls to themselves, and loyalty to* MATTHEW.)

DENISE: Ach, God love him . . . he's lovely.

CAROL: He looks dead sad . . . do you think he's mad at us?

JOHN: No . . . he's fine . . . (*Glancing at* LES) He's all right.

LES: Maybe we can fix something up for another night. You can bring . . . what was her name . . . Bridie?

DENISE: (*As they start to laugh again*) God . . . you want to see Bridie . . . she's a big fat lump, near forty and man mad.

CAROL: She's got a moustache.

DENISE: She's got dead thick legs. We had her with us one night, and a fella asked her if she'd got her legs on upside down. (*Laughter. Pause. They shift seating and pair off.* CAROL *and* JOHN. DENISE *and* LES.)

LES: Where are you two going off to?

CAROL: Oh now . . . it's top secret.

DENISE: We are though . . . we'll have to leave in about half an hour.

JOHN: You're kidding . . . can't you put it off?

CAROL: No can do . . . it's very important. (*A slight gloom descends on* JOHN *and* LES.)

JOHN: I thought heaven was supposed to last for all eternity!

LES: No, mate . . . you're mixing it up with army service. (*Return to laughter as they hail a waitress.*)

18. EXT. THE STREET

MATTHEW *on the street. He looks a rather sad, dejected figure. He looks along the street, there is a lighted chip shop ahead of him. A police Land Rover is sitting by the kerbside. Two policemen emerge from the chip shop, one is carrying a couple of bags of chips, the other carries a gun. They clamber into the Land Rover and it speeds off.*

MATTHEW *then notices* MARION *walking towards him. She turns into the chip shop. When he reaches the shop he, too, goes in. Hold.*

19. INT. THE PUB

LES *and* JOHN *are regaling the girls with tales of their exploits. The girls are wide-eyed.*

CAROL: (*To* LES) Did you get a medal?

LES: I got a bollocking.

DENISE: Why . . . sure you'd saved his life?

LES: Not from him . . . from the CO. It was a sensitive mission . . . we weren't supposed to be there . . . officially.

CAROL: And were you supposed to leave your friend to die?

JOHN: (*Blowing himself up*) The risk of our game, love. If it had been one of us we'd have expected to have been left, to take our chances.

DENISE: Even if you're badly hurt?

JOHN: Tough.

LES: We're all volunteers in our unit . . . the day you sign on, you write your will.

(*Hold, and then out on the girls' admiring glances.*)

20. INT. THE CHIP SHOP

Inside the chip shop. MARION *is waiting at the counter. The* GIRL *is making tea. There is another couple in the shop, the man is quite obviously a soldier. The counterhand is bored, scruffy and chewing gum with a wide open mouth.*

GIRL: (*To* MATTHEW *as she prepares* MARION's *tea*) Yes . . . what do you want?

MATTHEW: I'd like a fish supper, please . . . and some tea, please.

(MARION *looks at him when she hears the accent.*)

Do you do bread and butter?

GIRL: Aye . . . one piece or two?

MATTHEW: Two pieces, please.

GIRL: Right . . . if you just take a sate I'll bring it over to you.

(*As she sets* MARION's *tea on the table,* MATTHEW *hands her a fiver.*)

MATTHEW: I'll just pay you now.

(MARION *stares at him again as she lifts her tea and walks away.* MATTHEW, *aware of* MARION'*s stare, glances after her. The* GIRL *gives him his change. He goes and sits down opposite* MARION. *She keeps gazing at him. He finds it disconcerting. At one point he catches her eye. Her face is expressionless, staring at him. He smiles at her. She doesn't respond. He drops his head, slightly embarrassed, then glances up at her again. He sees that she is crying . . . tears coursing down her cheeks. He doesn't know what to do for a moment, then rises and crosses to her.*)

MATTHEW: Excuse me . . . are you all right? (*Pause.*) Can I help? Will I join you? (*Pause.*) Look . . . would you like to talk?

MARION: Are you Scotch?

MATTHEW: A Scot . . . yes. (*Pause.*)
(*She blows her nose, tries to compose herself.*)

MATTHEW: (*Tentative*) Do you mind? (*He sits.*)

MARION: If you like.
(*He is sympathetic, concerned.*)
Are you a soldier then?

MATTHEW: Is it that obvious?
(*She just looks at him. Pause. He smiles warmly at her. She returns a weak smile. He feels ill at ease, awkward.*)
Do you come here . . . (*Smiles.*) . . . what I mean is . . .

MARION: No . . . I don't come to pick up soldiers, if that's what you think.

MATTHEW: No . . . no . . . I never dreamt, really . . . (*Pause.*)
Are you from around here?

MARION: No . . . (*Pause.*) . . . no, I live in Belfast. I have a flat (*She hesitates, unsure. Pause.*) My mother's in hospital . . . I've . . . I've been up visiting her.

MATTHEW: I see. I'm sorry . . . I didn't mean to pry . . . is she?

MARION: (*Nodding her head*) She's very bad.
(*The waitress comes across with* MATTHEW'*s food.*)

MATTHEW: (*As she leaves*) She doesn't look too happy at her work. She doesn't look very clean either. Would you like something to eat?
(MARION *shakes her head.*)

Are you sure?

MARION: No, really . . . I've no appetite . . .

(*He takes the remarks to be linked to her mother's illness, and nods knowingly and sympathetically.*)

MATTHEW: I can understand that.

MARION: I'm sorry . . . I'm being a real misery . . . I must look a sight.

MATTHEW: Not at all . . . no, no. (*Pause.*) Sometimes it's good to have someone to talk to . . . or someone who'll just listen. (*They lapse into silence as he eats.*)
Fish and chips never seem to taste as nice as they smell from a hundred yards away.

MARION: The tea's not bad. Usually in places like this it tastes like dishwater. (*She sounds tearful again. Pause. With a great effort at control.*) How long have you been in the army?
(*As he is about to reply she bursts into tears again.*)
I'm sorry . . . (*Struggling to her feet*) . . . I'd better go.

MATTHEW: It's all right . . . listen . . . sit down . . . look . . . I'll ring for a taxi . . . it's all right . . . I'll see you get home. Just sit there for a minute. (*He crosses to the counter.*) Do you have a telephone I can use?

GIRL: It's not a public phone.

MATTHEW: (*Glancing back at* MARION) Well, look, could you call a taxi for me, please?

GIRL: (*Holding out her hand*) That'll be twenty pence.
(*He gives her the money.*)
Is she pregnant?

MATTHEW: I beg your pardon?

GIRL: It's happening all the time. You soldiers don't seem to be able to control yourselves. What's your name?

MATTHEW: Pardon?

GIRL: For the taxi . . .

21. INT. THE PUB

They are at the arms around each other stage.

CAROL: (*To* JOHN) You can make up your minds while I go to the loo.

DENISE: I'll come with you.

(*They take their bags and go.*)

JOHN: Why do women always go to the loo in pairs?

LES: To decide on tactics . . . who's getting what, when, and how often. What do they have in their bloody bags?

JOHN: Make up . . . a small tin of talc . . . to sprinkle down the knickers.

LES: What about this party?

JOHN: No . . . I don't like that idea at all.

LES: You're not going to just let them walk away, are you?

JOHN: Let's try and talk them out of it . . . it's too risky.

LES: I think they're genuine. Come on, we're on to two good ones here . . . you know what they say about nurses.

JOHN: If they're that keen why do they want to go to a party?

LES: Well you coax them then . . . it seems worth the risk to me.

JOHN: Don't be so daft . . . you don't believe those stories we tell about ourselves, do you? Apart from the risk from them . . . goodness knows who else'll be there. (*Pause.*) Here they come. If they insist then let's just make another date.

(*The girls arrive back.*)

CAROL: Well, are you coming . . . because we'll have to go.

JOHN: You don't have to go for goodness' sake . . . it's only a party.

DENISE: We've promised to go . . . it's our friend's twenty-first.

LES: It's not that we don't want to go . . .

JOHN: No . . . we do . . . we'd love to, but . . .

LES: We can't really discuss it . . . but we've something on . . .

JOHN: Very early in the morning, and we have to be back. But couldn't we make another date? Tomorrow night, or anytime.

DENISE: We're in here quite often . . . we'll probably see you.

LES: We can ring you at the hospital . . .

CAROL: No . . . at least don't ask for Sister Donnelly . . . we're not supposed to take calls at work.

JOHN: I'll say I'm your brother.

CAROL: With that accent, don't be daft.

DENISE: Don't ring us at all . . . look, we'll see you in here

tomorrow night . . . half-seven. Come on, Carol.
(*They call them back for a parting kiss then* LES *and* JOHN *slump gloomily into their chairs.*)

JOHN: I don't believe they're sisters at all.

LES: I don't give a shit what else they are . . . they're available.

JOHN: Of course we're not captains either.

LES: Slip of the tongue . . . corporal. (*Pause.*) One for the road, and then home to tuck in jolly old Jock.

22. INT. LIVING ROOM OF THE BAXTERS' HOUSE IN SCOTLAND

The ironing is sitting neatly piled up. JANET *enters from the kitchen. She has a full baby's bottle in her hand. She checks around the room, yawns, goes to the door, and switches off the light on her way out. Hold.*

23. INT. MARION (AND MARK'S) FLAT

MARION *and* MATTHEW *are sitting drinking coffee. He is ill at ease . . . not quite sure what to make of the situation.*

MARION: Have you ever shot anyone over here?

MATTHEW: Me? I have never shot anyone anywhere.

MARION: I'll bet you have. What does it feel like to pull a trigger, and actually kill a man?

MATTHEW: I don't know . . . seriously . . . I've never done it.

MARION: I'll bet you've killed people here. I've heard the Scots are the toughest ones in the whole army.

MATTHEW: You'll hear lots of things about the Scots that aren't all true.

MARION: It must be wonderful . . . adventure, excitement . . . I think if I was a man I'd be in the army. Do you ever think about the people you shoot . . . Afterwards, I mean? I suppose you'll say it's a war, that you're just doing your job . . . and never think of them again. As far as you're concerned they're probably all terrorists . . . who deserve to die. Kill them before they kill you . . . isn't that it? How would you feel if you shot an innocent man?

MATTHEW: Marion . . . I don't shoot men, innocent or no . . .

203

the only weapons I use are a pen, and a typewriter.

MARION: Of course you never admit to making mistakes . . . you never think that some of the people you kill might be innocent.

(*She glares at him fiercely. He looks back. She crumbles.*)
I'm sorry. (*Pause.*) Would you like some more coffee?

MATTHEW: No, thank you. I'd better be thinking about getting back. (*Pause.*) Will you be all right? Isn't there anyone. . . ?

MARION: (*Cutting in*) No . . . I've nobody . . . (*Looking at him.*) . . . nobody. (*Rising quickly.*) I must go to the bathroom . . . then I'll leave you to the door.

(*She goes. He sits looking after her. Uncomfortable.*)

(*Cut to: the bedroom in the Baxters'.* JANET *is asleep. Pause. The baby starts to cry. The crying builds up.* JANET *stirs. She gropes out a hand and switches on the bedside lamp.*)

JANET: (*Sleepily*) It's all right, pet, it's all right.

(*She switches the bottle heater on, and places the full bottle in it. Gets out on to the edge of the bed, the crying continues.*)
All right, pet . . . all right . . . Mummy's coming.

(*Cut to: close up on* MATTHEW. *The bathroom door opens and he looks up. He smiles, but then the smile freezes on his face. He seems about to say something and rises . . . A shot rings out. His body jerks . . . convulses and then lies still. Pause. A trace of blood seeps from the corner of his mouth.* MARION *stands, just gazing at him, the revolver hangs from her hand. Close up on* MARION.)

(*Cut to: a close up on* JANET. *She is in bed, nursing the baby. It is sucking contentedly on its bottle.*)

(*Cut to:* MARION *still standing rigid, frozen, gazing at* MATTHEW. *Pause. She moves towards him, realizes she still has the gun and sets it down. She goes to the body and starts to undress it. Hold.*)

(*Cut to: the bathroom. We see* MARION's *reflection in the mirror. Her*

*face is quite impassive. She gazes at herself, fills the wash-hand
basin and rinses her face in cold water. She comes back through
to the bedroom.* MATTHEW *is propped up in bed, his eyes staring.
She goes and takes a photograph from the dressing table drawer.
It is her wedding photograph. She sits on the edge of the bed,
gazing at it. Pause. She turns it to* MATTHEW, *as if for him to
look at it.*)

MARION: He even looks like you . . . and you still killed him.
This is our anniversary . . . one year to the day we were
married . . . one year to the day he died. We were on our
way to Donegal. We were stopping over with his aunt in
Derry. He only went out for cigarettes. You shot him . . . a
Scotch soldier . . . you said he was armed . . . stood up in
court and swore it . . . all your mates . . . all with your
voice . . . all telling lies. And I had to sit and listen. (*Pause.*)
Why do you all tell lies? (*Pause.*) We spent weeks getting this
place ready . . . for what? All those people you killed . . .
and never once said you were sorry . . . it was you wasn't it?
You killed him . . . my Mark. (*She looks at the photograph
again.*) Matthew, Mark . . . Matthew, Mark . . . Matthew,
Mark . . . Oh my God . . . Oh my God . . .
(*She starts to sob. After a moment she replaces the photograph.
She stands and looks down on* MATTHEW.)
How will they know? How will they know where to find you?

24. INT. THE BARRACK ROOM

JOHN *is standing by* MATTHEW's *unslept in bed,* LES *enters.*

LES: He's not in the telly lounge . . . and he's not on the bog.

JOHN: Did you check the phone? Maybe more teeth have
arrived.

LES: I wonder did he get back all right?

JOHN: Of course he did. If he was normal you'd assume he
picked up a woman.

LES: He's answered one question for me . . . I think I know now
what the Scots wear up their kilts . . . their marriage
licence . . . and a big sign saying, 'Do not touch'.

JOHN: (*Laughing*) A big sign saying 'Keep off the ass!' (*Pause.*)

Should we tell someone?

LES: Let's give him until we've had breakfast and got to the office. He's that bloody daft . . . he's liable to go straight there, and be sitting grinning up at us.

25. INT. THE BARRACK ROOM

LES *and* JOHN *ready to go to the office.*

LES: He didn't come back.

JOHN: Where has the daft Scots git got to?

LES: What'll we do?

JOHN: Maybe he did get a bird . . . oh shit. We shouldn't have left him. If anything's happened we'll be in the shit.

LES: I'm more worried about him than me at the moment. I think he's got a bloody haggis for a brain.

JOHN: Maybe he's gone AWOL . . . over to check that bloody tooth.

LES: How would he get anywhere at that time . . . I mean, Scotland!

JOHN: (*Kicking* MATTHEW's *bed*) Where are you, you stupid bloody Jock?

(*Cut to: classroom.*)
    (JANET *in the classroom.*)

JANET: Right . . . and what do we call that person?
    (*Hands shoot up.*)
    Marion.

MARION: The Prime Minister.

JANET: Good girl . . . the Prime Minister . . .

(*Cut to: the clerks' office,* LES *and* JOHN *sitting working.*
    MATTHEW's *desk is empty. Pause.* SERGEANT BELL *enters. He looks stunned. They both look up at him.*)

SERGEANT BELL: They've found Corporal Baxter.

(*Cut to: classroom, there is a knock on the door.* JOHN CLARKE *enters,* JANET *looks at him, realizes something is wrong.*)

JOHN: Excuse me, Mrs Baxter. (*To the class*) Now boys and

girls . . . I want you to go quickly and quietly into Miss
Gibson's room . . . Off you go now.
(*He stands, avoiding* JANET, *as they quietly file out. As the
children file out,* JANET *just sinks slowly into her chair. She has a
piece of chalk in her hand. She slowly rolls it through her fingers.*
JOHN *is still reluctant to look at her. When he does she looks up
at him.*)

JANET: (*Quietly*) Am I a widow?
(*Hold.*)

26. INT. JANET'S LIVING ROOM

JANET, *stunned, dazed. An* ARMY MAJOR *is with her.*

MAJOR: I am sorry Mrs Baxter . . . we had to tell you . . . before
the press get hold of anything.
(*She shows no sign of comprehension.*)
It is . . . possible . . . they are capable of . . . well, fixing
things . . . it is their line of country. (*Pause.*) We don't need
to discuss the funeral arrangements just at the moment.
(*Pause.*) Mrs Baxter . . . soldiers away from home . . . you
mustn't think . . .
(MATTHEW'S FATHER *enters. The* MAJOR *stands, awkward.
The old man approaches.*)

FATHER: What for, sir? What for . . .
(*He breaks down. The* MAJOR *drops his head.*)

JANET: She didn't know him, Major . . . she didn't know him.
No one who knew my husband could have killed him.

27. INT. DERRY HOUSE, AND BAXTER HOUSE

MARION *in the house in Derry. She has her wedding photograph in
her hand. She props it up on her dresser. Looks at it. Cut to* JANET
standing looking down at her wedding photograph.
Cut to MARION *in the house with three newspapers. They each
carry a photograph of the Baxters' wedding day. The headlines read:
'Army Clerk Lured to his Death': 'Clerical Officer Slain': 'Unarmed
Soldier Murdered'.* MARION *is looking at these with disbelief, reading
through the stories with incomprehension, stunned. She looks at her
wedding photograph.*

MARION: (*Addressing the photograph*) He told me . . . he told
    me . . . why do they always tell lies . . . why?

28. EXT. THE BAXTERS' COTTAGE

JANET *has just got out of the funeral car.* JOHN CLARKE *holds the
gate for her, but she refuses to let him come any further.* MATTHEW'S
FATHER *is visible in the car.* JANET *walks up to the house. She turns
her key in the door, then watches them until they drive away. Pause.*

Cut to: JANET *entering the empty house . . . totally alone. She stands
inside the door. She gazes across the room to where their wedding
photograph and others sit. She walks slowly into the room, removing
her coat as she does so. Half-way across, the coat just off her
shoulders, she can go no further. She slumps to the floor. Her body
heaves with sobbing. Across her shoulder the photographs can be seen.
She looks up and goes across on her knees. She holds a photograph of*
MATTHEW *in front of her and then hugs it to her chest. Hold.*

29. INT. THE BARRACK ROOM

LES *and* JOHN *are dressed in civvies; they are going home for a short
leave.* LES *is placing Matthew's personal effects into a series of
envelopes and a plastic bag.* JOHN *is just sitting on* MATTHEW'S
stripped bed, watching. SERGEANT BELL *enters.* JOHN *rises.*

SERGEANT BELL: (*As* LES *hands the stuff over*) That everything?

LES: Yes, Sergeant.

SERGEANT BELL: Not much, is there?

LES: Shouldn't we check things, Sergeant?

SERGEANT BELL: We put them in sealed envelopes and hand
    them over to his wife.

LES: The girl . . . I mean . . .

SERGEANT BELL: You were mates . . . you should know.

LES: We didn't know him that well . . . I mean we thought he
    never bothered.

SERGEANT BELL: You think there might be something in here?

LES: There might be . . . What's it matter now? Why let her be
    hurt any more?

SERGEANT BELL: Let me give you two a bit of advice. If you ever get married, while you're in this job . . . bring the missus with you . . . get quarters. If she's got a job, like Mrs Baxter . . . make her give it up.

JOHN: What was it for, Sergeant?

SERGEANT BELL: For what we're paid for, lad . . . You sign your own names . . . we don't forge them. (*As he goes with the bag.*) I'll mention it to the Major . . . Let him decide. (*Goes.*)

30. INT. THE BAXTERS' LIVING ROOM

JANET *ushers* LES *and* JOHN *in.*

JANET: Sit down, please. Would you like some tea?

JOHN: No thanks, not for me.

(LES *shakes his head.*)

JANET: Matthew talked about you two quite a lot.

JOHN: We were good friends.

LES: We're very sorry.

JANET: Thank you for the letter and the flowers. There were quite a lot of wreaths . . . one from the RUC . . . I thought that was nice. People have been very thoughtful. They closed the school for the day of the funeral.

JOHN: He talked about you a lot . . . and the children.

JANET: Yes . . . well he was very much a family man.

LES: We were kept up to date on all the news . . . Ricky's teeth, all that.

JANET: Nicky.

(JOHN *nods.*)

LES: Always on about them.

JANET: I suppose that's one small consolation . . . a complete family, one of each.

JOHN: Are you still teaching?

JANET: No . . . no, I haven't gone back yet . . . I don't know that I will. There'll be enough for us to live on. You realize at a time like this how precious the time with your children is.

LES: We're not married . . . it must be great . . . children and that.

JANET: I know you're not married . . . he told me all about you. His letters were full of news . . . just everything . . . he wrote it all down. I'll miss them. The postman'll notice the difference. It's a bit of a walk up from the road . . . he'll not have to make it as often now.

LES: Are Matthew's parents. . . ?

JANET: Just his father . . . he's pining away . . . An only child.

LES: I suppose parents never outgrow . . . well, stop worrying about their children.

JANET: I suppose at his age he never thought his son would go first . . . I don't suppose you do.

JOHN: You got all his things?

JANET: Yes. Did you do that? Thank you.

LES: We only packed them up . . . I mean the army sent them on.

JANET: They're very good . . . they can't do enough for us.

JOHN: Well why not? He was serving King . . . Queen and Country.

JANET: Still . . . the major who comes out is really very helpful and considerate.

(*They lapse into silence.*)

JOHN: We meant to get a photograph together . . . never got around to it.

JANET: Funny thing . . . I don't have a photograph of him in uniform. He wasn't really fond of uniforms . . . he never wanted photographed in it. His father was always asking for one . . . He's an ex-soldier. I suppose it would have been nice for the children . . . when they're up a bit.

LES: He was shy . . .

JANET: He was very quiet . . . even when we had a row . . . he never really shouted.

(*Pause. There is lying between them a great deal that is unspoken. This is evident in the looks they give each other.*)

JOHN: Maybe . . . I mean our train back's at half-five.

JANET: Yes . . . it's not a very frequent service. We're a bit out in the wilds I'm afraid.

LES: It's a beautiful place . . . a bit like Ireland . . .

JANET: Yes . . . Matthew said that.

JOHN: (*Handing over bag*) We brought a few things . . . for the

kids . . . we ah . . . we forgot one of them is a girl.
(JANET *takes the bag and breaks down. They're not sure what to do. In the end* LES *goes to comfort her. She takes a while to recover. Pause.*)

JANET: Who was she?
(*This is the moment they've dreaded.*)

JOHN: We honestly don't know.

LES: We do know that he wasn't involved with her . . . I mean . . .

JANET: That's not the impression from the papers.

JOHN: Those bastards . . . sorry . . . they don't know what they're talking about.

LES: We used to coax Matthew to go out with us . . . and he never would. Honestly . . . it was the first time . . . we'd met these two girls . . . He didn't want anything to do with it, honestly.

JOHN: He left us to go back to camp . . . apparently he met somebody in a chip shop . . . there was nothing more to it than that. They could have rigged it all up.

JANET: He was in bed, naked . . . I suppose I'll have to wait until they catch her . . . I'll never know whether I'd have been able to forgive him or not.
(*Nothing more is to be said. They rise. She goes to the door with them. She carries the bag of toys. She stops at the door as* JOHN *and* LES *walk to the bottom of the path. They look back at* JANET, *framed in the doorway. They walk slowly away. Hold on* JANET. *Close, numb and hurt.*)

31. INT. AND EXT. MARION AND JANET
The room in Derry, MARION *looks as if she hasn't slept for days. The newspapers lie on the floor. She washes her face, stops and looks at the papers, bundles them up in a fury, crams them into a wastebin; starts to get ready to go out.*

Cut to: JANET *by the churchyard wall, looking in at the grave, still covered in flowers.*

Cut to: MARION *gazing at her photographs, the engagement, the wedding, the grave. She is ready to go out.*

Cut to: JANET *walking past the school. There are children in the yard; she stops to watch them.*

Cut to: MARION *walking along the street. Men stop to look at her.*

Cut to: JANET *at home, going through the envelopes the army sent.*

32. INT. POLICE STATION
MARION *entering a police station. There are three policemen behind the desk. When she enters they watch her across the room.*
PC: Good morning, love . . . What can I do for you?
MARION: I'd like to see someone . . . an inspector.
PC: Can you tell us what it's about, love?
MARION: It's important.
PC: (*Glancing at his colleagues, who haven't taken their eyes off* MARION) Is it about a serious crime?
MARION: Yes . . . I know something about a murder.
PC: I see . . . you'd better see the detectives. Just sit down in that corridor for a moment. (*He watches her go.*) Sometimes you just wish you were a detective.
(*The other two* PCs *snigger.*)
I know the sort of interview I'd like to give that one. (*He lifts the telephone.*)

33. INT. INTERVIEW ROOM
MARION *is in an interview room. A detective,* JOE, *is with her. He has been writing furiously. He looks at her, rises and leaves. She sits, looking around the room. Another detective,* PETER, *enters.*
PETER: Now, Miss . . .
MARION: Mrs. I'm a widow . . . My husband's dead.
(*He looks at her.*)
He was shot . . . murdered.
PETER: (*Obviously thinking she's unstable*) You say you saw the Scottish soldier the night he died?

MARION: The night my husband died?

PETER: What? No . . . no . . . you say you saw the Scottish lad the night he was murdered?

MARION: I've told the other one all that.

PETER: (*Checking notes*) Yes . . . you have . . . but there are a few details I'd just like to go over with you. (*Pause.*) Now . . .

34. INT. THE STATION FOYER

Both detectives are standing, with the PC who first spoke to MARION.

PC: Did you get any sense out of her, Peter?

PETER: Sense, yes . . . but about what? How do you read her, Joe?

JOE: Disturbed . . . a crank . . . but one I'd like to crank.

PETER: One track mind.

JOE: She's some honey . . . What do we have on the Scottish murder?

PC: Him and his two friends were invited to a party . . . the two women said they were nurses. Donegall Pass are handling that one.

JOE: Right . . . I'll go in again . . . Do we try to get something sensible out of this one . . . or just thank her and send her home?

PC: She looks familiar . . . I just can't recall . . . but she does look familiar.

JOE: Yeah . . . but we've all had that dream.

(PC, PETER, *and* JOE *all laugh. A shot rings out. Stunned silence.*)

PETER: Where the hell did that come from . . . it sounded like it was inside.

JOE: (*Walking slowly*) It sounded like the interview room.

35. INT. THE INTERVIEW ROOM

MARION *lies on the floor, a pool of blood around her head. All her photographs and the press-clippings (headlines) about* MARK *are there too. One of the headlines about Matthew is there, 'Army Clerk Murdered', she has scrawled 'Liar' across it in lipstick. The policemen just stand frozen. Hold.*

44. INT. THE BAXTERS' LIVING ROOM
JANET *and* MATTHEW'S FATHER *are sitting at the table, two uneaten meals in front of them. Both are absorbed in their own thoughts, pushing the food around their plates. Hold.*

Cut to: JANET *by the graveside. She is looking across the grave to* MATTHEW'S FATHER.
JANET: She was beautiful . . . (*Pause.*) . . . I'll never know now . . . Will I?
(*He just stands, his head bowed. She slowly walks away.*)

Cut to: JANET, *still walking, thinking. She is walking through the village. The village is deserted, shops are closed.* JANET *walks. Fade out.*

THE MILITARY WING

Cast:

JOYCE MORPETH	Gwen Taylor
CLAIRE WILLIAMSON	Veronica Roberts
YVONNE DUNCAN	Gaylie Runciman
JOHN ANDERSON	Mark Drewry
STEPHEN PATTERSON	James McKenna
EVANS	Richard Huw
LUGS LOCKHART	Adam Blackwood
WINTERS	Gary Bleasdale
LIEUTENANT ARCHER	John Skitt
JILL BURNS	Frances Low
CORPORAL WYNNE	Karl Howman
MRS SMALL	Rynagh O'Grady
WRAC (DOT)	Sally Watts
SERGEANT	John Forgeham
DOCTOR	Osmund Bullock
CECIL	Tim Potter
NURSE JONES	Anné McCartney

1. INT. BATHROOM

JOHN ANDERSON *is just finishing off. He is cheery, lively, singing softly to himself: 'Show me the way to go home/I'm tired and I want to go to bed/Well I joined the army many years ago/Now I wish that I was dead'. He starts doing a few exercises just prior to leaving the bathroom, touching his toes, running on the spot, etc. Packs his toilet bag, puts his dressing gown on. Just as he's at the door he stops, his manner changes and he leaves the bathroom as someone with severe back pain.*

2. INT. JOYCE'S WARD

STEPHEN PATTERSON, *is propped up in bed and has just finished shaving.* SISTER MORPETH *approaches, doing a round of the ward.*

JOYCE: Good morning, Private Patterson . . . How are you feeling this morning?

PATTERSON: (*Slight trace of a Scot*) Marvellous, Ma'am . . . they can't keep me in here much longer. No word of the tests yet?

JOYCE: Not yet . . . It takes time, I've told you.

PATTERSON: I could do a twenty-five mile route march this morning . . . but they won't even let me walk to the bathroom.

JOYCE: Be patient . . . we'll know soon.

(JOHN ANDERSON *starts making his way slowly and painfully down.* JOYCE *stands by the foot of his bed until he arrives. She just looks at him, without speaking. He looks at her.*)

ANDERSON: It's bad this morning, Sister . . . it's very bad.

(*She just looks at him.*)

I hardly slept at all last night.

JOYCE: Didn't you? Well then the night staff must have . . . There's no mention of your inability to sleep in their report.

ANDERSON: You don't sleep when you're in pain like this, Sister.

219

JOYCE: I wouldn't know, Private Anderson. If we find people who are really in pain, and unable to sleep, we can usually give them something to help them. (*Pause.*) Did you ask for anything to help you to sleep?

ANDERSON: You know me, Sister . . . I don't like to give anybody any trouble.

JOYCE: I think they should operate on you.

ANDERSON: (*With just the hint of a snort*) There isn't much point them operating on me unless they've some idea of what's wrong . . . and what they're looking for.
(*Pause. She just glares at him for a moment, then walks away. He sits himself gingerly on the bed, replaces his stuff in the locker.* EVANS *from the next bed is looking at him.*)
What is it, Taff?

EVANS: She doesn't like you, does she?

ANDERSON: How do I know what she likes . . . it's her problem.

EVANS: I don't think she believes you . . . About not sleeping like.

ANDERSON: No . . . Well that's her problem too, isn't it?

EVANS: I think they reckon you're working your ticket.

ANDERSON: Why don't you go choke on a leek . . . thick Taff git.

3. INT. THE SISTERS' HUT
It is partitioned off into three bedrooms, a bathroom, and a toilet, a small kitchen, and a small sitting room, with television. YVONNE DUNCAN *is just being shown in by* SERGEANT SMALL, *portly, middle thirties. She is in her twenties, blonde, a Scot. He is carrying her suitcases, she a large handbag-cum-shoulder bag. He stops outside one of the bedrooms. The door is wide open. The room clean and neat.*

SERGEANT SMALL: Here we are. Welcome to the dream hut.
(*She just glares at him.*)
The other two sisters are almost as pretty as you are . . . so all the men dream about getting in here.
(*A silly grin, as* YVONNE *stares stonily at him.*)

YVONNE: So what do you dream about, Sergeant?

SERGEANT SMALL: (*Misunderstanding*) What . . . (*Grinning*)
What do you mean, love?

YVONNE: I mean when the . . . men . . . are dreaming about
being in here . . . Sergeant.
(*He is embarrassed.*)
Put my cases into the room and piss off.

SERGEANT SMALL: (*Doing so*) Do you want me to show you
round?

YVONNE: Captain.

SERGEANT SMALL: Captain.

YVONNE: I think I'm capable of finding my own way around.
Although I come from Scotland, I've become quite good at
recognizing things like bathrooms and toilets. Just leave the
cases and get out, Sergeant.

SERGEANT SMALL: (*Going to the door, angry*) Now listen,
love . . .

YVONNE: (*Cutting in sharply*) I am not your love . . . I am a
captain. I am also a Scot, and a woman. I don't like fat
Englishmen trying to amuse me by telling me daft
anti-Scottish jokes . . . nor patronizing anti-woman jokes.

SERGEANT SMALL: I was only trying to be friendly . . .
(*Meeting her fierce gaze.*) . . . Captain.

YVONNE: You don't have to be friendly, Sergeant . . . This is
the army . . . all I require from you is respect and
obedience.

SERGEANT SMALL: Yes . . . Captain. (*Handing her over a set of
keys.*) One of them's . . .
(*She slams the bedroom door in his face as he's talking.*)
. . . for the bedroom, the other one is for the front door.
(*He stands for a moment, then leaves.* YVONNE *starts
wandering about, getting to know the place. She tries a bedroom
door. It is locked. She tries the other, it is open. She hesitates,
then enters, it is* CLAIRE's *room. She looks around, opens
drawers, wardrobes, etc., inspects photographs. There are a
number of* CLAIRE *with various people, always women. One
features* JOYCE *and her on holiday. Hold.*)

4. INT. CLAIRE'S WARD

CLAIRE WILLIAMSON, *at the bedside of* MRS SMALL. MRS SMALL *is the wife of* SERGEANT SMALL. *She is from southern Ireland. A rarely happy person who is always moaning.*

CLAIRE: You wanted to see me, Mrs Small?

MRS SMALL: Oh you are on . . . I thought perhaps you were on a day off.

CLAIRE: No . . . but I've been very busy. (*Pause.*)

MRS SMALL: My breakfast was wrong . . . I ordered kippers. I got bacon and sausage. The bacon was over-cooked and the whole lot was cold.

CLAIRE: I'm sorry about that. Are you sure you ordered correctly?
(MRS SMALL *glares at her.*)
It is easy to tick the wrong place.

MRS SMALL: I ticked what I wanted, Sister . . . but I didn't get what I ticked.

CLAIRE: Why didn't you send it back?

MRS SMALL: I wasn't going to wait until lunchtime for my breakfast. Anyway, I'm not one for complaining all the time . . . and if you complained about everything that's wrong in here you would be complaining all the time.

CLAIRE: If you're unhappy about things, you should let someone know. There's not much I can do about your breakfast by the time I come on. What did you do with it?

MRS SMALL: I ate it, what do you think? We get little enough to eat in here, without leaving the bit we do get.

CLAIRE: Well we'll make sure you get what you order tomorrow morning. Did you sleep well?

MRS SMALL: I wouldn't say it was a great night's sleep. There's too much noise about this place.

CLAIRE: There's not much we can do about the noise outside I'm afraid.

MRS SMALL: It's not all of it outside. Some of them night nurses, they never shut up chittering . . . endless nonsense they talk . . . about men . . . that's it all night long. Men . . . men . . . men . . .

CLAIRE: If the night nurses were talking too loudly, I'm quite sure they would have toned it down, if you'd asked them to.

MRS SMALL: Oh it doesn't do to say too much . . . you get the reputation of moaning all the time. Nobody's in here because they want to be you know. You nurses don't seem to realize that . . . it's not very nice, not being well.

CLAIRE: We've all had some experience of that Mrs Small . . . even nurses. (*Pause.*) However . . . You're healing up nicely. You'll be out within the week now.

MRS SMALL: He'll have to be told I need to rest after this . . . a good holiday's what I need . . . I can't be running after him the minute I get home. (*Pause.*) I just hope you're going to tell him that, Sister.

CLAIRE: Sergeant Small will be fully informed of your condition. I'm sure he'll realize you need to rest . . . he'll not expect you to run after him.

MRS SMALL: You don't know him . . . Sergeant by name and Sergeant by nature . . . barking out his orders night and day, as if he's still on the parade ground. My mother warned me. My dad was a soldier. They're all the same she used to say . . . they parade around all day and then expect their wives and children to parade about after them half the night. Army wives . . . huh . . . sometimes I think they only want us around until they can find a real enemy.

5. INT. THE SANGAR

Inside the sangar. LUGS *and* WINTERS. LUGS *drawing.* WINTERS *is writing a letter. A half-finished game is on the solitaire board.*

WINTERS: What are you drawing this time, Lugs?

LUGS: (*Looking up, then out through the observation slot*) The view.

WINTERS: Great . . . you never draw anything else.

LUGS: There's not much more to draw up here.

WINTERS: But if you've drawn it once you've drawn it . . . haven't you?

LUGS: It changes . . . well, a bit.

WINTERS: Which bit? I've never seen any changes in it . . .
boring . . . boring . . . boring. They just shove us up here
because they can't think of anything else to do with us, if
you ask me. I hate it.

LUGS: Who're you writing to this time?

WINTERS: The wife.

LUGS: I didn't know you were married?

WINTERS: I'm not . . . she's somebody else's wife.

LUGS: That's a dangerous game . . . Another soldier's wife?

WINTERS: Give over . . . who wants to screw another soldier's
wife? They're all promiscuous that lot . . . they'd go to bed
with anybody. No, mate . . . this is a bit of class . . . a
solicitor's wife . . . a successful one too . . . but she prefers
a man of action.

LUGS: I see . . . so why did she pick you?

WINTERS: Go to sleep, you flop-eared freak.

6. INT. JOYCE'S OFFICE

JOYCE *is just about to start sipping her tea when* CLAIRE *enters. She
pours a cup for* CLAIRE, *who puts a spoonful of sugar into it.* JOYCE
nibbles a biscuit.

CLAIRE: I thought you'd stopped eating biscuits?

JOYCE: I thought you'd stopped taking sugar?

CLAIRE: After that woman Small I need something sweet.

JOYCE: What's she complaining about this time?

CLAIRE: Ask me the short question . . . What is she not
complaining about?

JOYCE: You have her and I have that hateful John Anderson . . . I
cannot stand that man. Why don't they just throw him out and
have done with it. . . ? He's useless anyway.

CLAIRE: They'd have to pay him a pension if they did that.

JOYCE: If that's all they're worried about I'll tell them I'll pay it to
him . . . just to get rid of him.

CLAIRE: Ignore him . . . Why should you worry if he wants out?

JOYCE: I don't worry about that . . . it's his dishonesty. I know
he's putting it on . . . everybody knows he's putting it on.
It makes me really angry that I have to nurse people

who are not genuinely ill.

CLAIRE: You're just tired and irritable . . . we did have a very late night last night.

JOYCE: I know . . . let's have an early one tonight.

CLAIRE: I intend to, don't worry. (*Pause.*)

>(*There is a knock on the door. It is opened, and* YVONNE DUNCAN *enters. She is still in her civilian clothes.*)

YVONNE: Hello . . . I'm Yvonne Duncan . . . the new sister.

>(*They rise and greet her, etc.*)

JOYCE: Sit down.

>(YVONNE *does.*)
>
>There's some tea in the pot . . . I'll just have to go and get you a cup. (*She goes.*)
>
>(YVONNE *and* CLAIRE *just gaze at each other intently for a moment.*)

YVONNE: You two are good friends?

CLAIRE: (*Surprised by the question*) Well, yes . . . we are. (*Pause.*) When do you start?

YVONNE: Tomorrow.

CLAIRE: They don't waste time, do they?

YVONNE: I prefer to get stuck in straight away . . . I like to get things started as quickly as possible.

CLAIRE: Have you been in Belfast before?

YVONNE: Aye . . . but it was years ago, when I was a child. My grandmother's from Belfast.

CLAIRE: So, do you still have relatives over here then?

YVONNE: No, well I probably do . . . but none I know about.

>(JOYCE *returns with a cup.*)
>
>My grandfather was a Glasgow Protestant . . . my grandmother was a Catholic. He'd been a soldier over here. I think it caused a bit of bother between the families.

CLAIRE: So what's new?

7. INT. THE SECURITY DESK AT THE ENTRANCE TO THE WARDS

It is manned by two military police personnel, and a male medical orderly. JILL BELL *is a young, very pretty military policewoman.*

225

BOB WYNNE *is in his late twenties, quite good-looking, a Corporal. He is married and has two children. His wife is at home in England. He is having an affair with* JILL. *To him it is just an away from home adventure, but to her it is an intense love affair. They are alone as the scene opens, and the atmosphere between them is rather strained.*

JILL: You've been telling me lies, haven't you?

BOB: What lies?

JILL: What lies . . . what lies . . . Lies about you and her.

BOB: No . . . I've told you the truth.

JILL: The truth! When we started together you were supposed to be getting a divorce. Now you're back to family holidays.

BOB: Jill . . . you knew I was married when we started.

JILL: I knew what you told me when we started . . . you were getting unmarried.

BOB: Keep your voice down . . . people are going to notice. Let's talk about this when we're out tonight.

JILL: We never talk when we're out. You're only interested in one thing when we're out.

BOB: Shut up . . . people are watching us.

JILL: I don't care.

BOB: Well I do. I'm a married man . . . as far as people are concerned a respectable one.

JILL: Don't make me laugh. (*Pause.*) I don't know if I want to go out tonight.

BOB: Suit yourself.

JILL: Right, I will . . . I won't.
     (*Pause.*)

BOB: (*Looking puzzled*) Does that mean we are or we aren't?

JILL: It means what I said.

8. INT. THE SANGAR

WINTERS *is pacing in the limited space there is available. He stops and looks over* LUG's *shoulder.*

WINTERS: Bloody hell . . . what's that supposed to be?

LUGS: Out there.

WINTERS: Where? (*Peering out*) It's just a load of squiggles.

LUGS: Don't be daft . . . it's abstract.

WINTERS: You what?

LUGS: The colours represent different things out there . . . the layers represent significance to the eye.

WINTERS: (*Pointing*) What's that then . . . that blob?

LUGS: It's a nurse . . . she walked across.

WINTERS: A nurse! Piss off. I know some of them ain't anything to write home about, but stroll on.
(*Pause.* WINTERS *moves away. Regards* LUGS.)
Here, Lugs . . . you ever had it then?

LUGS: Course I have, what do you think I am?

WINTERS: What, here . . . with a nurse?

LUGS: Not here . . . not a nurse . . . a WRAC.

WINTERS: I see . . . but have you ever had it with a woman?
(*Pause.*) We going to go to the pub tonight . . . see what's around?

LUGS: If you like.
(LIEUTENANT ARCHER *enters. He is young and keen. They spring to attention.*)

LIEUTENANT ARCHER: (*Saluting*) Carry on.
(*He looks around the sangar, inspects the views, etc. He looks at* LUGS's *sketch pad then at* WINTERS's *solitaire board.* LIEUTENANT ARCHER *lifts the cover of* WINTERS's *writing pad.* WINTERS *almost makes a move to stop him, but checks himself.* LIEUTENANT ARCHER *glares at him and indicates the solitaire and the writing pad.*)
Are these yours, Winters?

WINTERS: Yes, sir.

LIEUTENANT ARCHER: (*Flicking the writing pad open again*) Do you always choose the time you're on watch to write to your mother?
(LUGS *gives a suppressed laugh.*)
What's amusing you, Lockhart?

LUGS: Nothing, sir, sorry, sir.

LIEUTENANT ARCHER: (*Inspecting the sketch pad*) What's this supposed to be?

(WINTERS *sniggers in the background.*)

LUGS: It's an abstract of the view, sir.

LIEUTENANT ARCHER: (*Turning it this way and that*) Rubbish, that's what it is. Tell me, Lockhart do you know why you're up here?

LUGS: Observation, sir.

(*Pause.* LIEUTENANT ARCHER *thinks, inspects the pad again.*)

I do that when I'm observing, sir. It helps me to concentrate. It trains the eye. (*Pause.*) It helps me to notice the details, sir.

LIEUTENANT ARCHER: (*Impatient*) All right, Lockhart, you don't have to go on.

(*Annoyed at being bested, he crosses to the solitaire board, to* WINTERS.)

I suppose you'll say this helps you to concentrate, Winters?

WINTERS: It does, sir. We have a method . . . we take it in turns to try and keep ourselves alert. It stops us getting bored, sir.

LIEUTENANT ARCHER: Nonsense, man. You're trained, professional soldiers. You're not supposed to get bored. Do you think we'd spend thousands of pounds training you, if it was as simple as giving you sketch pads and games of solitaire? (*Pause, annoyed.*) Well?

WINTERS: They do help, sir.

LIEUTENANT ARCHER: And writing to your mother . . . is that another part of the therapy? (*Pause.*) Now you two had better pull yourselves together . . . and start behaving like soldiers. I want you sharp and alert . . . I want you concentrating only on the job in hand. There should be no distractions . . . understood?

(*They nod and respond.*)

If I catch either of you at this sort of nonsense again I'll put you on a charge . . . dereliction of duty. Is that clear, Lockhart?

LUGS: Yes, sir.

LIEUTENANT ARCHER: Winters?

WINTERS: Yes, sir.

(LIEUTENANT ARCHER *moves towards the exit. He moves back and gathers up the sketch pad, writing pad and solitaire.*)

LIEUTENANT ARCHER: You can collect these from the company office later.

WINTERS: Excuse me, sir . . . (*Pause.*) . . . My letter, sir . . . That's my private business, sir.

LIEUTENANT ARCHER: (*Tearing the letter from the pad*) You had better watch your step, Winters. (*Hands him the letter.*) I'll have my eye on you two from now on. (*Moves to exit.*) Carry on. (*Goes.*)

WINTERS: That wanker thinks we're thick.

LUGS: (*With a smirk*) You should write and tell your mummy on him.

9. INT. THE WARD

EVANS, PATTERSON and ANDERSON *sitting around the table. They've just finished their lunch.*

PATTERSON: It's funny how weak you feel after a few days in bed. I thought I was great.

ANDERSON: It depends what you've been doing in bed.

EVANS: I know what I'll be doing . . . and not a worry in the world.

ANDERSON: I think you're daft. I mean, suppose you meet a girl and she really wants children. What do you do then?

EVANS: Tell her I can't have any, what do you think?

ANDERSON: What if you're in love with her?

EVANS: Tell her I love her, but I can't have children.

ANDERSON: You thick Taff git.

EVANS: Don't call me that, I don't like it.

ANDERSON: What's this, Welsh liberation . . . who cares what you like, Taffy?

EVANS: I'm warning you, boyo. Call me that again and bad back or not, I'll batter you.

ANDERSON: Oh yeah?

EVANS: You bet, boy.

PATTERSON: Cool it you two . . . Sister's up there.

ANDERSON: If I didn't have this bad back, Taffy, I'd have you.

PATTERSON: You don't have a bad back, John, you're bluffing.

ANDERSON: What's this . . . all you foreigners going to stick together?

EVANS: Everybody knows you're trying to work your ticket.

ANDERSON: And everybody knows you're as thick as a leek.

(EVANS, *outraged, jumps up. He grabs* ANDERSON *and pulls him to his feet.*)

EVANS: I've bloody warned you, boyo.

PATTERSON: (*Rising*) For goodness' sake, you two . . . Are you both daft?

ANDERSON: You mind your own business. Come on, Taffy . . . you hit me and I'll see you court-martialled.

PATTERSON: Here comes the nurse.

(*As the nurse approaches* EVANS *lets go.* ANDERSON *swings and catches* EVANS *with his full force, on the point of the chin.* EVANS *collapses.*)

10. INT. JOYCE'S OFFICE

ANDERSON *is standing in front of* JOYCE'*s desk.* BOB WYNNE *is also there.*

JOYCE: (*Furious*) Stand up straight, Anderson.

ANDERSON: I can't, Ma'am, my back's hurting.

BOB: (*Barking*) Stand to attention when you're told, soldier.

ANDERSON: (*Resting with his hands on the desk*) Ma'am, I've got to sit down . . . I'm in agony.

JOYCE: (*Furious but defeated*) Pass him that chair, Corporal.

(BOB *does so.*)

Corporal Wynne, I want you to get a full report of this incident to the Guard Commander immediately . . . and to Private Anderson's Commanding Officer, I want him charged.

ANDERSON: He grabbed me, Ma'am, he was going to hit me, and I couldn't defend myself with my back.

JOYCE: Private Patterson and Corporal Jones both stated that he had released you when you struck him. It was a cowardly assault. I will not tolerate brawling on my ward.

ANDERSON: I need to lie down, Ma'am . . . this thing is going mad. (*Pushing himself to his feet.*) I don't think I can make it back to my bed . . . can you give me a hand, Ma'am? (*Pause.*)

JOYCE: Corporal Wynne, would you call Corporal Jones for me please?

BOB: (Gazing at ANDERSON's *back*) Yes, Ma'am. (*He goes.*)

ANDERSON: I'm going to need something for this pain, Ma'am. (*Holding out his hand*) I think I've broken my knuckles as well.

JOYCE: Private Anderson . . . as from this moment I am going to move heaven and earth to have you transferred to a hospital on the mainland. I won't be happy until I've seen the back of you.

11. INT. THE SISTERS' SITTING ROOM

JOYCE *is sitting watching television, still in uniform.* CLAIRE *enters, dressed to go out.*

CLAIRE: Are you sure you don't want to come with us?

JOYCE: No, thank you. I can't bear that place. Anyway I'm tired . . . and we did plan an early night.

CLAIRE: You're not annoyed with me for going, are you?

JOYCE: No, not at all.

CLAIRE: She did ask . . . and with her being new . . .

JOYCE: Claire . . . it's all right. I don't mind in the least.

CLAIRE: What do you think of her?

JOYCE: Pardon?

CLAIRE: Yvonne, she's nice, isn't she?

JOYCE: I hardly know her, she seems fine.

CLAIRE: I like her.

JOYCE: Obviously.

CLAIRE: You are annoyed, aren't you?

JOYCE: Will you stop it. I am not annoyed. I am not upset. I think she's probably a very nice woman. I hope you both have a great time tonight. (*Pause.*) I'm just very tired and very fed up. It's Evans and Anderson. They were brawling on my ward today. I despise them. I don't want to feel like that. What really annoys me is that I let it show . . . I let them see it. Anderson just undermines me . . . he does it quite deliberately.

CLAIRE: Evans will be gone soon . . . and you've said yourself you're going to get rid of Anderson.

JOYCE: I've told him that . . . so he'll probably beat me on that one as well.

12. INT. A LOUNGE BAR
LUGS *and* WINTERS *are sitting drinking.*

LUGS: This place is boring.

WINTERS: What, Belfast?

LUGS: This place . . . this bar . . . the hospital. I don't mind Belfast, it's just this duty.

WINTERS: Are you going to leave the army when your time's up?

LUGS: Haven't thought about it.

WINTERS: Do you like it then?

LUGS: It's all right. There's worse. At least you get some change. You could be doing something as boring as this in a factory. And have to do it for years and years.

WINTERS: You should do the recruiting ads, mate. (*Pause.*) Course your ears are too big for telly. Could you not get them fixed?

LUGS: Fixed! . . . I can hear with them . . . that's what they're for.

WINTERS: What about the birds? I mean how do you pick them up?

LUGS: How many birds do you have then?

WINTERS: I've had them, mate . . . dozens of them.

LUGS: Where are they now? I've never seen you with a bird.

WINTERS: You want to see my address book?

LUGS: That proves nothing.

WINTERS: It proves more than yours.

LUGS: I don't have one.

(WINTERS *sneers.*)

Tell you what. I used to have this woman . . . beautiful she
was, married. Funny thing, her husband was a solicitor
too . . . Great it was . . . straight up.

WINTERS: (*Looking at him, uncertain*) Yes . . . so what
happened?

LUGS: She dropped me.

WINTERS: (*Smirking*) Why . . . were you not good enough?

LUGS: She met this other bloke . . . said he did more for her.

WINTERS: Yeah . . . what sort of things?

LUGS: You know . . . kinky things.

WINTERS: So tell me . . . what sort of things?

LUGS: (*Moving closer, conspiratorial*) Used to write to her . . .
and call her Dear Mummy. (*Laughs at* WINTERS*'s fury.*)

WINTERS: You'll have even bigger lugs if I slap you on them.
(LUGS *just laughs more.*)
Here . . . (*Surveying the place.*) . . . what do you reckon to
those two over there? (CLAIRE *and* YVONNE.)

LUGS: (*Gazing over*) Untouchables.

WINTERS: Rubbish . . . what do you mean?

LUGS: They're from the hospital . . . the one on the left's a
sister . . . a captain.

WINTERS: She'd certainly make me stand up straight.
(*Fade up on* CLAIRE *and* YVONNE.)

YVONNE: I don't think this will become my favourite night spot.

CLAIRE: Sorry.

YVONNE: Why . . . did you build it? Do you go into the city
much?

CLAIRE: Now and again . . . shopping. I never go in at night.

YVONNE: Maybe we should investigate it . . . dances and
things. Do you think they're nurses over there?

CLAIRE: Probably . . . or just girlfriends.

YVONNE: Lesbians you mean?

CLAIRE: No . . . soldiers' girlfriends. I don't know. I've only
actually been here once before.

YVONNE: With Joyce?

CLAIRE: Yes . . . she hated it.

YVONNE: Does that mean you have to hate it too?

CLAIRE: It doesn't mean anything, except that she didn't like it. I can't say I care for it much myself though.

YVONNE: Do you fancy picking something up?

CLAIRE: What . . . men?

YVONNE: Unless you fancy those two nurses over there. What about those two over there? (LUGS *and* WINTERS) You can have the one with the ears.

CLAIRE: They're just private soldiers.

YVONNE: You want an Officer and a Gentleman. Looking around here I'd say we can't afford to be too particular; they're men.

CLAIRE: I'm not interested.

YVONNE: (*Looking at her*) In them . . . or in men?

CLAIRE: You like asking questions that you think will embarrass people, don't you?

YVONNE: I like asking questions. Have I embarrassed you?

CLAIRE: You've tried to, and I just wonder why you do it.

YVONNE: I'm interested in you . . . I want to find out about you.

CLAIRE: Maybe there are things I don't want you to know.

YVONNE: So don't tell me. (*Pause.*) Do you fancy chatting those two up? (*She indicates* LIEUTENANT ARCHER *and another officer.*)

CLAIRE: I certainly do not.

YVONNE: I don't mean seriously . . . just for a laugh.

CLAIRE: I wouldn't find it in the least funny.

YVONNE: You've no sense of humour. I could always do it on my own . . . get them fighting over me.

(CLAIRE *just looks at her.*)

13. EXT. A PARK

JILL *and* BOB *are walking together. They sit down on a bench. They look quite comfortable and quite happy together. Hold.*

JILL: I never wanted to join the army you know.

BOB: So how come you're here. . . ? It's not compulsory.

JILL: It was Tony . . . that boyfriend I told you about. We had a row . . . just as we were passing the army recruiting office . . . so I went in and joined up.

BOB: Rubbish . . . I don't believe a word of it.

JILL: Honestly. They didn't take me straight away . . . but that's how it started. I'd never thought about it until then.

BOB: You poor sod. What did he say?

JILL: We didn't speak again for a while . . . by the time we did I'd committed myself . . . so he called me a fascist headbanger . . . and here I am.

BOB: You never told me any of this before.

JILL: No . . . there are lots of things I haven't told you. I did tell you about Tony . . . and that I joined up after we fell out.

BOB: If you were a man you'd have joined the Foreign Legion.

JILL: Huh, sometimes I think I have (*Pause.*) Where are you going?

BOB: You what?

JILL: On holiday . . . where are you going?

BOB: I don't know . . . I'll let her arrange that. I'm only going for the sake of the children.

JILL: You have been honest with me, haven't you?

BOB: Of course I've been honest with you. You have a wonderful opinion of me.

JILL: Sometimes I think you've no opinion of me at all. I just can't trust you.

BOB: Now listen, Jill . . . when I said I was prepared to leave her, you said you didn't want me to.

JILL: I said I didn't want you to leave just for me. I didn't want to be accused of breaking up your marriage. That's not the same thing. Anyway, you'd never really any intention of leaving.

BOB: I said it, didn't I?

JILL: You've said lots of things.

BOB: You really do think I'm a shit, don't you?

JILL: Of course I do . . . and you are. I just want to see some evidence of your supposed good intentions.

BOB: We always get into this conversation. No matter where we go, this is what we end up with. Come on, love, we're having a good time . . . let's not spoil it.

JILL: I see . . . talking about our future spoils things . . . that's nice for me.

BOB: Come on . . . don't you think I want to sort things out . . . I'm not happy the way things are.

JILL: Of course not . . . you'd like me to stop complaining.

BOB: I'd like you to realize that we'd both like the same thing. (*They sit quietly.*)

JILL: It's so quiet and peaceful here. We could be anywhere. (*Pause.*) If you took a photograph of us, and put it in one of those television quizzes . . . how many people would guess this is Belfast?

BOB: My wife for one . . . and she'd wonder who the hell you were.

JILL: There now, you see . . . why did you bring that up? I was quite contented and you've ruined it all. What am I doing with you?

14. INT. JOYCE'S OFFICE
She is there with the DOCTOR.

JOYCE: So do you tell him, or do I?

DOCTOR: It might be better coming from you.

JOYCE: It will certainly be better for you.

DOCTOR: I'm not dodging it . . . I'm thinking of him really. I think it will seem less ominous coming from you.

JOYCE: He isn't a fool you know. He keeps asking about the results. He's going to guess the worst.

DOCTOR: We don't know if it is the worst . . . Get him back to the mainland, he might respond to treatment.

JOYCE: Surely we should tell him that . . . instead of total lies.

DOCTOR: We can tell him the tests are not conclusive. That's true in a sense . . . and he'll undergo a lot more when they get him over there.

JOYCE: (*Not very happy about things*) What about Anderson?

DOCTOR: Sometimes I wish he'd catch something for real. (*She glares at him.*) Sorry . . . that was silly. He's a problem. No matter what we do no matter what we say, he goes on insisting he's in pain. What can we do?

JOYCE: Throw him out and have done with it.

DOCTOR: Yes, I suppose that's what will happen in the end . . . but until it does we're stuck with him.

JOYCE: I don't want to be stuck with him . . . I want him off this ward. Send him back to the mainland as well . . . otherwise I might be sent back . . . to stand trial for murder.

DOCTOR: I will try . . . I have tried. He knows what he's doing . . . a real barrack room lawyer . . . perfectly well aware of the limits of our powers. (*Pause.*) At least we'll have Evans off your hands in no time. (*Pause.*) This new sister's quite a character.

JOYCE: So they tell me.

DOCTOR: You don't like her?

JOYCE: I don't know her.

DOCTOR: She's not going to take any nonsense anyway. A real tough little Scot.

JOYCE: Have you asked her out yet?

DOCTOR: Not yet, I'm still assessing the quality.

JOYCE: That white coat is not nearly as impressive as you think.

DOCTOR: It's what's under the white coat that I hope to impress with.

JOYCE: Take my advice . . . sneak up on them from behind.

DOCTOR: Thank you, Joyce. No doubt you'll speak well of me, if she asks you.

JOYCE: Absolutely. (*Pause, gazing at him.*)

DOCTOR: What is it?

JOYCE: You want me to speak well of you to our little Scot . . . how would you like to return the favour?

DOCTOR: Of course . . . I'll tell her you're wonderful . . . but I didn't know you were like that.

JOYCE: Wouldn't a tough little Scot be just the person to look after John Anderson?

DOCTOR: How could we land him on her . . . on what grounds?

JOYCE: On the grounds that she's a tough little Scot?

DOCTOR: I'd like to help you, Joyce . . . in order to help myself . . . but I don't think it's on.

JOYCE: We could always do it on the grounds that we can't risk him and Evans together . . . after what happened.

DOCTOR: For as big a favour as that, I'd expect you to come out with me yourself.

JOYCE: If I go out with you you'll transfer Anderson?
(*He nods.*)
Maybe I've misunderstood Anderson . . . maybe he's not really as bad as I think.

DOCTOR: (*Going*) Maybe I'll just talk to our Scots friend on my own behalf.
(*They both laugh as he goes. Pause.* JOYCE *takes up the notes from her desk . . . the test results for* PATTERSON. *She looks troubled.*)

(*Fade to: the ward.* EVANS *sitting with* PATTERSON.)

EVANS: As soon as this is over, and I'm ready to go . . . I'll have him.

PATTERSON: You'll get yourself thrown in the cooler. Best to forget about it.

EVANS: No way, boyo . . . I'll make him into a real patient.

PATTERSON: He only did it to help himself to get out . . . it was nothing personal.

EVANS: He nearly broke my jaw . . . that's personal.

PATTERSON: You know what I mean . . . it could just as well have been me . . . or anybody . . . he wants out.

EVANS: If I give him a good enough going over, maybe it'll help him. Where is he anyway?

PATTERSON: Gone for more x-rays. They're putting the pressure on him again.

EVANS: They really hate him . . . natural I suppose. It must be hard to treat people who've lost an arm, or a leg . . . or had their brains blown out . . . and then have to watch him play-acting the whole time. They want to nurse people who are really sick, don't they?

PATTERSON: You're not really sick.

EVANS: I was . . . I've had an operation . . . that was real.

PATTERSON: But why did you want to have a vasectomy? Why are you doing it . . . Don't you ever want to have any kids?

EVANS: I've got plenty . . . five.

(PATTERSON *looks questioningly.*)

My lady . . . she was married before like.

PATTERSON: What age is she . . . she must be ancient.

EVANS: Forty-three . . . not too old.

PATTERSON: You go with a bird who's forty-three . . . stroll bleeding on. What d'you want a bird that age for?

EVANS: I didn't ask her her age when I met her, did I?

PATTERSON: But she must have looked old.

EVANS: She doesn't look forty-three . . . she only looks about in her thirties.

PATTERSON: Even so . . . and five kids . . . from a bachelor to the captain of a five-a-side football team in one go. (*Sniggers.*)

EVANS: What age is your bird then?

PATTERSON: She's not bleeding forty-three anyway . . . except maybe round the chest. Twenty . . . beautiful. A hairdresser. We're getting engaged the next time I go home. (*Pause.*) Be married by this time next year.

EVANS: You going to stay in the army after you're married?

PATTERSON: Of course I'm going to stay in the army . . . this is my life, mate . . . I love it.

(*Fade up on: Sister's Office. The* NURSE *has just brought in the tray, with just one cup on it.*)

NURSE: Sister Williamson was over when you were with the doctor, Ma'am. She said she was going over to Sister Duncan's ward this morning.

JOYCE: (*Surprised*) Oh . . . I see. (*Pause.*) That's all right, Corporal, thank you.

(*As the nurse goes.*)

Oh, Corporal Jones . . . would you tell Private Patterson I'd like to see him after I've had my tea . . . in about fifteen minutes.

(*The* NURSE *replies and goes.*)

15. INT. THE SECURITY DESK

JILL *is sitting, glaring unhappily at* BOB *chatting and laughing with* YVONNE, *some way away.* CECIL SMART, *the orderly, is with* JILL.

CECIL: I'd watch that one, dear . . . a real maneater if ever I saw one.

JILL: Huh . . . I don't see anything special about her.

CECIL: My dear . . . they're the deadliest of all. She also has three pips going for her. That can make an impression on a mere corporal.

JILL: Look at him . . . men are so damned gullible. What's he giggling about . . . like a big silly schoolboy?

CECIL: Maybe she's very funny, dear. From what I've seen of you two here you're not exactly a barrel of laughs. Perhaps you should look and learn.

JILL: (*Nasty*) Are you queer?

CECIL: Not at all, dear . . . I don't know any queer gays . . . you hetros have all the queers.

JILL: Very funny.

CECIL: I don't want you taking it out on me, because your boyfriend decides to chat up another woman.

JILL: He's not chatting her up . . . they're only talking.

CECIL: (*Throwing his head up*) Physician heal thyself.

16. JOYCE'S OFFICE

STEPHEN PATTERSON *is with* JOYCE. *She has just told him he is to be sent back to England, and will undergo further tests and treatment there. From his point of view this is the worst possible news. He is very gloomy, gazing, unseeing, at the desk. She is watching him, torn, but knowing she has said all she can say. Pause.* CLAIRE *knocks and enters.* PATTERSON *doesn't stir.* JOYCE *gestures to* CLAIRE *and she goes, having taken in the situation. Hold. Close on* PATTERSON. *Hold.*

17. INT. JOYCE'S OFFICE

CLAIRE *is there. She is reading through the report on* PATTERSON.

When she's finished she pauses a moment.

CLAIRE: There isn't much doubt, is there?

   (JOYCE *shakes her head.*)

   What did you tell him?

JOYCE: The truth, I suppose.

   (CLAIRE *looks questioningly.*)

   Not in words . . . but my manner, my expression. I'm not
   a very convincing liar.

CLAIRE: Few of us are. Sinton should have done it himself. He's
   the doctor.

JOYCE: He's busy with other matters.

CLAIRE: Chasing after nurses, as usual.

JOYCE: I think it's Yvonne he's interested in at the moment.

CLAIRE: I don't think he'll have much luck with Yvonne.

JOYCE: That won't stop him trying . . . it never has in the past.

CLAIRE: Maybe this will cure him. Yvonne'll not be as polite as
   the rest of us. (*Pause.*)

JOYCE: Thank you for coming over. I don't know whether I
   really needed you, or just missed seeing you today.

CLAIRE: I'm sorry . . . I did think you'd have joined us for
   lunch though.

JOYCE: I decided to take a late lunch. I haven't had a great day
   today . . . I wouldn't have been the best of company.

CLAIRE: Maybe you need a break, a few days away.

JOYCE: Do you want rid of me?

   (*Pause.* CLAIRE *looks at her, surprised.*)

   I don't know why I said that. I've just become so used to
   having you around when things aren't going well . . . and
   these past few days you haven't been. Forget I said it. It's
   silly really.

CLAIRE: But I have been around.

JOYCE: No you haven't, Claire . . . you know you haven't . . .
   not the way you were before. I'm afraid if I try to talk to
   you, she'll burst in . . . or you'll dash off to get ready to go
   out with her.

CLAIRE: Joyce . . . she's only been here for a couple of days.

JOYCE: And you've barely been apart for a single moment of it.

I feel uncomfortable in the hut. I feel like an intruder. She
has a way of looking at me which makes me feel like that.

CLAIRE: Anyone would think you were . . . (*Pause.*)

JOYCE: Finish it . . . anyone would think I was what?

CLAIRE: It doesn't matter.

JOYCE: (*Slapping the table, surprising* CLAIRE) But it does
matter . . . it matters to me (*Quieter*) What were you going
to say?

CLAIRE: It's a silly thing . . . and I don't mean it. (*Pause.*) I was
going to say that anyone would think you were, jealous.
(*Pause.*)

JOYCE: Well, I am jealous. We've been such close friends.
We've done everything together, spent most of our time
together and suddenly I'm frozen out. I know it's only been
a couple of days, in a way that makes it even worse.

CLAIRE: You haven't been frozen out. Yvonne's new, she's still
settling in. You haven't been falling over yourself to be
friendly with her.

JOYCE: I don't normally fall over myself to be friendly with
people I don't know.

CLAIRE: (*Upset*) I don't know what this conversation's about.
You refused to come out with us the other night. You
refused to join us for lunch. You haven't been exactly full
of chat in the hut.

JOYCE: I need time to get to know her . . . and she's not exactly
opening her arms to me either.
(*Pause.*)

CLAIRE: We're going into the city tonight . . . why don't you
come with us this time?

JOYCE: By the time I finish here I'm not fit to go anywhere. I
just want to sit and unwind. It's what we used to do . . .
and talk over the day.
(*The door knocks and the* NURSE *enters.*)

NURSE: Excuse me, Ma'am . . . (*Handing* JOYCE *a package.*)
Evans's notes, he's just back.

JOYCE: Thank you, Corporal. What's Private Patterson doing?

NURSE: He's back in bed, Ma'am.

242

JOYCE: Well just let him be for now. We've told him he has to
   go back for treatment in England, so he's feeling a bit
   depressed. I'll talk to you in a few minutes.
   (*The* NURSE *takes her leave.*)
CLAIRE: You'll be getting rid of Evans anyway. (*Pause.*) Will
   you come with us tonight?
JOYCE: I don't know . . . maybe another early night is what I
   really need.

18. INT. CLAIRE'S WARD
MRS SMALL *is propped up on top of her bed.* DOT, *a young*
WRAC, is sitting beside her, on a chair.
DOT: It's so boring in here.
MRS SMALL: They're just shoving me out you know, and they
   don't really know what was wrong with me. I still feel
   weak.
DOT: That's just with lying in bed.
MRS SMALL: I've had to lie in bed . . . I've been ill.
DOT: I know, but it makes you weak. It'll pass in a couple of
   days.
MRS SMALL: A couple of days! He'll expect me to be hop,
   skipping and jumping after him before a couple of days.
   (*Pause.*) When will you get out?
DOT: I don't know. Sister's trying to coax them to let me go
   home for a week.
MRS SMALL: She must like you . . . she's never done anything
   for me . . . except talk to me as if I was retarded.
DOT: I think she's lovely. She's been dead nice to me.
MRS SMALL: They're trying to push me out far too soon you
   know. They should let me gather my strength in here,
   before they push me out.
DOT: Does your daughter help you about the house?
MRS SMALL: Thon one, a lazy lump. She takes after her father.
   It's an argument to get her to do anything. The young ones
   nowadays have no time for a sick mother. (*Pause.*) Who was
   that was rushed in next door, did you hear?
DOT: A soldier who shot himself . . . it was just Cecil on the

desk who told me. Severe head injuries he says.

MRS SMALL: Huh, when you look around here you think they do themselves more harm than the IRA.

DOT: It was accidental. He's critical. He's on the new Scottish sister's ward.

MRS SMALL: I see her hanging about here a lot. She's a stern looking one.

DOT: I think she's nice.

MRS SMALL: You think everybody's nice. You'll learn.

DOT: She's got a very interesting face.

MRS SMALL: I didn't notice anything interesting about her. It was my husband showed her in when she arrived. He says she wouldn't be out of place as the mob leader at a Celtic and Ranger's game.

(CLAIRE *is making her way down.*)

DOT: I think they need to be tough to do this job.

CLAIRE: (*At the bed*) All ready for tomorrow, Mrs Small?

MRS SMALL: I hope that doctor knows what he's doing. I don't feel all that great.

CLAIRE: Well it will take a few days I'm sure . . . but you'll be yourself again in no time. Is Sergeant Small bringing your clothes up tonight?

MRS SMALL: God knows what he'll bring up. I'll probably go out looking like a beggar.

CLAIRE: How are you, Dorothy?

DOT: I'm fine thank you, Sister. I hear that one who shot himself's still serious?

CLAIRE: Well you tend to be when you shoot yourself. You're just after gossip. I'll maybe have good news for you tomorrow.

MRS SMALL: Do you not feel they're rushing me a bit, Sister?

CLAIRE: I don't think so, Mrs Small. You'll recover all the better for being in your own surroundings.

MRS SMALL: Surrounding of dirty dishes, and piles of dirty clothes. That's some convalescing.

DOT: Severe head injuries the soldier has. I've heard he'll be lucky to live.

CLAIRE: Where do you get all this information from, Dorothy?

DOT: There's not much goes on here that isn't known about.

MRS SMALL: They rush us through that quick, it's a wonder we've time to pick up any gossip.

CLAIRE: (*Trying to be good-natured*) Are you two conspiring to keep me from getting home? (*Pause.*) I'll see you both in the morning.
(*As she walks away there is a tremendous explosion.*)

19. INT. THE SANGAR
LUGS *and* WINTERS *on their feet, panicking as another explosion occurs.*

LUGS: (*As they both strain to see through the observation slot*) Bloody hell . . .

(*Cut to: the camp from the sangar's point of view. There is another loud thud, and a bomb appears to explode on one of the billets.*)

(*Cut to: sangar interior. Total panic.*)

LUGS: It's the camp . . . the bastards are attacking the bloody camp.

WINTERS: We'd better get out of here, before they hit us.

LUGS: (*Shaking*) Shouldn't we stay here until we're told?

WINTERS: It's rockets or mortars . . . if one hits this place we're dead . . . come on, you daft bugger. (*They scramble to get out.*)
(*They rush out of the sangar as the air fills with the wail of sirens.*)

19 CONT. EXT. BOTTOM OF THE LADDER TO THE SANGAR
As they reach the foot of the ladder they are confronted by an angry
LIEUTENANT ARCHER. *They automatically spring to attention.*

LIEUTENANT ARCHER: Just where do you two think you're going? Who told you to leave your post? You're shaking . . . pull yourselves together.

WINTERS: It sounds bad, sir . . . we've got mates . . .

LIEUTENANT ARCHER: (*Cutting in*) We've all got mates,
Winters. Just calm down . . . pull yourselves together.
We're under mortar attack . . . this is no time to rush about
in a blind panic. Return to your post until you're ordered to
do otherwise.
(*They both stand shaking, shocked, terrified.*)
Guards, attention . . . stand at ease . . . attention . . . (*He
shouts these commands at least half a dozen times. Then
commands them to stand at ease.*)

LUGS: Sorry, sir.

LIEUTENANT ARCHER: Shut up, Lockhart. Atten . . . tion.
Now, you two listen to me . . . this is what all those
months of training were all about. You're supposed to be
professional soldiers . . . not bloody boy scouts. You don't
desert your post in the middle of an enemy attack. I could
have you both court-martialled for this . . . is that clear?

LUGS: Yes, sir.

WINTERS: Yes, sir.

LIEUTENANT ARCHER: You'll return to your post until such
times as the situation is clear and you can be relieved.
(*Pause.*) Stand at ease. (*They do.*) I'll come and see you as
soon as I find out what is going on. If we can't get you
relieved soon, I'll see you get something to eat. (*Pause.*)
Carry on.

(*Cut to: interior of the sangar.* WINTERS *and* LUGS *inside.
Quieter, but still tense and frightened.* LUGS *is looking out.*)

LUGS: How many do you reckon copped it?

WINTERS: How the hell do I know? Listen to those bloody
sirens . . . dozens by the sound of that.

LUGS: (*A tremble in his voice.*) Oh Christ, it must be bad . . .
they're bringing in civilian nurses.
(LUGS *rushes to the door. Pause. We hear him retching outside.*
WINTERS's *face shows disgust.* LUGS *returns slowly . . .
wiping his mouth on his sleeve. He looks at a disgusted*
WINTERS.)

LUGS: I couldn't help it.

WINTERS: I just hope they send us sandwiches, and not bloody
    stew.

20. INT. THE DESK
*BOB and JILL are trying to keep the area clear to facilitate the
movement of stretchers. They do what they can to assist nursing staff
who are treating the less seriously injured. BOB is trying to keep a
record of names and details. JILL starts to serve tea. YVONNE
appears briefly and checks some of the stretchers coming in. She chats
briefly to BOB. JILL sees them together and glares at BOB, as
YVONNE returns to the casualty department. There are some dazed
and shocked SOLDIERS who wander in and have to be kept clear of
the main area of activity. CECIL is wheeling in stretchers.*
BOB: (To JILL) We've got to keep this area clear and not let any
    others wander into casualty.
JILL: (Nastily) Orders from Yvonne?
BOB: This is an emergency, you silly little bitch.
    (*They just glare at each other and return to their various tasks.*)

21. INT. JOYCE'S WARD
*Part of it is screened off. There is a lot of activity behind the screens.
EVANS is lying in bed awake, feeling sorry for himself, but quiet.
ANDERSON and PATTERSON are sitting together, quiet. Their
silence is almost reverential. As nurses move to and fro they just sit,
mute. Inside ANDERSON's head a lot is happening. Close on his
face, strained, tight, emotional. MRS SMALL and DOT wheeling a
trolley, on which are pots of tea. They are serving the other patients.
They approach ANDERSON, PATTERSON and EVANS. EVANS
props himself up, feeling very fragile. A pillow falls and ANDERSON
picks it up and props it behind EVANS. Hold.*

22. INT. THE DESK
*BOB is sitting writing into a book. A number of SOLDIERS are still
sitting around. Some looking dazed and shocked, with wounds
dressed, arms in slings, etc. The only sounds are those related to
essential activity. JILL passes through with a trolley containing
implements, etc. BOB and she gaze at each other, but neither face*

registers anything. Pause. BOB *rises and goes and starts to use a mop which has been sitting.* JILL *returns wearily and goes slowly towards the desk. She sits watching* BOB *mopping the floor.* CECIL *approaches.*

CECIL: Look at me, covered in blood and gore. What a night. I'll tell you, dear, I hope if they ever use cruise missiles, they do it on my day off. And those sisters . . . sergeant majors could learn a few things from them. (*Pause.*) Here, you look a little pale, dear . . . would you like some tea? I'll go in a minute and rustle us up two cups . . . and a few biscuits. Frantic activity always gives me the urge for chocolate biscuits. Penguins. I'm always partial to a Penguin after such a spurt. (*Pause.*) How they all survived's a mystery to me. They say three were killed. These bloody Irish . . . and they're such nice people when you're on holiday. I fish you see. It's a wonderful country for fishing. Beautiful rivers and lakes . . . an abundance. Why can't they do that. . . ? A bit of fishing would calm them down, instead of all this bloody nonsense . . . and no pun intended, dear.

(*Pause. He looks over at* BOB.)

Look at the goes of him with that mop. You're going to get a real treasure there, love. Fully house trained by the looks of him.

(JILL *is becoming more and more upset. Tears are beginning to form.*)

I counted three legs in there. Did you see any yourself, dear? That young coloured fella lost his foot as well. It's the suddenness of it all. Out of a clear blue sky and zap. Eight human beings reduced to butcher's meat. Terrible. Then there's the three dead . . . and the minor injuries. I saw a splinter six inches long coming out of a knee. It would nearly put you off your food.

(JILL *has started to sob.*)

You'd wonder how these nurses have appetites at all . . . yet anything like the food they can shift. (*Pause.*) I suppose they just get used to it. You get used to anything I suppose.

(JILL *has risen to her feet.*)

If there's another war, goodness knows what I'll be left to carry about on stretchers . . . You can't afford to be squeamish, can you?

(*He looks at her. She bursts into hysterical crying.* BOB *comes running across.*)

BOB: What's wrong with her? What is it?

CECIL: Shock . . . it's shock . . . we were just chatting away there . . . as normal as you like . . . then this. Go and get a sister . . . Go on, don't just stand there with that silly bloody mop.

(BOB *rushes off.* CECIL *sits* JILL *down and tries to soothe her.*)

He'll be all right for mopping your floor, dear, but not a great deal of use in an emotional crisis, I'm afraid. You may save those for when you've visitors.

(BOB *returns with* YVONNE. JILL *rises again, hysterical.*)

JILL: Don't let her near me . . . don't let her touch me.

CECIL: It's the sister, dear, it's the sister. (*To* YVONNE) She's upset, Ma'am.

YVONNE: (*Forcing* JILL *down.* JILL *struggles and screams.*) Come on, come on. Just sit and try to relax.

(JILL *struggles to her feet again.*)

JILL: You keep away from me, you dirty Scotch bitch . . . you leave me alone.

(YVONNE *slaps her face hard and presses her down into the chair.* JOYCE *appears.* JILL *quietens, whimpers.* JOYCE *crosses to her.*)

JOYCE: Come on, Jill . . . just relax.

(*She does.*)

That's it . . .

(*To* BOB.)

Corporal, get her a cup of weak, sweet tea.

(BOB *goes,* JILL *just cries quietly.*)

(*To* YVONNE) She'll be all right.

(YVONNE *goes.* JILL *quietens down, heaving with silent sobs from time to time.*)

23. EXT. SOMEWHERE IN THE COMPOUND
LUGS *and* WINTERS *just strolling and breathing deeply.*
LUGS: Listen . . . quiet . . . you'd never guess anything had
    happened, would you?
WINTERS: I thought we were never going to get relieved.
LUGS: I don't feel tired now, do you?
WINTERS: I feel exhausted, but I don't feel like sleeping.
    (*Pause.*) I'll bet there'll be some of those poor buggers
    who'll lie awake in agony.

24. THE SISTERS' HUT
The three are sitting. CLAIRE *is in a very upset state. She is
shivering.*
CLAIRE: I just went to hold his hand, to comfort him, and that
    was it. I was left holding it . . . the wrist just dripping
    blood.
JOYCE: Let's try not to talk about it any more.
YVONNE: (*To* CLAIRE) You're shivering. (*She holds her.*) Joyce is
    right . . . just leave it for tonight.
    (CLAIRE *huddles into* YVONNE. JOYCE *looks hurt, distanced
    from them.*)
JOYCE: We'd all better get some sleep. We're going to be very
    busy on the wards tomorrow.
YVONNE: You go on, I'll look after Claire.
    (*She hugs her closer and* CLAIRE *huddles even tighter.*)
JOYCE: (*Rising*) I'll see you both in the morning.
    (*She goes hesitantly, reluctant, but the others don't even appear
    to notice her now.* YVONNE *is burying her face into* CLAIRE's
    head. JOYCE *goes. Pause.* CLAIRE *looks up into* YVONNE's
    face, they slowly kiss. Hold.*)

25. INT. JOYCE'S OFFICE. NEXT MORNING
The door knocks and when JOYCE *calls 'Come in'* JOHN
ANDERSON *enters. She asks him to sit. Pause.*
JOYCE: What's this all about, Private Anderson?
ANDERSON: I want to be discharged, Ma'am.
JOYCE: (*Considering*) Are you fit?

ANDERSON: I've always been fit. We both know that.

JOYCE: You realize you could face very serious disciplinary charges?

ANDERSON: I hope I do. (*Quite emotional*) I watched you last night, Ma'am . . . you and the others. I've never seen anything like it. I felt so totally worthless and ashamed. I've never admired people so much in my life.

(*She sits quietly for a moment. She checks his notes.*)

JOYCE: What are you going to say?

ANDERSON: I'll just tell them the truth. I hated the army and was prepared to do anything to get out. It was all lies and I'm prepared to serve my time, if they'll have me.

JOYCE: They might offer you a discharge.

ANDERSON: I'd prefer to serve on.

JOYCE: Do you think you'll like it any better?

ANDERSON: (*Controlling himself*) I'll just try and remember what I saw here last night . . . those lads being wheeled in and the way you nurses worked.

JOYCE: I think you're wrong. You're being emotional about it all and that won't last.

ANDERSON: Are you asking me to stay here?

JOYCE: Certainly not . . . I'm throwing you out. No, if they offer to discharge you, I think you must go. (*Pause.*) I'm sorry if I appear harsh, but I've lived through nights like last night before and sometimes even worse.

(*Pause.* ANDERSON *rises and goes slowly to the door. Turns at the door.*)

ANDERSON: Thanks for the advice, Ma'am.

(*She says nothing. He goes.*)

(*Fade up on the ward.* PATTERSON *is writing a letter.* EVANS *is sitting beside one of the injured soldiers. He looks up and sees* ANDERSON. *He nudges* PATTERSON *and they both watch* ANDERSON *walking normally down the ward.*)

26. INT. SISTERS' HUT. LATE AT NIGHT

JOYCE *emerges from the kitchen, in her dressing gown, a cup of*

*cocoa to take into her bedroom. There is talking from within Claire's
room.* JOYCE *pauses outside the door. Hold.*

27. EXT. BENCH IN PARK. EARLY EVENING
BOB *and* JILL *are sitting. Both look down.* JILL *rises and starts to
walk away. He just watches her go. Hold.*

28. INT. LIVING ROOM IN THE SISTERS' HUT
CLAIRE *is sitting.* JOYCE *comes in.*
JOYCE: Hello, Claire . . . Yvonne said to tell you . . .
CLAIRE: I know . . . she's discovered one of her long lost
    relatives and gone to make a visit.
    (JOYCE *sits. Silence for a moment.*)
JOYCE: Claire. . . ?
CLAIRE: I know.
    (CLAIRE *looks at her.*)
JOYCE: (*Pause.*) It's a bit like old times, isn't it?
CLAIRE: I'd like it to be a lot like old times. I don't want my
    relationship with Yvonne to destroy that. (*Pause.*) I don't
    want you to approve, or disapprove. I just want you to
    recognize that I do have other needs . . . normal needs and
    ones that our relationship couldn't satisfy.
    (*Pause.*)
JOYCE: (*Considers, smiles*) Let's turn the telly off and chat.

29. EXT. A PARKED CAR
BOB *and* YVONNE *are together.*
YVONNE: I thought you and Jill were a serious thing?
BOB: No, not really.
    (*She gives him a searching look.*)
    It was just a casual thing.
YVONNE: And your marriage . . . is that just a casual
    thing?
BOB: (*Smiling*) Let's say it's not an on-going thing.
YVONNE: I don't know if I like you, Corporal . . .
BOB: I'm hoping you'll get to . . . Captain.

30. INT. SISTERS' SITTING ROOM

JOYCE *is sitting.* YVONNE *enters the hut and then the sitting room.*

YVONNE: Hello, Joyce, where's Claire?

JOYCE: She's on late, she's not in yet.

YVONNE: Of course, I forgot. Will you tell her I had to go out . . . but I'll see her later? She can go to bed.

JOYCE: Keep it warm for you?

YVONNE: Jealous?

JOYCE: Concerned, for Claire. More relatives?

YVONNE: Cousins.

JOYCE: Kissing cousins.

YVONNE: You're a bit sharp. Have you lost a patient today?

JOYCE: I have as a matter of fact. He's not dead, not yet. We sent him back to England to let him do it there.

YVONNE: Sad, but he's better amongst his own.

JOYCE: Aren't we all?

YVONNE: I'm a simple Glasgow girl, Joyce . . . if you have a message for me, send it direct.

JOYCE: All right . . . stop messing Claire about.

YVONNE: Piss off, sweetheart. Is that a threat?

JOYCE: I doubt if you're that simple a Glasgow girl and I'm no fool. Claire's a friend . . . my dearest friend and I don't like to see her hurt.

YVONNE: I think I keep Claire quite happy. She's not complaining. You may be her dear friend, but there is a side of her nature you can't satisfy.

JOYCE: You know you could ruin her career? (*Pause.*) Does she know about you and Corporal Wynne? Young Jill Burns was in to see me today.

YVONNE: Not to arrest you I hope.

JOYCE: She's in love with Bob.

YVONNE: Tough on her.

JOYCE: What if I tell Claire?

YVONNE: It won't help Jill. It won't really make any difference to Claire . . . and I'll smash your head in.

JOYCE: You would too.

YVONNE: You're damned right I would. If you want to be a

253

mother confessor to everybody that's your business. I know you're well qualified . . . you've had a hard life, a broken marriage, and disastrous love affairs.

JOYCE: (*Rising*) How dare you.

YVONNE: If you're standing up to invite me to knock you down again I will.

(*Pause.* JOYCE *sits.*)

I've been through it too, you know. I'm not going through it again. What I've got left of this life I'm going to enjoy. If others get hurt too bad. They're going to have to look out for themselves the same as I had. (*Pause.*) You're a nurse, Joyce . . . keep your healing powers for that. The rest is outside your scope.

31. INT. SITTING ROOM

JOYCE *and* CLAIRE *in the sitting room.*

JOYCE: Did I tell you about John Anderson?

(CLAIRE *shakes her head.*)

He's being discharged . . . and then he's coming over here to join the RUC.

CLAIRE: You're joking?

JOYCE: I'm not. I doubt if they'll have him, but that's what he says.

CLAIRE: Have you heard anything about Stephen Patterson?

JOYCE: Just that he's pretty bad. I wish I could have been honest with him.

CLAIRE: You were, as far as you could be.

JOYCE: Yes.

CLAIRE: He's a very sick man; nothing you said or didn't say would have changed that.

JOYCE: No . . . I suppose you're right.

(*They rise.*)

32. INT. THE DESK

The three sisters arriving at the desk.

YVONNE: I'll arrange the tea in my office this morning.

(BOB *is pretending to busy himself.*)

CECIL: (*Wheeling in a stretcher*) You've a new arrival this
morning, Sister Williamson.

CLAIRE: Who's that, Cecil?

CECIL: (*With a sideways glance at* BOB) Young Jill . . . she
overdid it with the sleeping pills last night . . .
(JOYCE *and* CLAIRE *walk away after* CECIL. YVONNE *just
gazes after them.*)

33. INT. CLAIRE'S WARD

JILL *is lying beside* MRS SMALL. *The screens are drawn around her
bed.* CLAIRE *is in with her.*

MRS SMALL: (*To* DOT) Why am I always shoved next to the
suicides. . . ? It's creepy. I've enough depression in my
own life, without being next to that.
(*Pause.* CLAIRE *emerges, business-like.*)
Can I be moved, Sister?

CLAIRE: (*As she goes*) We'll get you something for your bowels
later, Mrs Small.

MRS SMALL: (*To* DOT) My bowels . . . what is she talking
about? There's nothing wrong with my bowels.
(DOT *smiles.*)

34. INT. JOYCE'S WARD

JOYCE *doing her ward round. Checking charts, greeting patients, etc.*

JOYCE: (*Stopping by a bed*) I think you'll be away soon Private
Thompson.

PRIVATE THOMPSON: Thank goodness, Sister . . . it's boring
me to death.

JOYCE: That's a word we don't use on this ward.

PRIVATE THOMPSON: Sorry, Sister . . .

JOYCE: Boring . . . we'll have to see if we can find a little job for
you.
(*Hold.*)

35. EXT

Under titles see JOYCE *and* CLAIRE *walking towards the home.*